JUST DYING
to Glamp

To Penny —
Blessings on this trip we call life —
April Ooker ♡
Philippians 4:13

Also by April Nunn Coker

*I'm Dreaming of a Black Christmas:
A Holiday Survival Guide*

Night Keeper

THE KEEPER SERIES

The Keeper

Keeper II: The Storm

Keeper III: Blackout

Ellie and the Alphabet Zoo

Just Dying to *Glamp*

Book 25
of the
Magnolia Bluff Crime Chronicles
By the Underground Authors

April Nunn Coker

Copyright © 2024

All rights reserved. No part of this book may be reproduced, stored in a retrieval program, or transmitted by any form or any means, electronic or mechanical, including photocopying, recording, or otherwise except as may be expressly permitted by the applicable copyright statutes or in writing by the author and publisher.

Book Cover Design: Crispian Thurlborn, Wyldwood Books Bespoke Book Designs and Services.

Just Dying to Glamp is a work of fiction. Names, characters, places, and incidents are either the product of the author's imagination or are used fictitiously. Any resemblance to actual persons, living or dead, or events is entirely coincidental.

Just Dying to Glamp/April Nunn Coker

Mystery – Fiction

First printing

To Dixie and the Get'away Gals:
Thank you for showing me how to glamp,
and for supporting my writing habit.
See you down the road…

"...for the Lord thy God walketh in the midst of thy camp, to deliver thee, and to give up thine enemies before thee..."   Deuteronomy 23:14

Chapter One

MAMIE BRAKED HARD and whipped her SUV into the parking lot of Applewhite Auto Sales #2, just outside of Leander, Texas. The driver in the car behind her honked but she didn't care.

"A vintage camper!" she cried to her Boston terrier Babs, who was napping on a dog pillow in the front passenger seat. The dog raised her head, wagged her bobbed tail, and rested her big brown eyes on her owner.

The sixties-era trailer in the back of the car lot was just what Mamie had been wanting. What a coincidence there was one for sale right there in town.

Ever since she had read an article about glamping in her favorite online woman's magazine, she had been dying to go "glamping," a term probably coined by some smart businessperson by combining the words "glamour" and "camping." She had learned about a glamping craze that had prompted women to buy vintage campers and fix them up with chandeliers, fancy linens, and cute graphics. Glampers towed unique, refurbished campers, and even dressed in vintage clothing to match the era. She had been dying to find a cute camper and try glamping herself.

The used car salesman who had dashed out of the small office as soon as she pulled up in her SUV danced with impatience after unlocking the trailer and inviting her to see inside. "I'll give you a few minutes to look around and think about it," he said before greeting another customer.

What would West do? Her late husband had known about her desire to get a vintage camper, and he would have known if the price was reasonable. He would have looked the trailer over, top to bottom, underneath and inside, searching for evidence of water leaks and rotten wood. He would have known what to look for and whether it was worth what they were asking. But West wasn't here anymore, and she needed to decide. To her inexperienced eyes, the trailer was perfect, just what she had been looking for.

The salesman finished talking with the other customer and hot-footed it back to Mamie. "What do you think? Do you like it? You could take her home today. I've had a lot of interest in this little trailer. It won't be here long."

She examined the young man's bristly face for signs he was being truthful. The expertise she had gained from teaching high schoolers didn't help. There was no way to know if he was giving her the facts or just trying to make a sale. Even though she was almost hopping with excitement, she refused to be swayed by a rapid-fire, smooth-talking car salesman. *I can't let him see how much I want it.*

"How do I know if my car will pull it?"

The salesman glanced at her SUV. "This trailer weighs a little over 2000 pounds. It can be pulled by almost any SUV, especially one with a tow package."

"I'm not sure what a tow package is, or if my car has one. My husband bought it for me." She crossed her fingers behind her back. *Lord, please let my car be able to tow this trailer.*

"Why don't you call him and ask?"

She shook her head. "I wish I could, but he passed away last year."

The salesman cleared his throat, looked down, and shifted his feet. "I'm sorry to hear that, ma'am. I'd be happy to look at your owner's manual and see."

Sadness quickly replaced her excitement. Mamie swallowed the lump that had formed in her throat, the one that appeared every time she spoke of her husband. She wasn't supposed to have been left alone this soon. They were supposed to grow old together—retire, travel, enjoy grandchildren. Now none of that would ever happen. Blinking back the tears that threatened to spill over, she returned to her car a few yards away and opened the front passenger door.

"Babs, stay," she ordered the dog as she reached into the glove compartment for the owner's manual. Now her hands were shaking with sorrow instead of excitement.

Mike, according to his name tag, seemed not to notice as he took the manual from her and flipped through it. "Says here your vehicle is rated up to five thousand pounds." He grinned, seeming to forget about her husband. "It can pull that trailer with no problems at all. You won't even know it's behind you." He closed the booklet and handed it back to her. "Shall we make a deal?"

Not so fast, buster. "Isn't there something else my car needs? Some kind of thing on the back so it can pull a trailer? Like a hitch or something?" She knew that at least, and her excitement was back.

"You don't have a trailer hitch?" He walked to the rear of her car to check. "Nope, you sure don't. Yep, you'll have to take it someplace where they can add one. I recommend Star Hitches. I can call and make an appointment for you if you like and keep your trailer here until you can pick it up. We'll just have to fill out some paperwork first."

This is all happening so fast. Isn't he being just a tad pushy? Or maybe he's just being helpful. Her head swam with the pros and cons of signing on the dotted line.

"If you'll come inside, we can get that paperwork taken care of. I'll need your driver's license, insurance card, and a down payment." Mike headed toward the office.

Her feet froze. She had never made a major purchase like this by herself. Except for that time she bought living room furniture without consulting West. He hadn't been happy about that, either. But he had gotten over it and even ended up liking it.

Evidently aware that she hadn't followed, Mike turned. "Coming?"

"Could I have a minute, please?" Mamie asked. She needed to think and maybe get a second opinion from someone who hadn't fallen in love at first sight like she had with the camper.

"Sure thing. I'll be inside when you're ready unless a customer comes along and then I'll have to help them. Take your time, though." He grinned and headed inside the tiny office building.

She snapped some photos of the camper with her phone before dialing her friend Starla, who agreed to look at the photos and give her opinion.

"Oh my gosh, what a darling camper! Yes, you should buy it and start camping. I'd even go with you if you asked. Heck, maybe Dave will let me find one to buy."

"You agree that I should get it? You don't think I'm rushing into it?"

"Absolutely not. You're a free woman now, and you've mourned West long enough. It's time for you to get out and have some fun. And if you can afford it, why not? Plus, these cute vintage trailers don't come along every day, so you don't want to miss your opportunity."

That settled it. Starla had confirmed it. *She's right. If I let this one go, there might not be another one. And I need something to do, something to occupy my time, something to look forward to. It's really not even about the money, and if thousands of other women are doing it, so can I.*

"Thanks, Starla. You always give such great advice. And you're so right. I'm going to do it." She shoved her phone in her jeans pocket and moved toward the office. It was time to put on her big girl panties—or drawers, as West would say—and go for it. And even if Starla hadn't answered the phone or hadn't liked the trailer, she would have bought it anyway. She had already made up her mind.

By the afternoon of the next day, a new hitch had been installed below the back bumper of Mamie's car and Mike was showing her how to hook up the trailer. He told her it would take practice, but with the backup camera on her vehicle it would be much easier than it used to be. The thought terrified her, but she figured if other women could do it, she should be able to learn as well.

Now something else troubled her: would she be

able to unhook it once she got home? She jotted notes as Mike explained what to do. If nothing else she could call on a neighbor to help. Her hands shook as she drove out of the car lot, the little vintage trailer in her rearview mirror. It reminded her of a bumper sticker she had seen once: *I go where I'm towed.* She might have to get one for her trailer. The thought brought a smile to her face, replacing the grimace of anxiety that came from towing a trailer for the first time in her life.

It followed her home without coming undone, without jackknifing, without wrecking, though the hitch seemed to make more noise than she expected. She lived on a one-acre tract of land with enough room to avoid having to back in. She pulled into her driveway and drove off the pavement to circle under the trees and park next to her garage. Low-hanging tree branches brushed the top of her car and trailer.

When she was satisfied with where she had stopped, Mamie exited the car and retrieved a scrap piece of wood left over from one of her husband's projects to rest the tongue jack on. Then she started checking things off the notes she had made. She placed the wheel chocks Mike had thrown inside the trailer around the tires before disconnecting the power cord for the trailer lights and unhooking the safety chains. Next, she unlocked the hitch ball cover before hand-cranking the jack. When it released the ball with enough clearance to pull out from under the hitch, she hopped back in the car and drove forward a bit. Then she got out again and cranked the tongue jack down until she thought the trailer looked level.

"I did it!" she cried to Babs, who had been deposited

into the backyard and was watching her through the chain-link fence. The trailer was parked and the car was ready to move into the garage. She clapped in glee, feeling like a kid who had just hit his first home run.

Yes, she had plunked down a sizable check to purchase the trailer, but now it was hers, free and clear, title and all. Her kids would think she was crazy, but this was her life, and she intended to live it to the fullest. It was time to get out of her comfort zone and try something new. West would be proud of her. Starla sure was.

"I'm so proud of you, Mamie. I know you'll have a lot of fun with that camper."

"Thanks, Starla. I guess we'll see. She needs redecorating in a bad way, and I already have a few ideas. Want to come over for lunch tomorrow? You can help me brainstorm. I could use another opinion."

After hanging up with Starla, Mamie rummaged through the utility closet in the laundry room until she found a heavy-duty extension cord. Time to plug the camper in and see if everything—or anything—worked.

"Whatcha got there?" Mr. Benson, her inquisitive next-door neighbor, appeared in her yard as she plugged the cord into the outlet on the outside of the trailer.

"Hi, Mr. Benson. I decided to get this little camper I saw at Applewhite's."

"Is that the one that was at Applewhite's?" Either he didn't listen, or his hearing was going bad.

"Yes, sir," Mamie replied, increasing the volume of her voice. A smile teased her lips.

"Whatcha gonna do with it?"

"I thought I might go camping." She walked over to her garage to plug in the other end of the extension cord.

"Gonna be kind of hard to get your family in that tiny thing. What is it, anyway?"

"Oh no, the kids won't be going with me. It's just for me."

"Going by yourself?"

Mamie straightened to look at him. She really hadn't given that a thought. All the articles she had read about glamping talked about single women camping alone or with friends or family.

"You know, it may sound silly, Mr. Benson, but I really haven't thought that far ahead. I just saw this trailer and had to have it. I'm sure I will figure something out, though. And I think the salesman said it's a 1962 Scotsman Scottie."

None of her friends had campers that she knew of, and it would be pretty cramped bunking with someone in a 14-foot trailer. From what Mamie could tell, the bed was only a twin. The dining table and benches were supposed to convert into a bed, but she had no clue how to do it. Maybe Starla's husband would let her buy a camper so they could be camping buddies. *Not likely since he just bought a new boat,* she thought.

"She's unique with that little bump-out in the front. Reminds me of Elvis and that pompadour of his. Maybe you could join a camping group," said Mr. Benson. "Marla and I belonged to one years ago when the boys were still home. I'll see if she remembers the name of it."

"A camping group? That's a great idea. I'll have to do some research. I'm sure there are groups of women who go camping together."

"I'm sure there are. Mind if I take a gander?" He stepped closer to the trailer.

"Not at all." Mamie held the door open for him to peer inside. He wouldn't be able to see much. She hadn't turned any lights on yet.

"Looks pretty cozy," he observed. "If you need help fixing anything on it, let me know. It's been around a while, and I'm pretty handy."

"That is awfully kind of you, Mr. Benson, and I may take you up on that offer."

"Any time, Ms. Mamie, any time. I know you widow ladies need a man to help sometimes."

Her face warmed. *Widow lady.* He was doing his duty as a kind neighbor, but it felt funny to be called that, even if it was exactly what she was, minus the orthopedic shoes and hairnet. She fixed a smile on her face as he turned to go.

"You're very kind, Mr. Benson. Please give my regards to Mrs. Benson."

Hoping he would take the cue to go home, she closed the camper door and took a couple of steps toward the garage.

"Will do. Take care now."

A sip of water might help soothe the ache in her stomach, the knot that had formed when she remembered she was a widow. She entered her kitchen from the garage and filled a glass with cold water from the refrigerator.

"Am I being crazy, West? Have I just wasted a chunk of money? Can I really do this?"

The kitchen walls echoed with her unanswered questions. He was probably laughing at her, but then again, he had always told her she could do just about anything she put her mind to.

"It doesn't matter, does it? It's a done deal. I'll make it work. I can do this. Right, Babs?"

The ever-present pup, who had entered the house through the doggie door from the backyard, grabbed a nearby rubber toy and shook it with a playful growl, obviously wanting Mamie to take it from her and throw it.

"You silly girl. Let me have it." Mamie pried the toy out of the dog's mouth and tossed it across the kitchen into the living room. The dog bounced after it, tackled it, and brought it back. Mamie obliged by tossing the toy twice more, then said, "Okay, girl, I have to get back to work."

Babs followed her owner outside but remained inside the fence when the gate was opened and then closed.

On the other side of the fence, Mamie opened the camper door again and heaved herself up.

"I'm going to need a stepstool," she told no one in particular. She flipped the switch that was supposed to turn on the exterior light. "It works!" She laughed.

She tried two more lights, pleased to see that they worked as well. She had light, but no air conditioning, and it would be hot working in this little trailer in the summer. Next on her list: an air conditioner and someone to install it. *Wonder if Mr. Benson would do that?*

She opened drawers and cabinets, discovering all kinds of goodies, such as kitchen towels, plastic dishes, even pots and pans. The cushions on the benches and bed had seen better days. She would need to replace those, or at least the covers, and she was no seamstress. *Wonder who could sew me some new seat covers?*

She ran her fingers along the curtains. They were cute with their Route 66 map theme, but they weren't at all her taste. Everything inside the camper was beige or brown. Not good. She needed color and lots of it.

The paint on the outside of the trailer--white with blue and yellow arrow designs down the sides--seemed to be in good shape. Maybe the décor inside should complement the outside. What she needed to do first was clean the whole trailer, inside and out. *I'll get on that early tomorrow morning before it gets too hot,* she decided.

After a quick shower and then a prepared freezer meal for dinner, Mamie settled in her chair with her laptop to investigate she-sheds, glamping, and camping groups. Social media abounded with ideas for décor, but what caught her eye was the variety of camping groups. She scrolled through several, looking for anything that might stand out as a group she might want to join.

After sending requests to several ladies' camping groups, she sipped tea while searching Amazon for camper steps, curtains, bedding, and air conditioners.

She was finally feeling excited about life again.

Chapter Two

"**MOM, WHAT DID** you do?" Mamie's twenty-three-year-old daughter Junie burst through the front door and, like she had done all her life, dropped what she was carrying—today her heavy work backpack—on the floor in the foyer. Having just graduated from college with an MBA the previous spring, Junie worked for a wealth management company in nearby Round Rock. Still single, she felt free to drop in on her mother unannounced at any time, especially around mealtime.

Mamie looked up from her laptop where she searched for upcoming campouts with a ladies' group she had joined called Gals Gone Glamping. "Hello to you, too, Junie. What do you mean?"

"That camper by the garage. Is it yours?" Junie plopped down on the sofa next to her mother.

"I just got it, yes."

"It's very cute. I'm jealous. What are you going to do with it? Hello to you, too, Babs," she said to the dog who had jumped into her lap and was covering her face with wet kisses.

"Camp. I joined a ladies' camping group."

"No way, really? That's great, Mom! I've heard about those. Sisters on the Lam and such. Which one did you join?"

"Gals Gone Glamping. I'm looking at upcoming campouts now."

"Do you know anyone?"

"Not a one." Mamie scrunched up her face and glanced sideways at her daughter, expecting a scolding.

It didn't come. "You're so brave, Mom. I'm proud of you." Junie pushed the dog off and wrapped her arms around her mother. "Dad would be proud, too. He would want you to live your life. And not just your life. Your best life."

Those ever-ready tears pricked the backs of Mamie's eyeballs. "Thank you, sweetie. That's what I thought, too. I'm tired of staying in the house. It's time I ventured out and made new friends and saw new places. Thank you for understanding."

"Just promise me one thing, Mom."

"Okay?"

"Please be careful."

"Of course! Always."

"Good. Will you be taking Babs with you?"

"I wouldn't think of leaving her home by herself."

"You bought a camping trailer?

Mamie and Junie's attention riveted to the door through which Junie's older brother Tyler had entered without knocking. He slammed it like he always did. It was a wonder he hadn't worn out the hinges on that heavy front door, the one that had been installed when Mamie and West built the house before the kids were born. Tyler's habit of slamming doors had been a sore spot with his father. His mother decided to overlook it. The door had survived this long—Tyler would soon be

...yler. Fancy having both my children here at ...e. If I had known, I would have prepared a ...rt or something." She patted the sofa next to her. "Come have a seat."

Tyler obliged as his mother explained how she came to be the new owner of the old trailer.

"That's great, Mom. Why don't you show it to us?"

After they followed her outside, Mamie proudly showed off her new acquisition as Tyler brought her up to date on her four-year-old grandson.

"I can't wait to hear about your shenanigans, Mom. When is your first campout?" he asked.

"I'm still looking for one close by. I'll let you know."

"You better," both of her children said, kissing her on each cheek.

After Junie and Tyler left, Mamie resumed her search for campouts and found that one was being held less than an hour away that very month. Carefully following the online instructions, she signed up, hoping to get in. She had learned that campouts were limited to a certain number because campgrounds only had so many sites and their meeting rooms had certain capacities. Maybe she would get in this time. Magnolia Bluff. Even though it was fairly close, she had never been there before.

Wanting to play, Babs would not leave her alone as she scrolled through an online superstore searching for bedding, curtains, and fabric. She insisted upon her owner's attention by placing her paw on the edge of the laptop.

"What do you think, Babs? What color scheme should we go with?" After clicking through hundreds of thumbnails, Mamie finally decided. *I think I'll do a cheery yellow theme with blue accents to go with the outside of the trailer. But first, I better take some measurements.*

Cooler temperatures and longer shadows marked the end of the June day, but Mamie opened the camper door and pulled herself inside, realizing that she hadn't looked at camper steps while shopping online. She flipped on a light and made quick work of measuring the windows and bench cushions, jotting the measurements down as she went. Before leaving the camper, she remembered to pick up the key lying on the table so she could lock it up for the night.

"Goodnight, sweet little camper," Mamie said as she turned the light off. She couldn't wait to get back to her laptop to finish her order and see if she had been accepted to the campout. It was like Christmas in June.

For the first time in a long time, she crawled into bed without feeling like loneliness was crawling into bed with her. Even with Babs snuggled beside her, she usually felt it more keenly at night than at any other time.

Tonight was different. Buying the camper and ordering things online for it had given her a new sense of purpose she had lacked since West's death. She fell asleep imagining the camper after it was fully decorated, and all the adventures she would have with it. Anticipation had replaced the dread of getting up in the morning.

***

Mamie downed her coffee and breakfast cereal

before heading outdoors. She couldn't recall when she had gotten out of bed so early. The morning air was pleasant, punctuated with a cool breeze and the sounds of birds greeting each other in the trees. *Maybe I should get up early more often,* she mused as Babs followed her outside. A school bus lumbered by and came to a stop at a house down the street, reminding Mamie of former days. The sounds of children talking and laughing floated in the air as the bus driver closed the doors and continued on his mission. She didn't miss getting up and going to work every day, but she did miss the kids. Not enough to go back as a substitute teacher, though.

    She gathered car washing tools from the garage and prepared to wash the trailer. As she made her way around to the back side, she noticed a few light dents near the roof that she hadn't noticed earlier. She stood on a stepladder and ran across them lightly with her fingers. What had caused this? Of course. The tree branches she had driven under. They had dented the skin. Who knew how delicate it was? *That's why it's called skin*, she supposed. She would have to be more careful.

    Upset with herself at damaging her little Scottie, Mamie washed the outside gently but thoroughly, soaking herself almost as much as the camper, and using muscles she had long forgotten were there. She would pay in the next day or two when they made their presence known. When she finished, she stepped back to admire her work. Shiny as a new penny, it gleamed in the sunshine.

    "What a pretty little camper you are!" She laughed, wondering if Mr. Benson was listening on the other side of the privacy fence between their properties.

When Starla arrived for lunch, she caught Mamie scrubbing the inside of the camper, her clothes wet and her shoulder-length blonde hair escaping the ball cap she was wearing.

"Look at this!" Starla exclaimed as she slammed her car door shut.

"Ow," Mamie said as her head hit the corner of the cupboard above her.

Starla poked her head inside the door. "Sorry about that. Am I too early?"

Mamie straightened, pulled her rubber gloves off, and threw them in the sink. She wiped sweat off her forehead and grinned at her friend. "I almost forgot. I asked you over for lunch, didn't I?"

"Don't tell me you're going to make me starve."

"Never. But look at my new toy! What do you think?"

Starla smirked. "I think you may have morphed into a boy, talking about your new toy."

Mamie laughed. "You may be right, but isn't she cute?"

Starla surveyed the interior of the 14-foot trailer, taking in the bed, table, benches, cupboards, sink, and everything else. "You really think you can sleep in here?" She adjusted the pink *Dog Mom* baseball cap holding her brunette ponytail.

"Cute cap. I need one of those."

"Thanks. I thought it was appropriate for a woman with three chihuahuas."

"Absolutely, and yes, I do think I can sleep in here. It'll be like my very own little playhouse," Mamie said. "It'll be so pretty when I get my new bedding and curtains in it, and I'm going to look for someone to make new cushion covers. It's in such good shape that I don't even need to paint the inside. It'll be perfect for Babs and me."

"Good thing you're short. I can't imagine staying in such a tiny place with my long legs, especially with an animal. You need a chihuahua."

"Plenty of room for Babs and me. It'll be fun. Open the cabinets and you'll see all the storage. Plus, there is storage under the bench seats and under the bed. I'll keep my Boston, thanks."

Starla dutifully opened a cabinet door and peered inside. "I'll take your word for it. Now, what's for lunch?"

We've been friends since college and raised our children together. Couldn't you be a little more excited for me, Starla Gleason? Mamie's disappointment must have shown on her face.

"Aw, Mames, I'm sorry. I'm glad you've found something to be excited about. I bet you're going to have a blast with this little camper. And maybe I'm a bit jealous that I'm not as brave as you. I could never pull a trailer. Dave would never agree to me even having one."

Mamie smiled. "You could do it, Starla. Lots of women do. It's really not as hard as it looks."

"I'll let you have the adventures and tell me about them."

"If you say so. And since you're mostly interested in lunch, I have fresh chicken salad and sourdough bread,"

Mamie said with a smile on her face.

Chapter Three

THE DAY OF reckoning had arrived. Mamie's request to join the Gals Gone Glamping group had been officially approved with a welcome message from the founder, and she had also been accepted to the campout. Although she hadn't been to church since West had gotten sick, she remembered a lady in her church who sewed, and had agreed to make new seat cushion covers if Mamie promised to come back. Mamie did but made no promises as to when. Her new seat covers had been finished and put on just in time for the campout. The camper was ready for her maiden voyage.

Mamie had spent every available hour for the past few weeks scrubbing, decorating, researching, and practicing. The grocery store parking lot after hours had been a perfect place to practice backing up and turning. She felt like she was ready to tow Miss Maisie, the name she had given her camper, the forty miles to the RV resort.

Mamie had not been able to sleep for all the thoughts running through her mind—going over her lists again and again, reciting the steps of hitching the trailer to her car, wondering how her dog might do on the trip, and what her fellow campers might be like.

"I can't believe I'm really going to do this," she told Babs.

Babs watched her owner make several trips loading luggage, bags of food, and her cooler. The last time she had used that cooler was on vacation with West and the kids. It had graduated to vintage, much like herself. While it sported scuffs and dents, she sported wrinkles and extra pounds. No matter. Vintage was good.

As Mamie finished checking off everything on her lists, she noticed Babs lying on the kitchen floor, her head on her front paws, dejection all over her furry face. Mamie grinned and went to the laundry room to retrieve the dog's harness and leash from their hooks by the back door. Babs's head popped up. She could always hear the jangle of the metal parts from any area of the house.

"Want to go?" Mamie said.

"Go" being the magic word, Babs suddenly became a wriggling mess, twisting and turning so much that Mamie had to pin the dog between her knees to get the harness on her. She finally settled down and waited at the back door as the leash was clipped on. "This would be a lot easier if you could be still, you silly girl."

It only took a few short minutes for Mamie to realize she should have hitched up before loading up. In fact, it might have been a good idea to hitch up the night before. Even so, with the help of the car's backup camera she was able to get the hitch lined up to the trailer jack, but then she realized that she needed to crank the jack high enough for the hitch ball to fit under the coupler. She unlocked the padlock that secured the ball and then got into the car to back up.

It only took her a few tries to line the hitch and trailer tongue up and get the ball under the receptacle, but as she cranked up the jack, it wouldn't drop over the ball. *Haven't I done everything right? What have I done wrong, West?* She already felt the whole neighborhood had been watching her back up, get out of the car, look at the hitch, get back in the car, pull forward, back up, repeat.

She got out of the car again to look at the hitch. She even tried to rattle the coupler, hoping it would grab the ball. There was no rattling the coupler, and nothing happened. Now what?

She glanced at Babs curled in a ball in her dog bed in the front seat. "You're no help."

Digging her phone from her purse, she opened the YouTube app. There had to be a video about hitching a camper to an SUV.

"Need any help, Missy?"

Babs popped up and barked as Mamie almost dropped her phone.

"Mr. Benson!" He stood next to the passenger side window that she had rolled down. He must have been watching her from his living room window.

She got out and followed him as he inspected the back of her car.

"You gotta lift up this latch here so the ball can go in." He flipped the lever on the coupler, and as soon as he did there was a thump as the ball popped under it. "Now you need to lock it. Want me to do it?"

Mamie swallowed, feeling the heat of embarrassment coloring her face. "Sure," she murmured. *Oh, for Pete's sake.* Beads of perspiration rolled down the small of her back.

"There," he said as he closed the padlock. "Don't forget to hook up your chains and lights."

"Oh yes," Mamie said, her face coloring again. How could she have forgotten those? "Thank you, Mr. Benson."

"Any time. I'm gonna go refill my coffee mug, but I'll come back to help you check your lights, okay? I've already seen the *Perry Mason* episode that's showing right now. Don't go anywhere until I get back."

"Okay, I won't." Mamie shook her head as he headed to his house. It was sweet of him to be concerned about her. *My resident dad. Maybe he isn't nosy at all. Maybe it's just genuine fatherly concern.* She finished plugging in the trailer lights, secured the safety chains, and straightened. Yep, this was too much work to do just before leaving. Next time she'd definitely hook up the night before. If there was a next time, after all the trouble.

As she got back in the driver seat, she noticed that Babs was napping again. Maybe she would be a good traveler. This trip would be the test.

A quick check of the brake, turn signal, and marker lights—with Mr. Benson's help—and Mamie was ready to hit the road. Adrenaline surged through her veins as she wheeled out of her driveway, heading to Hayden's Resort on Burnet Reservoir in Magnolia Bluff.

"Here we go, Babs! Our first camping trip! Woohoo!"

The dog opened her eyes, glanced up at her, and closed them again. At least she was a faithful companion.

As her tires rolled onto the street, a scraping, thumping sound met her ears. In the rearview mirror the trailer rocked side to side as it rolled onto the pavement. Uh oh, she had bottomed out. Should she stop and check for damage? *Yes,* she answered herself as she pulled over to the curb and opened the car door just in time to see Mr. Benson trotting toward her. She hadn't realized he could move so fast at his age.

"Whoa! Did you raise the jack?" he said.

Mamie didn't know what to say. Raise the jack?

Her neighbor shook his head as he cranked the jack all the way up. "Good thing it didn't bend when it hit the street," he said. "You sure you know how to pull this thing?"

Heat flamed in her cheeks. "I guess I forgot that."

"You probably won't forget ever again, now that you've seen what can happen. You're lucky you didn't damage your jack, or your trailer, for that matter. Maybe the city won't charge you to fix that hole in the street." He chuckled as he turned to head back to his house. "Women," Mamie heard him say under his breath.

Babs, who had been sitting up in her dog bed watching the conversation, curled up as Mamie got back into the driver's seat. Maybe Mr. Benson was right. Maybe she didn't know what she was doing. But that last comment had lit a fire under her. She would learn one way or another, and neither way meant she'd stay home, afraid to try.

Chapter Four

IT WAS A short trip from Leander to Magnolia Bluff, with no need for a pitstop. Traffic had been light on the state highway, with only a small section of construction. Mamie felt proud every time someone passed her, especially if they waved. She used to wave or do a thumbs-up at people pulling vintage trailers. Now she was the one others waved at, the one with the cool vintage trailer.

The dog sat up as Mamie's car came to a stoplight in the small town of Magnolia Bluff. As Mamie accelerated, Babs lay down in her bed, content to sleep as her owner navigated new territory. Just complete trust, and no *Are we there yet?* like the children used to ask, which reminded her of another bumper sticker she had seen: *RV there yet?* She smiled, patting the dog's soft fur.

After a few minutes of driving down a winding country road along the Hill Country shores of Burnet Reservoir, a large sign appeared ahead. Hayden's Resort and Campground.

"We're here!" Mamie said. Babs popped up, sniffing and looking out the window. She rolled it down a bit so Babs could get some good smells.

Another large sign, professionally painted and set in a wildflower and cactus bed surrounded by rocks, welcomed them into the campground. She pulled the car and camper up to the designated area next to the office and stopped. "Stay here, baby girl. I'll be right back."

She rolled down the windows, hopped out of the

car and went up the wooden steps onto the porch of the rustic log cabin sporting a sign that read *Office. Campers register here.*

"Howdy. Welcome to Hayden's Resort and Campground. How can I help you?" An older gentleman with a friendly smile greeted her from behind the counter as she opened the old-fashioned screen door. A small box television was showing an episode of *Murder She Wrote*, one of the classic TV shows Mamie and West used to watch together. He had always reminded her not to tell him who the culprit was, because she usually figured it out before he did. He had also told her she should have been a detective instead of a teacher.

"Hello, I have a reservation," she said, swallowing the lump that had formed in her throat. Another grief trigger.

"Are you with them Gals Gone Glamping?" He looked and sounded like a bonafide Texas country boy, complete with plaid shirt, denim overalls, and a toothpick hanging out of his mouth.

"Yes, I am. I'm Mamie West."

"All right then. Let's get you fixed up."

Mamie filled out the campground paperwork, paid her balance, and received her campsite assignment with a map showing her where to park. She was relieved when her host told her there was someone waiting outside to lead her to it.

"If you need anything, the store's fully stocked, and there's ice outside for $3.50 a bag. We open at 7:00 am and close at 8:00 pm. There's an emergency phone number on your map for after hours. Enjoy your stay."

"Thank you." Mamie returned to her SUV where Babs waited patiently. A handsome young man in a golf cart motioned for her to follow him. Winding through the campground shaded with tall oak and pecan trees, he stopped in front of a campsite, but her heart sank when she realized she would have to back the trailer in. After he pointed to where she would park, he wheeled around to return to the office. He must have seen the expression on her face because he stopped outside her car window.

"Can you do it, or would you like some help?" he smiled. He couldn't have been more than twenty years old. Blond curls escaped a ball cap that had seen better days.

Mamie hesitated. Should she try to do it herself?

He took his cue from her pause. "I don't mind backing it in for you if you want. Or I can help you."

"It's just that I've never backed her up before. I mean, I practiced in a parking lot, but never at a campground."

"Let me help guide you. The only way to learn is to do it and then keep practicing."

Practical wisdom from such a young man. "Okay, I guess you're right. Just tell me what to do." She glanced at Babs who looked at her, probably wondering when she would be allowed out of the vehicle. "Cross your fingers for me. Or paws, or paw toes. Whatever."

But the dog laid her head down and closed her eyes as Mamie followed the young man's instructions to pull forward and use her door mirrors to help guide her into the spot. He told her to turn her steering wheel in the direction she wanted the trailer to go, but that didn't seem to help much. Using the side mirrors and looking out her window helped most of all. With his coaching she had the trailer in its spot in just a few minutes, although a couple of times, he'd had to yell at her to stop when she got too close to a tree. He never lost his cool, though, not like Mr. Benson.

"You did it, ma'am! Good job. You'll be a pro in no time." The young man wiped his brow with the back of his hand and sat in the golf cart.

"I couldn't have done it without your help. Maybe I should write a book called *Glamping for Dummies*."

He laughed. "Believe me, there are people way more qualified to write that book than you are. You did great."

"You're very kind. What's your name, by the way?" Mamie asked as she got out of the car.

"Brady. Brady Hayden. It was my pleasure. I'll be seeing you around. Let me know if you need anything."

"Hayden. As in Hayden's Resort?"

"Yes, ma'am, my aunt owns the resort. My uncle built it, but he passed away a while ago."

"I'm sorry to hear that. Thank you for your help, Brady. Nice to meet you." Mamie waved as he took off. She glanced around her campsite, noticing there were other campers nearby, but not too close. Though the campsites were unpaved, they were packed hard and seemed to be level. Picnic tables and firepits were also provided at each site. Mamie was pleased to see the bathhouse just a few yards away, handy for a gal with no bathroom in her trailer.

It was time to disconnect the trailer and set it up.

But first Babs needed a break. She let the dog out and followed her down the lane past some other campers. Other ladies were milling about setting up their sites, some visiting and chatting and laughing. Maybe soon Mamie would be able to do the same. She decided to take the initiative and waved at a couple of ladies nearby who had glanced up as she walked toward them.

"Hello," she called.

"Hello!"

"Are y'all with the Gals Gone Glamping group?"

"The Three Gees? Yes, we are. Are you?" The one nearer her approached. Babs wiggled, wanting to make a new friend. *Three Gees. Cute name for the group.* Mamie thought. *Catchier than Gals Gone Glamping.*

"I just joined. This is my first camping trip." As the dog sniffed the woman's shoes, Mamie said, "This is Babs. She doesn't bite, but she may jump on you and scratch you without meaning to."

"It's fine. I'm a fur mama, too. She's just smelling my dogs." The woman extended her hand. "I'm Lou and this is Florence." The other lady had joined them.

"I'm Mamie." She extended her hand to them both. "Pleased to meet you."

"Where is your campsite?"

"Just a couple of spaces down. Number 31, I believe."

"Oh my gosh, is that your cute little camper?" Florence cried.

"Yes, I just got her."

"I just love vintage campers. One of these days I'm going to get one for myself. What kind of trailer is yours?"

"She's a 1962 Scotsman Scottie. This is my first trip with her."

"Could we take a look inside?"

"Let her get set up, first, Florence. If you don't mind, we'd like to have a peek later on," Lou said.

Mamie beamed. "Certainly! I just finished decorating the inside, so I'll be happy to show it off."

"Do you have a special name for it?" Florence asked. "Lots of ladies give their campers names."

"I do, actually. Her name is Miss Maisie."

"Love it! How did you come up with that?"

"Good grief, let her go, Florence. If you need help setting up, unhitching, anything, just holler," Lou said as Mamie coaxed Babs on.

Friendly ladies. She hoped everyone else was just as warm. After Babs had walked a bit and relieved herself, Mamie put her back in the car and went about unhitching. Unplug lights, disconnect chains, unlock hitch, chock trailer tires, crank jack down until hitch ball clears, pull out from under coupler, crank jack down, eyeball to see if the trailer looks level, lock hitch, set trailer stabilizers in place. Done!

And all by herself. Except for Mr. Benson's help. And Brady's. But she was here now, ready to get set up. First things first. Plug in to the power pole and make sure she had electricity.

After plugging in the extension cord, she entered

the trailer and flipped the switch to her outside light. Nothing. She flipped another switch for one of the lamps inside. Nothing. The electricity was not working. Mamie broke out in a cold sweat. *Oh no! Now what?* All that work and she would have to change campsites. Her power pole wasn't working.

She went outside to get Babs out of the car and then stood in place, wondering what she should do. Should she walk all the way back to the office and tell them the power wasn't working? It was at least a hundred-yard walk. She went to the power pole to make sure the cord hadn't fallen out. No, it was still plugged in. She had plugged her extension cord into a 30-amp adapter just like the lady on the YouTube video had advised and plugged that into the 30-amp outlet. Was the adapter defective?

It was at that moment that Brady just happened to ride by on his golf cart with a load of trash on the back. He waved and she motioned for him to stop.

He rolled into her campsite and braked, leaning across the seat with his left arm draped over the steering wheel. If she had been thirty years younger, he wouldn't have had a chance. "What can I do for you, ma'am?" he drawled.

"I don't seem to have any electricity at this campsite," Mamie said, trying to ignore the youthful muscles in those tanned arms of his. His white tank top, wet with sweat, clung to his toned torso. There was no fat on this guy. No tattoos, either. Clean cut, all-American boy.

"Let me check that for you." He clambered out

of the golf cart and walked to the power pole, Mamie following him. "I see what the problem is. You have to switch this breaker to the *on* position. Like this."

He stepped back so she could see what he did as he flipped the switch. She felt her own blood betraying her as it rushed to her cheeks. "Oh," she said. What else could she say? Something so simple, but no one had told her. West was probably laughing himself off his cloud.

"It's a common mistake new campers make," Brady said, patting her shoulder.

"Today has been a learning curve, for sure. Thank you for being so nice about it. I feel like such a dummy."

"No worries. Everybody has to learn sometime. Let me know if there is anything else you need."

As Mamie watched Brady get back into his golf cart, her mind went wistful with memories from years ago when another strapping young man named West stole her heart. *What I wouldn't give to feel those strong arms around me again,* she thought as Brady drove off.

A bloodcurdling scream shattered her thoughts. Babs let out a fearful bark as goosebumps popped out on Mamie's skin. What in the world?

Chapter Five

MAMIE PUT BABS in the camper, switched on the air conditioner, locked the door, and sprinted toward the source of the scream.

"What's going on?" she asked as she joined the ladies gathered at the back of one of the RV sites a couple of loops from hers. The campsites in the RV park were situated in rows with loops of road between the rows. What was everyone looking at? She followed the eyes of everyone staring at something on the ground.

"The only good snake is a dead snake," the woman in the center of the circle said. She held a long metal rod in one hand as she stared at the creature she had killed.

Snake? Mamie moved closer to see what appeared to be a copperhead lying near the water faucet. Of course, she was no snake expert, but West had killed one in a flowerbed once, and she remembered its coloration. Her skin crawled. Camping meant getting close to nature, but it had never occurred to her that she might be getting close to snakes and other varmints, too. Weren't wild creatures afraid of humans? Why would they be in a campground where there were lots of people?

"I hope there aren't any more around here," one lady said. "I didn't bring my snakebite kit."

Snakebite kit? Was there such a thing? Mamie shuddered at the thought of being bitten by a snake. She would die of fright before the venom got her.

Brady rolled up in his golf cart. "What's going on, ladies?"

"I found this in my campsite," said the woman pointing at the dead snake with the metal rod. Mamie noticed she was wearing a name tag that said *Darla.*

Brady got out to inspect the snake and confirmed Mamie's suspicions. "Copperhead. We've found a few this year. Everyone all right?" He scanned the group with his long-lashed, bright blue eyes.

Some of the women murmured "yes" while others nodded their heads. Darla poked the dead snake with the rod.

"I'm glad I had this awning crank rod in my hand. As soon as I saw it, I smacked it as hard as I could. Like I always say, 'The only good snake is a dead snake.'"

Mamie noticed Brady roll his eyes and shake his head before gesturing for Darla to give him the rod. She frowned as she handed it to him. He made fast work of looping the dead creature around the end as the women backed up a few feet.

"Watch where you step, ladies," Brady said as he tossed the snake into the back of his golf cart, "especially around logs, rocks, or leaves. Although all snakes aren't dangerous, there could be more of these guys around. Cooler temperatures bring them out. Coldblooded creatures like the warmth of sunshine."

"Great," one woman muttered as she turned to leave. The others followed, each headed in a different direction toward their respective campsites.

"You mean there may be more?" one woman said, surveying the ground around her.

"I'm afraid so. Just watch your step."

Mamie watched the athletic young man climb back into his golf cart. How he must have loved telling his friends about the silly old women at the campground. As he drove away with a smile and wave, she wondered about his family. Did he live with his parents? Did he have a girlfriend or brothers and sisters? He was certainly patient with women, but then he was paid to be helpful, or at least he should have been. Hopefully his aunt paid him to work. The niceness was a bonus.

"He's a cutie, huh?" Lou said from behind her.

"And nice, too," Mamie replied. "I'm glad no one was bitten. Wonder what he will do with that dead snake?"

"Probably throw it in the lake," Lou said. "That's what I would do with it."

Darla slapped the ground with the awning rod that Brady had returned to her. "I might have been bit if I hadn't been watching. Them copperheads love hiding in leaves. He ain't gonna bother no one now." She laughed.

The ladies who had gathered around Darla's trailer had dispersed, leaving Mamie and Lou with Darla.

"I guess we should all be on the lookout," Lou said. "Good catch, Darla."

"Thanks. Are you new?" Darla asked Mamie.

"Yes, this is my first campout. I'm Mamie."

"We usually don't have such a dramatic beginning to our weekend." Darla laughed. "Where are you from?"

"Leander. Not too far from here. Where are you ladies from?"

"Daingerfield," Lou said.

"Avinger," Darla said.

"Very nice to meet you, and yes, that was certainly exciting. I think I'll go back to my campsite to check on my dog and finish setting up. I'll see you at dinner."

"Let us know if you need any help setting up. We're old pros," Lou said. "And watch that dog in the leaves and weeds. I'd hate to see it get bit."

"Me too!" Mamie said with a shudder.

Babs was curled on the bed when she entered the camper. The small a/c unit had cooled it to seventy-two degrees. The weather was mild enough that Mamie turned off the a/c and cranked open the jalousie windows to let the breeze blow through. Huge live oak trees around her campsite shaded her trailer, making the interior pleasant enough for Babs when she had to be left alone.

As Mamie rolled out her new patio rug and set stabilizer pins underneath the trailer, Babs curled up in her dog pillow on the rug, happy to be near her mistress. She watched Mamie set out folding chairs and a bowl of water.

"There you go, sweetie pie."

Sitting in a camp chair, she checked her phone, not really expecting any messages, but one never knew. Her parents were getting up in years, and she wanted to be available if they needed her. She also wanted to know if her children tried to get in touch with her. It didn't hurt to check, but there were no missed calls or texts.

After checking her email and social media, Mamie decided to take Babs for a walk around the campground.

"Want to go for a walk, baby? Dinnertime isn't for a couple of hours, so let's explore." Babs's wiggling bottom made it almost impossible to get her harness and leash on her, but Mamie managed. She had to giggle at the dog's excitement even if it caused some back strain. Holding Babs's leash, Mamie locked her camper door and headed toward the nearby lake.

The water lapped gently at the shore beyond the office and marina where Mamie had entered the RV park. Burnet Reservoir spanned hundreds of acres and provided hours of recreation for anyone who enjoyed boating, fishing, camping, water-skiing, picnicking, or swimming. The campground had its own swimming area designated by buoys, the sandy beach dotted with colorful umbrellas and lounge chairs. A few young children splashed in the water while their parents hovered nearby, and several women lay stretched out on loungers, no doubt working on their tans. Mamie wondered if they belonged to Gals Gone Glamping. She decided to find out.

"Hello, ladies," she said as she approached.

They turned, one lady holding on to her straw hat as the breeze picked up.

"Hi," said another.

"Are you all a part of Gals Gone Glamping?" Mamie asked. Babs became a wiggle-bottom again as her owner kept a tight grip on her leash. She would have jumped all over the ladies in her excitement to make new friends.

"The Three Gees? Yes, are you?" the lady with the hat said.

"I'm new to the group. I just wanted to introduce

myself. I'm Mamie West and this is my dog Babs."

"Cute dog! Why don't you pull up a chair and join us?" the hat lady said.

One of the others got up and dragged a chair closer. "Here you go. I'm Marlene, and this is Sissy and Bertie." Bertie was the one with the hat.

So far, every woman Mamie had seen in the group seemed much like her—middle-aged or older and eager to make friends. She settled into the chair Marlene had offered, keeping Babs away from the others.

"We were just talking about how this group has grown in its two years of existence," Marlene said, settling into her chair and extending long legs under knee-length denim shorts. Shiny gray strands of hair punctuated naturally blond shoulder-length hair. Jackie O-style sunglasses rested upon her freckled face. Red lips framed unnaturally white teeth. Mamie noticed the nails on her hands and feet sported matching red polish. In her bright white button-down shirt, Marlene was an attractive middle-aged lady. Mamie suddenly felt a bit self-conscious as she glanced down at her own unmanicured hands.

Sissy carried a bit more weight than the others, but she was attractive with short white hair, minimal makeup, and a touch of color on her lips. Mamie couldn't tell if she was wearing eye makeup under her aviator sunglasses. Her fingernails were bare, as were the toenails visible in Birkenstock sandals. A pink pullover polo shirt and khaki capri pants comprised her outfit.

Bertie sat in her lounger in rolled-up overalls and a tee shirt with rubber flipflops on her feet. No makeup or nail polish on this lady. Her short gray hair was topped with a baseball cap.

"Marlene and Sissy founded the group," Bertie said. "I joined a couple months afterwards."

"Where are you ladies from?" Mamie said.

"We're all from the Dallas area," Sissy said. "I'm from Allen, Bertie's from Grapevine, and Marlene is from Plano. Marlene and I went to high school together in Plano, and we've kept in touch. I moved to Allen when my husband got a job there."

"Bertie, how did you meet them?" Mamie wanted to find out everything she could about the group.

"I was looking for a camping group and I came across them on social media."

"How many ladies were at your first campouts?"

"Only about five," Sissy said, "but we grew quickly when word got out. Now we have about two hundred ladies in the group. Of course, they don't all camp at once."

"We're so happy you've joined us," Marlene said. "I hope you are happy with us after the campout is over. We're a bunch of crazy old women." She laughed.

"Not everyone is old," Sissy said.

"That's right, we do have some younger ones. But it's mostly us older ones who have the time to do it. The younger ones work and have young families," Marlene said.

"What about you? What do you do?" Bertie asked Mamie.

Mamie swallowed. Should she tell them about West? Was she ready to share him with total strangers? She glanced at Babs, who had settled on the sand watching birds fly over the lake. As if sensing her doubts, Babs looked up at her. Mamie patted her on the back, warm from the sunshine.

"I was a schoolteacher, but I do tutoring from home, now," Mamie said.

"We were teachers, too!" Bertie said with a smile. "What did you teach?"

"High school English."

"I taught first grade," Bertie said.

"Junior high science," Marlene said.

"High school home economics," said Sissy. "There are a lot of teachers in this group. I guess teaching makes you want to travel. Or it just makes you crazy." She laughed.

"Do you have family at home?" Marlene asked.

This was it. She had to tell them. "No, my children are grown and gone, and I lost my husband last year," Mamie said.

Marlene leaned over and placed her red-tipped hand on Mamie's arm. "I am so sorry to hear that, Mamie. We have several widows in this group. You have lots of support with us."

"What was his name?" Bertie asked.

"Bertie," Sissy said with a warning in her voice.

"No, it's fine. His name was West. Dalton West, but everyone called him West." Tears sprang to her eyes as she received their looks of sympathy. She shouldn't have told them. She didn't want everyone feeling sorry for her. She got up. "I think it's time to walk Babs some more. It's been a pleasure meeting you. I'll see you at dinner."

They all glanced at each other before Marlene said, "Pleasure meeting you too, Mamie. Let us know if you need anything. See you in a little while."

Mamie forced a smile as she pulled Babs along with her. Heading down the shoreline, careful to avoid getting her shoes wet, she let Babs stop and sniff whenever she wanted to. The ladies were nice, but talking about West to people she didn't know was unnerving. She didn't want to come across as needy. "Let us know if you need anything," Marlene had said. Had she seemed needy?

Mamie walked to the end of the beach, a quarter mile from where the ladies still sat sunning themselves. She didn't want to walk back their way, so she continued up a rocky hill where tall grasses interspersed with large rocks. A great place for snakes. Maybe Babs would find them before the snakes found Mamie and Babs.

Chapter Six

A TRAIL WOUND its way through a patch of trees and undergrowth, and Mamie followed it, thinking it would end up at the campground. She and Babs had covered quite a bit of territory, though, and no RVs were in sight. Should she turn back? She checked her phone. There was still an hour before dinner, but she needed to get back and put her potluck dish together. She had decided to bring garlic rolls, but they were in the cooler and needed to be warmed.

"Are you lost?" A gravelly voice behind them caused Babs to pull on the leash and bark as the fur on the back of her neck stood at attention. Mamie's heart leaped while her adrenaline surged. She whirled around to see who had spoken.

A grizzled older man wearing dirty jeans, a stained and holey tee shirt, and worn-out hiking shoes stood in the pathway. He carried a cane fishing pole and tin bucket. One bristly cheek bulged as a toothless grin dripped tobacco juice. Something about him made the hair on the back of Mamie's neck stand on end. His eyes raked over her, making her feel uncomfortable and exposed.

"Beg your pardon?" Mamie said. Babs continued barking.

"That's a loud dog," the man said. "Do you know where you're going?"

"Yes, we're fine," Mamie said, trying to sound more convinced than she felt. She wanted to ask if the trail led to the campground, but she didn't want to engage with him more than she had to. Why had they come this way?

"All right." He spit to the side, which turned Mamie's stomach. "If you're lost, I can show you which way to go."

"I'm sure we'll find it," Mamie said, tugging on Babs's leash. The dog wouldn't budge. Her constant barking made Mamie's head hurt.

"Not this way, you won't," the old man said. "You passed a trail back yonder that you should take if you want to get back to the campground. This way takes you to the dam."

Mamie blinked. Should she thank him? Should she walk past him back to the trail? Why hadn't she packed her revolver with her? West had always said if she wasn't going to carry it with her, what was the point of having it? He was right. She would feel much safer if she had it with her. Now to figure out how to get past the man without Babs jumping on him or biting him.

She gripped the leash tightly, bringing Babs as close as she could and walked toward him, following the edge of trail, leaving as much space as possible between them and him. What if he grabbed her when she was within reach? There was no one else around to hear her if she screamed. Certainly no one had come to investigate Babs's incessant barking.

As she reached him, Babs tugged, trying to get at him, all the while barking. Baring her sharp white teeth, she leaped at him as best she could while being restrained by the leash. Mamie rushed past him, not caring if she seemed rude. Thank God he didn't touch her. He backed up to allow them to pass, those disgusting teeth grinning at her with brown liquid oozing through them.

"Thank you," she murmured as she passed him, every nerve in her body on high alert. Never again would she walk Babs without carrying her trusty revolver. Even if she never used it, its presence would be reassuring, and showing it might scare away a threat.

Mamie didn't dare turn around to look at him as she hurried Babs along the path in the direction from which they had come. She didn't want to know if he was following her. She just wanted to get away from him. Soon the path she had missed came into view, and as she rounded the corner, she sneaked a glance to see if anyone was following. No one was behind her. As grateful as she was, she didn't trust her own eyes. She broke into a trot and ran as fast as her middle-aged legs, hips, and knees would allow her to go, with Babs keeping up beside her. Almost out of breath, she was finally able to see the RV park. Past the beach where she had met the three ladies earlier, she collapsed onto a bench outside the clubhouse, needing rest before returning to her camper. Babs lay on her side on the ground beside the bench, panting. They both needed a good drink of water. And maybe she needed to join a gym. She was badly out of shape.

***

Potluck dinner consisted of an array of casseroles, main dishes, salads, vegetables, and breads, along with an impressive offering of desserts. Mamie's rolls disappeared before the line ended. After one of the women asked a blessing on the food, Mamie went through the line and then carried her plate to an empty chair at a table occupied by several ladies she didn't recognize.

"Anyone sitting here?" she asked.

"You are!" A bright smile belonging to a pretty lady about Mamie's age greeted her.

"Thanks," she said as she set her plate down and took the seat.

"Anyone need a drink?" another of the ladies asked.

Mamie realized she had forgotten to get hers. "I do," she said.

"Tea or water?"

"Tea, please."

"Sweet or unsweet?"

"Sweet, please."

"Got it!" The wiry little woman dashed off before Mamie could thank her.

"Are you new?" the woman with the pretty smile asked.

"Yes, this is my first campout."

"Welcome, then! I'm Sheila, this is my daughter Tessa, and the one who went to get your tea is Lanie."

"I'm Mamie. Pleased to meet you." She placed her napkin in her lap and picked up her fork.

The women proceeded to enjoy their dinner while asking Mamie the usual questions about where she was from and how long she had been camping. She learned that the three ladies were from the same hometown of Weatherford and camped together often. Sheila was a pastor's wife, while her daughter taught Sunday school classes with her husband. Lanie managed the church bookstore where they all attended. Mamie had stopped going to church when her husband became ill and had never returned, although she had always intended to. Guilt niggled at her. She needed to go back, and she had promised the lady who had sewn her cushions, but it would be so hard without West by her side.

Although Sheila had asked her if she was involved in church, she didn't press the issue when Mamie told her she hadn't been in a long time. The three ladies continued their lively chatter and invited her to join them around the campfire later that evening.

After everyone had eaten and the meeting room had been cleaned, the ladies dispersed--some meeting around campfires, others retiring to their campers, some staying in the clubhouse to play card games. Mamie went to check on Babs, put her leash on, grabbed a folding chair, and followed the smell of the main firepit near the office where about twenty women gathered. The lake, with its shimmering moonlit waves and the lights of lake houses on the opposite shore, was visible down the gradual slope from the office near the entrance. Whoever designed the campground made sure to provide lake views from every campsite.

"Join us, Mamie!" she heard as she set her chair next to Lou. Florence was seated next to her, and across from them sat Marlene, Sissy, and Bertie. Sheila, Tessa, and Lanie followed her and set their chairs next to hers. She had found her tribe. *This was a good idea, West*, she thought with a warm and fuzzy feeling. Babs didn't even try to jump on anyone. She just settled at Mamie's feet. It was apparently her tribe as well, even though she was the only four-legged fur baby present.

Darla and another woman Mamie hadn't met tended the fire, poking the logs with fireplace tools, and what looked like the same metal rod that Darla had used to kill the snake earlier. *The fire is cozy, but West's long-sleeved shirt would have been nice,* she thought. The flames cast a warm glow on the faces surrounding the firepit. She stared at the flickering tongues of fire while catching snippets of conversation that floated around her.

"I don't know where she is. She said she was coming. Maybe she had to call her daughter."

"I'll be so glad when I can retire. This job is about to drive me crazy. I have only two more years."

"Did you get a new car? That's not the one you used to drive, is it?"

"We had to put him in a nursing home. We just couldn't do it anymore."

Mamie's ears perked up with that remark as her chest tightened. The decision to place West in a care facility had been one of the most difficult decisions of her lifetime. She felt for anyone in that situation and cast a surreptitious glance at the woman who had said it, looking for signs of the strain she had known all too well. But the woman was turned away from her so that her face wasn't visible.

"So, Mamie, where do you go to church? I mean, when you go?" Sheila asked, breaking into her thoughts about West.

Mamie stalled, trying to come up with an answer, but in the end, all she could say was the truth. "I haven't been to church in a long time," she admitted.

"Oh." Sheila, Tessa, and Lanie glanced at one another as Mamie stared at the fire. She would have to tell them, too.

"My husband and I used to go, but then he got sick, and I couldn't go anymore because I had to take care of him."

"Is your husband still sick?" Lanie asked.

"No. I mean, he passed away last year."

Lanie put her hand on Mamie's arm, just as Marlene had done earlier. "I'm so sorry. I didn't mean to..."

"It's fine, Lanie. It is what it is." A lump formed in her throat. When would that stop happening?

"Can we pray for you?" Sheila asked, touching Mamie's shoulder.

"I suppose so," she said.

"Tessa, would you, please?"

Now? Mamie thought, her eyes growing wide. In the middle of the gathering around the campfire, the four ladies bowed their heads while Tessa prayed for strength and healing for Mamie, who couldn't stop the tears that rolled down her cheeks. She was glad for the shadows. Some of the other ladies glanced at them, but they kept on talking with each other, even laughing. They had no idea, and Mamie didn't expect them or even want them to.

"Thank you, ladies. I appreciate it," she said, wiping her face with the back of one hand.

"Any time," Sheila said. "And know that you will be

in our prayers." She stood. "May I hug you?"

Mamie nodded and stood, receiving a hug from each of the three women.

And then a shot rang out.

Chapter Seven

EVERYONE GLANCED AT each other, some crying out with alarm. Several jumped to their feet, taking off in the direction of the shot fired. It could be that someone in their group had been hurt or was being threatened. It seemed no one messed with the Three Gees.

The thought crossed Mamie's mind that perhaps they should take cover instead, but she quickly deposited Babs inside her camper and followed the others to a campsite about fifty yards from where they had been sitting. Between Mamie's campsite and the clubhouse on the edge of the woods surrounding the campground sat a newer RV where a small campfire smoldered, surrounded by several folding chairs.

Several ladies had already gathered in an overgrown area behind the late model RV parked there. Some were weeping while others appeared to be in shock. Mamie peered through the crowd.

Lying half hidden under the bushes and vines in the waning daylight was a woman in a solid pink tunic over cropped jeans, her feet clad in expensive sneakers. Her salt and pepper shoulder-length hair splayed around her head and her open eyes chilled Mamie to the bone. She gasped. She had never seen a dead body before, at least not outside a funeral home. Poor woman.

"Is it Sarah?" A slender woman with curly brown hair cried as she joined the group. "I was just talking with her about her daughter's wedding!" She collapsed and wrapped herself around the body, sobbing.

"Sarah's dead, Carly," another woman said after checking Sarah's neck for a pulse. With her fingers, she gently rolled the woman's eyelids closed.

"No!" Carly screamed as several of the other ladies sobbed. One held Carly as she wept.

The panic and sorrow Mamie had experienced when finding out West had passed away washed over her again. Tears sprang to her eyes as emotion threatened to overtake her. Her breathing grew shallow as she remembered how he looked the last time she had seen him in hospice. He had appeared to be asleep. The nurse had to tell her he was gone. She had grasped his hand while kissing his forehead for the last time. He had still been warm. But at the funeral home. . .she shivered. The old familiar knot formed in her gut.

If Sarah was still warm, maybe she could be saved. "Has anyone called 911?" Mamie asked, her voice sounding unnatural to her own ears.

Several of the women turned to stare at her. *Okay, Mamie thought, I guess that was a dumb question.*

"Come on, Carly. There's nothing we can do for her now," the lady who had been holding her said, taking her hand and helping the distraught woman to her feet.

"I'm not leaving her, Hattie."

The sound of sirens pierced the air. Apparently, someone had called 911. The authorities would have to deal with Carly. Mamie's heart went out to her.

"Who would have shot her?" Mamie asked. *Why isn't anyone asking that question? Isn't anyone concerned about a shooter on the loose? Is there a gun near the body?*

Could she have shot herself? Accidentally? On purpose? "Did she own a gun?" she asked aloud.

Carly sobbed even harder.

"What kind of question is that?" Hattie roared as everyone turned to stare at Mamie. "Sarah would never have inflicted harm on herself. I can't believe you would even say that. Sarah was the sweetest, most giving, most cheerful, most caring person you could ever meet."

Sheila took Mamie's arm and stepped aside. "Are you a detective?" she whispered.

Mamie stared at her new friend and shook her head. "No."

"Then why don't we let the authorities figure it out," Sheila said.

Mamie nodded. "You're right, and so is Hattie. I have no right to ask questions. I'm sorry."

The police, fire truck, and ambulance rolled through the park entrance with lights flashing. Although the sirens had been turned off before entering the park, people poured out of their RVs to see what the ruckus was about. Police officers exited their vehicles and approached the scene. Mamie wondered why all the lights if there might be a shooter lurking. The police, apparently unconcerned about being targets themselves, cleared everyone out of the way as they surrounded the area where Sarah's body lay. Yellow police tape went around the campsite as a tearful Carly went inside Sarah's RV and retrieved her Yorkshire terrier. As she held the tiny, confused pooch, Carly retrieved some contact information from her phone for the officer. Then there was a hush as the county coroner arrived to make his declaration.

Mamie figured there was nothing she could do so she said goodnight to Sheila, Tessa, and Lanie and returned to her trailer, praying that no one with a gun was watching her. She grabbed her pistol, stuck it in her pocket, and took Babs for a walk away from the commotion.

"Quite an eventful first campout, huh, Babs? We haven't been here one night and already there's a murder," she said to the dog, who seemed to ignore her as she sniffed along the path for the perfect spot to do her business. "No matter, sweetheart. We'll protect each other. We're fearless that way." Fearless. Even though being outside alone in the dark after there had been a shooting in the park was a little unnerving. *Hurry up, dog.*

After their short walk, she snuggled with Babs in her new bedding, her revolver within easy reach. Then she realized something. This night, her first one camping in her trailer, was supposed to be one to remember. It would certainly be that, but the memory wouldn't be pleasant like she had hoped. She had thought she would be celebrating but now all she wanted to do was shut out the thoughts of gunmen and dead bodies and sleep.

Sleep would not come, though. When she closed her eyes, images of all the people she had met that day flickered through her mind like a horror movie trailer. The toothless grin of the guy she had met on the trail merged with the man who had greeted her in the office, and then melted into young Brady's face. Sarah lay on the ground. When Hattie screamed at Mamie, Sarah opened her eyes. Then Hattie's face morphed into Sheila's. Mamie sat up in bed sweating, although the air conditioner blew so hard and cold that Babs had tunneled deep under the covers.

Mamie grabbed her phone to check the time. A couple of hours had passed since she had crawled into bed. Would she go to sleep tonight? Was the shooter lurking in the campground, searching for another victim? Who had shot Sarah? Was it a random shooting, or had there been a vendetta? Mamie needed answers. Or maybe she just needed to hook up and return home tomorrow. Maybe her new hobby was too dangerous. Maybe she should try pickleball.

No, thousands, maybe even millions of women, went camping all the time and didn't die. She wouldn't let one murder ruin her new venture. She peeked out of the window over her bed to see if any police cars remained at Sarah's trailer. They had all left. She buried herself under the soft covers, her overactive brain finally giving in and allowing her to fall asleep in the wee hours of the morning.

When Babs woke Mamie by pawing at her face —*ouch!*—the sun was already high, warming the small camper. Babs danced impatiently at the door as Mamie pulled one of West's old denim shirts over her pajamas, stuck her pistol in a small crossbody bag, and clipped on the dog's harness and leash. She noticed several women in pajamas sitting around with coffee mugs and felt better about leaving her camper with bedhead while still in her night clothes. What was that saying, "Camping hair, don't care?"

As she passed Lou's and Florence's campsites, Lou called out to her. "Had coffee yet? Join us!"

Mamie nodded. "Thank you! After I walk the dog, I will."

"Bring a chair and a coffee mug."

Mamie gave a thumbs up and followed Babs until she had finished her business. Then Mamie put her back in the trailer before grabbing a folding chair—the one she had forgotten at the firepit the night before and had miraculously appeared at her campsite—and stainless-steel mug and heading to Lou's camper. The Three Gees apparently took care of each other, even when it came to recognizing and returning a forgotten chair. As she had predicted, the conversation was all about Sarah.

"I can't imagine how her family must be taking it," Florence said.

"I talked to Hunter this morning. He's in shock, of course. The whole family is." Carly wiped her eyes and nose with a tissue while Sarah's Yorkie sat on her lap looking forlorn.

"Sarah's husband?" Mamie asked as she set her chair down. Everyone else seemed to know who Hunter was. Lou grabbed Mamie's mug and filled it from a coffee pot sitting on a table next to the camper door. She handed it to Mamie's outstretched hand.

"Thanks."

Lou nodded. "Heck of a way to end a thirty-year marriage. I just can't imagine who would do that to such a sweet woman."

Mamie's head buzzed with questions and possibilities. No one led a perfect life, and everyone had secrets. Maybe Sarah had known something that someone else wanted to keep quiet. Maybe her husband had a reason to get rid of his wife. Maybe he had gambling debts. Maybe he had a huge life insurance policy on her. Maybe she had been having an affair and he was the jealous sort, or maybe she had witnessed a murder. Mamie dared not voice her thoughts, but she was dying to know more about Sarah. She'd always been curious. Even as a child, her mother would warn her about curiosity killing the cat—which she hadn't understood until she was older. Now was not the time, though.

"Poor Dannie, with the wedding only six weeks away. She'll have to finish the preparations herself," said another lady Mamie hadn't met.

"Dannie?" Mamie asked.

"Sarah's daughter. She's getting married soon," Lou said. "Although she might not now that this has happened. That poor family."

Sheila, Tessa, and Lanie pulled up in an SUV with the window rolled down. "We're going into Magnolia Bluff to shop. Anyone want to go with us?" Sheila asked from the driver's seat.

Mamie glanced at the others. Was it heartless to go on a shopping excursion after their friend had been murdered? If it wasn't appropriate, would Sheila be doing it? Should Mamie want to leave? Then again, maybe she'd learn more about Sarah.

"I'll pass," said Lou, "but you go ahead, Mamie. You should have at least a little bit of fun on your first campout." The other ladies nodded in agreement.

"Are you sure? I don't want to be disrespectful. And I'm not even dressed."

"It's not disrespectful. It's what Sarah would want," Lanie piped up.

"She'd be the first to tell us to carry on. Throw on some clothes. We'll wait for you," Sheila said.

Mamie gathered her chair and coffee mug and hurried back to her camper while Sheila and friends got out to chat with the others while they waited. With her dog's eyes on her, she pulled on a pair of cropped jeans and a tee shirt, brushed her teeth, and ran her brush through her unruly hair.

"Don't worry, sweetie, I'll be back soon. Here you go." She tossed Babs a treat before grabbing her purse without the pistol inside and heading out. She could add lipstick in the car. It was time to get to know these ladies and find out what they knew about Sarah.

As she hopped into the back seat of the SUV, all three greeted her.

"We're so glad you could come with us," Sheila said. "We heard there are some cute shops downtown and we want to check them out, and then we thought we would grab lunch."

"Sounds fun," Mamie said. "I hope you don't mind my appearance. I figured camping meant no makeup, although I am about to apply some lipstick."

"Are you kidding? We're not divas. I never wear makeup on a campout," Lanie said.

"Me either," Sheila and Tessa said in unison. Everyone laughed as Mamie pulled her lipstick and compact from her bag. Normally she never went anywhere without foundation and lipstick. Maybelline and Cover Girl loved customers like her.

    Mamie listened as the ladies chattered among themselves. She learned about their church and their families and that they had similar backgrounds to hers. Sheila's husband was a Baptist preacher, Lanie's husband an electrician, and Tessa's an architect. Sheila and Lanie's children were grown, and Tessa's were in junior high and high school. Sheila spent much of her time leading Bible studies and attending church functions, while Lanie's time was consumed with attending her grandchildren's sporting events and hosting church functions. Tessa stayed home and coordinated her teenagers' activities and transportation.

    Mamie's ears perked up when Sheila pulled into a parking space in the downtown square and suggested they pray for Sarah's family before getting out of the car. Mamie listened to the sweet prayer, wondering how well these ladies knew the murder victim. Should she ask? Her curiosity overcame her.

    As they got out of the car, she said, "Was Sarah a good friend of y'all's?"

    Tessa spoke first. "She and I had a lot in common. We had lunch on our own a few times. Her kids are about the same age as mine. Sweet lady," she said as she tossed her long, thick, dark mane.

    "Why would anyone want to kill her?" Mamie said.

    "That's a good question. I can't believe someone could shoot a person in a campground and not be caught. It had to have been a drive-by," Tessa said.

    "A drive-by?"

"Yes, someone must have shot her from a vehicle. I hope the police will be able to find out who."

Mamie shuddered. "Was Sarah outside her camper setting up when it happened?" She'd had no idea.

"It could have been any of us," Tessa said as she held the door open to a women's boutique.

"I don't know about that. I think she was targeted on purpose," Sheila said, shaking her short curly light brown curls. She frowned, blue eyes squinting as she spoke.

"Really?" Mamie said, her curiosity scratching at her insides.

"Her husband has been in and out of jail so many times we've lost count," Lanie said.

That was a new tidbit of information. "Really? Is he a criminal?" Mamie asked.

"He's an alcoholic and has had several DUI's," Sheila said. "He also likes to gamble, so it's possible he has built up a gambling debt and someone wanted to teach him a lesson by killing his wife."

"I think you've watched too much TV," Tessa said.

"It's possible, Tessa," Sheila countered. "You know how the mob can be. And the mob owns the casinos."

"Let's not jump to conclusions," Lanie said. "Besides, we have some serious shopping to do." She opened the door to a shop and stood with one hand on the door and the other on her slim hip, waiting for everyone to enter.

"You've got that right," Sheila laughed.

Once inside the Bohemian Belle Boutique, everyone in the group headed in different directions to check out the clothing and accessories. Mamie stopped at a clothing rack, but her mind was not on the flowy tops she rifled through. Blaming Sarah's death on the mob seemed too easy. That wasn't how the mob operated, according to her knowledge of mafia killings, which derived from TV detective shows. Mobs were more likely to use methods that made people disappear, like tying cement to a body before dumping it into a lake or river. But what did she know?

Several shops later, including a stop for lunch at the Silver Spoon diner, the ladies returned to the campground to rest before that evening's gathering. That night was supposed to be pajama night, with the hostesses providing breakfast for dinner. Mamie had purchased a set of pajamas with little campers all over them and saved them for this campout. She was curious to see what everyone else would wear. If they all shopped at Walmart, they probably had the same pajamas, but she didn't mind. She liked them for herself.

Chapter Eight

MAMIE DIDN'T FEEL like resting, though she could tell by her dog's excitement that she had slept while her owner was away. She wrestled with Babs and finally got the harness and leash snapped on for a walk. Very few ladies were outside, many probably napping or shopping. Mamie waved at those sitting outside and was thankful no one asked her to join them.

She found a bench at the lake's shore overlooking the wide expanse of water. The gentle lapping sounds were so relaxing, she leaned back, stretched her legs out, and crossed her ankles. As Babs finished her sniffing and settled on the ground under Mamie's feet, she closed her eyes and concentrated on the nice breeze coming off the lake. It was a good opportunity to do what she had been needing to do since West passed—be in the moment.

She whispered, "Lord, please be with Sarah's family and friends. Give them comfort. Help the police find out who killed her and bring them to justice. Let me be a comfort to her friends here at the campout, and show me how I can help..."

Her eyes popped open. A jet ski roared dangerously close to a nearby dock. Laughter floated in the air as the two teens riding the machine veered it away from shore. She shook her head as Babs stood and stared at them moving across the lake. Silly kids. They thought they were invincible.

"I've told the lake authorities that the buoys need to be replaced," came a voice from behind her.

"They've gotten so worn out boaters can hardly see them anymore."

Mamie twisted on the bench to behold the young campground maintenance man behind her. He had driven his golf cart down the pathway to where she was sitting.

"Hi, Brady. Yes, I was afraid those kids were going to run into the dock."

"Some of the buoys have broken apart and are floating under the water. How are you doing, Miss uh. . ."

"Just call me Mamie," she said. "I'm doing great, enjoying the campground, especially the lake. The weather is perfect." Babs wagged what little tail she had as she watched him. A good sign. Dogs could usually tell if something wasn't right about a person.

"It's a good time of year for camping here. I'll get back to work. I just saw you sitting here and thought I would check with you, see if everything is okay."

What a sweetheart. She wondered briefly if Junie would like him. She'd love for that girl of hers to find someone to share her life with, now that she was settled in her career.

"Could I ask you a question before you go, Brady?"

"Certainly."

She glanced at his ring finger to make sure before she asked her next question.

"Are you single?"

The young man's face colored. He shifted in his seat and stroked his chin. "Um, why do you ask?"

"I was just wondering. I have a daughter you might want to meet, that's all."

Relief relaxed his expression as he smiled. "I thought you were asking me because you, you know—it wouldn't be the first time a woman hit on me. I am single, but I'm in a relationship. Thank you for asking, though."

It was Mamie's turn to be embarrassed. "No, that's not what I meant. I'm so sorry!" Her face felt like it could ignite. Flustered, she wished she could jump in the lake, literally.

He gave an easy laugh and wheeled his golf cart toward the campground road. "No worries. Have a good day. Let me know if you need anything, you know, camping-wise." He winked as he drove off.

She dropped her face into her hands. How embarrassing. He probably did have a proposition or two in his past. He was so cute and friendly, some lonely women would have no qualms about approaching him. But that wasn't something she would do. Her face burned as she stared at the lake. How would she ever live that one down? She prayed she wouldn't have to call on him for help. Her pride couldn't take it.

The sun dipped closer to the horizon, highlighting the gentle blue waves of the lake with shimmering crests as cicadas and assorted birds created an early summer symphony on shore. Mamie checked her phone. Time to change into her pajamas and join the ladies at the clubhouse for dinner and games. A missed call notification lit up the screen.

Back at her camper, she set her phone on speaker so she could simultaneously change clothes and return the call.

"Junie? I'm sorry I missed you. Is everything all right?"

"Mom! I just heard about the murder at your campground! Are you okay? Why haven't you called me?"

Babs' head popped up as she heard Junie's voice. The dog had curled up on the bed, having become comfortable in her new surroundings.

"I'm fine. I'm sorry I didn't call. I didn't think you would hear about it all the way over in Round Rock."

Junie gave an exasperated sigh. "You told me you would let me know you got there safely, anyway, remember? And now there's been a murder? It's been all over social media."

Social media. Of course. Where else did kids get their news these days?

"I'm sorry, Junie. I've been pretty busy since I got here."

"Are you coming home?"

"Not yet. Why?"

"Because there's a murderer loose where you are?" Her daughter's impatience came through loud and clear.

"They don't think it was a random murder, Junie. The woman had some domestic problems. We're quite sure the rest of us are safe. There's no need to worry."

"Who's 'we?' The police or a bunch of old ladies?"

"Beg your pardon?" Mamie bristled. "We are NOT a bunch of old ladies. There are younger women here—"

"I'm sorry. I admit that was rude. But Mom, how do you know it wasn't a random murder, that there's not some madman out there killing women? A ladies' camping event is a perfect place for victims, don't you think?"

She had a point, but... "If I thought I was in any danger, yes, I would leave."

"I wish you would just come on home," her daughter said, "but I know you have your mind made up. Just please be careful, okay? And call me with updates, please?"

"Don't worry, honey. I have to get ready for dinner now. I'll try to remember to check in tomorrow. Love you."

The girl had become a mother hen. She seemed to think that Mamie couldn't take care of herself, that she was lonely. She always second-guessed Mamie's decisions. She didn't need anyone's supervision or advice. Junie should be glad her mother was independent. She could be bothering her all the time. But she wouldn't let Junie's doubts ruin her adventure. She pushed those thoughts out of her mind and continued getting dressed, reminding herself to be happy she had a daughter who loved her.

She exited her camper, leaving Babs asleep on the bed. It felt silly walking around outside in pajamas, especially in the early evening, but she spotted some pajama-clad ladies in the distance entering the clubhouse. *At least I'm not alone in my folly,* she thought with a grin.

As she walked down the road toward the

clubhouse, she noticed that some of the police tape around Sarah's camper had fallen to the ground. She let her curiosity win and stepped into the campsite, scanning the area for anything that might offer clues to the murder. She was no sleuth, but maybe the investigators had missed something.

As Mamie neared the trailer, she noticed the door slightly ajar. A gust of wind could fling it wide open, so she went to shut it. Should she go inside? Would that be trespassing? A little peek before she shut the door good won't hurt. If someone caught her, she could just say that she had noticed the door open and wanted to make sure no one was inside before she closed it. That was the truth. Someone could be inside. Goosebumps popped up on her arms. *You're so silly, Mamie*, she thought, chiding herself.

It was a newer RV, so it didn't have the vintage charm of her camper, but it had a lot more space. Sarah had decorated it in a beach theme with lots of kitschy décor and bright colors. Curtains made of striped beach cabana fabric, the tablecloth, and bedcovering all matched. An open suitcase rested on the bed and a bin containing electrical cords and camping supplies had been pulled halfway from under it. A glittery stainless-steel mug sat on the counter, probably still full of water or whatever Sarah had been drinking. Mamie felt like an intruder, like she was treading on hallowed ground.

As she backed up to close the door, she noticed a familiar paperback book on the dinette a few feet away. It was one of the *Games We Play* mysteries written by author Linda Pirtle. Mamie had been reading the same series. She stepped inside to pick it up. As she flipped through the pages, a piece of paper fluttered to the floor. It was a handwritten note Sarah must have been using as a bookmark.

"Be careful what you wish for, honey. You may get more than you bargained for."

Mamie started as the door handle rattled, then froze as the door opened and a man stepped in. The man from the office. She hadn't caught his name when she checked in. Why was he here? She folded the note into her hand and tucked the book into the waistband of her pajama bottoms, covering it with her loose top, hoping he wouldn't notice.

"What are you doing in here?" he asked in a stern voice. A frown creased his otherwise friendly face.

Mamie hesitated as she struggled to come up with a reason for being inside Sarah's trailer. Her free hand went to the crossbody bag now containing her pistol again and rested on the top zipper. He waited, his eyes narrowing.

"I thought I might have left something in here," she lied. "I noticed the door was open, so I came in to look for it. And... it's not here, so I will be leaving now." She stepped toward the door, hoping he would back up and let her out. He didn't budge.

"What was it? I'll keep an eye out for it," he said, his expression and voice softening.

"No, I remember now where I left it." She moved closer to the door, but he still didn't move. There was no way she could get around his large frame. "Excuse me."

Finally, he backed out the door and down the steps to allow her to pass. Beads of sweat rolled down her back.

It was hot in that confined space with no air movement, not to mention being caught snooping. She gripped the bottom of her top where she had the book hidden.

"Thanks. Are you staying?" She was dying to know why he was there.

"Yeah, I think the lady had one of the keys to the bathhouse. I was just going to see if it was laying around in here. Did you see a key, by any chance?" He ascended the three steps into the trailer.

"No," she said, not believing him for a moment. Something was up.

"Mamie!" someone called from across the road. "Are you coming?" It was Sheila, Lanie, and Tessa, dressed in pajamas and heading toward the clubhouse. All three wore matching pajamas, just like hers. *More Walmart shoppers,* she thought with a smile.

"I'm coming," Mamie said, waving to the girls as she hurried in their direction, all the while wishing she could watch what Office Man did instead. What business had he in Sarah's trailer? Had he been a friend of hers? Was there something going on between them? What if he was the one who shot her?

When she was sure he couldn't see her, she slipped the book into her bag.

Lanie noticed. "What've you got there?"

"Oh, just a book I'm reading. I forgot to leave it in my camper," Mamie lied. She didn't like telling little white lies, but she certainly didn't want to confess to sneaking into Sarah's trailer. Maybe Lanie wouldn't press her.

"I see you've got good taste," Sheila said with a

chuckle. "Walmart?"

"You know it," Mamie said. To her great relief, the other ladies chattered about finding the pajamas in the right sizes for everyone, and Lanie seemed to forget all about the book, and the murder, for that matter. How was she supposed to enjoy dinner and make new friends when there was a killer on the loose, possibly in this very campground? Curiosity burned inside her like a wildfire, but she interacted with her new friends, who introduced her to others. She could only pick at her loaded breakfast plate. She was too preoccupied to eat.

"Is something wrong, Mamie?" Lanie asked, noticing her swirling the syrup on the pancakes with her fork.

"I guess I'm just not hungry," she replied. "I don't usually eat a large meal at night." Which was true. She didn't. It was tough trying to keep extra weight off at this age. She usually had a light snack instead of a full meal.

"Are you feeling all right?" Tessa asked.

"Yes, I feel fine," Mamie answered, wishing she could just go back to her trailer and think. Or see if Office Man had left Sarah's trailer. But she didn't want to be rude.

As the ladies finished dinner and disposed of their trash, tables were moved into place for the games. There would be two tables of about twenty women each. As they all pulled out their dollar bills and found seats at the table, Mamie hung back until Sheila noticed that she wasn't joining them.

"Come on, you have to play," she said. "It's so much fun! And you might win money!"

"I didn't bring any ones with me," Mamie said. "Besides, I'd rather watch since I haven't played before."

"It's so easy, you'll catch on. Come on, I'll lend you three dollars." Lanie pulled out a chair for her and slapped three one-dollar bills on the table in front of the chair.

Not wanting to make a big deal out of it, Mamie sat with everyone else, listening as Lanie explained the game.

"You roll dice to play, but they're not regular dice. They're three-sided and they have the letters 'L,' 'C,' and 'R' on them. If you get an L, you give a dollar to the person on your left. If you get a C, you put a dollar in the center of the table, and if you get an R, you give a dollar to the person on your right. The last one with a dollar at the end of the game wins all the money. It's fun, you'll see."

"So it's like gambling?" Mamie asked. Should she participate? She had never even bought a lottery ticket. If this game was gambling, maybe she shouldn't play.

"No, it's just an exchange. You're not placing bets," Tessa said with a wink.

So maybe just a mild form of gambling. Peer pressure won. She waited for her turn to roll the dice.

The best part of the game was the conversation around the table that went on when it wasn't one's turn. Some ladies ran out of money quickly but then gained a dollar or two just as fast when others had to pass dollar bills to the left or right. Finally, it was down to two ladies who still had money. When the last dollar was given, the winner was declared. Lou had won. She posed for a photograph holding all the bills, and then everyone at Mamie's table watched as the other table wound down their game. The winner of that table turned out to be a lady Mamie hadn't met yet. Two happy ladies came away with about sixty dollars apiece. Mamie couldn't remember when she had laughed so hard and for so long. This group was going to be good for her soul.

After saying goodnight, she walked back to her camper in the dark, glad she had remembered to leave her outside light on. She had almost forgotten about her encounter with Office Man, but as she passed Sarah's trailer, she saw a flash of light in one of the windows. Was he still in there? If not him, then who?

Chapter Nine

MAMIE SLIPPED BEHIND a tree at the edge of the campsite and waited. Maybe whoever it was would step out. Her skin tingled with nervous energy as she held her breath and watched the light in the windows moving from one end of the trailer to the other. The blinds were closed so there was no way to see inside. Should she sneak up and try to see around the blinds, or should she just wait? She decided to wait. She didn't need the intruder to discover her snooping outside the trailer. What if they had a gun? She watched the light bounce. Whoever it was seemed to be looking for something.

As the minutes crawled by, Mamie's lower back began to ache, reminding her of the long hours on her feet when she taught school. She didn't want to leave but she was so uncomfortable she had almost given up when the door of Sarah's trailer finally opened. The flashlight beam blinded her, but when the person turned to shut the door, the light shifted, enabling her to recognize the snooper. It was Carly, the woman who had been so distraught upon learning that Sarah was dead. A halo of dim campground lighting illuminated her shoulder-length blonde hair, large-framed eyeglasses, and the flowered pajamas she had worn to dinner. What would she be doing in Sarah's trailer? What was she looking for?

Carly headed toward her own trailer and Mamie waited until the woman was out of sight before heading to her camper. From what she could tell in the darkness, Carly hadn't been carrying anything except a flashlight and a drink mug. Either she had found what she was looking for and it was small enough to conceal, or she had not found anything. Mamie burned with curiosity. What if Carly was somehow involved in Sarah's murder? And what had the police found out, if anything? Should she turn in the note she had discovered? How could she do that without confessing to trespassing? Oh, the pickle she had gotten herself into.

***

The next day dawned bright and sunny with the sounds of birdsong in the air. She had not slept well, exhausted by her overactive imagination and the stress of getting caught snooping in Sarah's trailer. She threw West's denim shirt over her pajamas and leashed Babs before stepping outside. The humidity portended the hot summer just ahead.

The brilliance of the morning sun gleaming on the peaceful, still lake created a picture of paradise. The trees bordering the shore competed for the best shade of green as their reflections in the watery mirror doubled their impact. A lone flat-bottomed boat floated offshore, probably a retiree enjoying his golden years fishing. She let Babs lead the way, enjoying the mild breeze coming off the water. The morning would have been perfect if she'd had a cup of coffee in hand, but dog-walking came first.

When Babs had finished her business, they headed uphill toward the camper and that precious first cup of coffee. Now there was a police car at Sarah's campsite. Mamie led Babs there in hopes that the police might be able to tell her something. Probably not, based upon the detective shows she had watched, but it was worth a try.

As she neared the trailer, one female officer

stepped out of the car and walked around the back. Another officer, this one male, came out behind her and stopped to make some notes on an electronic tablet. Mamie approached him slowly.

"Excuse me, Officer?" she said.

He looked at her with the bluest eyes she had seen since she had gazed into West's. His dark brown hair accented with touches of gray on the sides was clipped short, almost in a buzz cut, but it suited him and gave him a look of authority. Not to mention the well-fitting uniform he wore. She had always thought men in uniform were attractive. *Wait. What am I doing?* Her face warmed as she anticipated his response.

"May I help you?"

Not exactly friendly, but he was working. She cleared her throat. "I wonder if you could tell me if you've found out anything yet."

"I can't talk about an investigation, ma'am." Even though his voice was stern, a smile teased the corner of his lips. He continued using a stylus on the tablet he held.

"Of course, I knew that. It's just that, you know, everyone is just dying to know what happened to Sarah—sorry, poor choice of words—and we're all kind of afraid for our own safety. You understand. We're all women here trying to camp and have a good time, and this happening during a campout—well, it's pretty scary." She was babbling and she knew it. She had also become acutely aware of how she must look, still wearing pajamas and not bothering to brush her hair.

The tiniest smile graced his lips as creases around his eyes deepened like West's used to do. There was kindness in those eyes. He was handsome in an all-American guy way, but not like West, whose countenance had been more rugged. Would she ever stop comparing every attractive man to West? A pang stung her heart.

The officer stopped what he was doing and gazed at her. "We are doing everything we can to find out who killed your friend. My advice to you and everyone else is to be alert to your surroundings and let us know of anything suspicious. Use common sense and stay in groups. Now if you'll excuse me, ma'am, I have work to do."

"My name is Mamie. Mamie West." She extended her hand. Should she tell him about Office Man going into Sarah's trailer? Or the note she had found in Sarah's book? No, it was probably nothing anyway, and she didn't want to get cited for trespassing.

"I'm Officer Vandegan. Nick Vandegan. Pleased to meet you. Now, if—"

"Of course. Good luck. I hope you figure out who the murderer is soon." She backed away, the dog's leash wrapping around her ankle. Babs yelped as Mamie's feet swept under her legs, knocking her over. Before she knew it, she herself was on the ground, pain radiating from her left wrist.

Officer Vandegan sprang into action, setting his tablet on the ground and kneeling next to her. "Are you injured?"

"Just my wrist." She winced, her other hand gripping the injured part.

"Let's get you up." His arm swept around her waist as his hand supported her elbow so she could stand. She stiffened at the close contact, noticing that his body was muscular and warm and manly. She untangled Bab's leash carefully with one hand, trying to ignore the pain in her other.

"Thank you, Officer. I'm fine, just need to have my wrist looked at, I guess."

"Allow us to take you to the emergency room, then," he said. "Officer Combs, we're done here," he called to his partner who had walked around the trailer toward them.

"I can drive myself, thanks," she said, her face aflame. Babs seemed fine, sniffing the feet of both officers. Mamie pulled her away and turned toward her campsite.

"What happened?" the lady officer asked.

"Ms. West here had a fall and needs to have her wrist looked at," Vandegan replied.

"Of course. I'll take her if you want to stay."

"No, I think we're done here for now. Can you help Ms. West with her dog? Then we can drive her to town."

"Of course."

Mamie wanted to crawl into a hole. Not only had she taken a tumble in front of the most attractive man she had met in a long time, but she was also wearing pajamas, her hair was unkempt, and she hadn't even brushed her teeth. She wanted to ask for time to change, but she figured the officers didn't have time to wait on her. Officer Combs allayed her fears by suggesting she take a few minutes to get dressed.

"Thank you, Officer." Babs seemed fine, so she left the officers and walked the dog back to her camper.

Though it was difficult to dress with her injured wrist, she managed to change into some leggings and a tee shirt, brush her hair and teeth, and apply some lipstick. Good thing she could still use her right hand. When she was ready, she joined the officers at their car.

As Officer Vandegan opened the car door for Mamie, Lanie pedaled by on her bicycle, did a double-take, and stopped.

"What's going on?" Lanie said, her eyes wide.

"Good morning, Lanie." Mamie said, realizing how it must look for her to be getting into a police car. But then she had an idea. "I got tangled up in Babs's leash and fell and injured my wrist. These officers were going to take me to the emergency room, but I figure they are much too busy to be bothered with that. Would you mind taking me?"

"Oh no, you poor thing. Of course, I'll take you. Let me get my car and I'll pick you up at your camper." Lanie took off on her bicycle.

"We really don't mind taking you," Vandegan said.

"Yes, but then you would have to wait for me and bring me back. There's no need when I have friends to help. Thank you very much, though, for the offer."

"We'll be checking on you, then. I hope it isn't broken."

Mamie hoped so, too. The pain didn't seem to be intense enough for a broken bone, but how would she know? She had never broken a bone before. It was throbbing, though. "Thanks. Me, too."

"You take care." Vandegan patted her arm, sending

a charge of electricity through her. Officer Combs opened the passenger door of the police car as he strode around to the driver's side. Mamie could have sworn he winked at her. Her stomach flip-flopped as she walked back to her camper to wait for Lanie. Did he find her attractive as well? She hadn't experienced that sensation in years.

Lanie wanted every detail about the fall and then she wanted to know if the police had revealed anything about the murder investigation. Mamie appreciated the conversation because it distracted her from the pain in her wrist. She tried to hold her wrist still and wished she had wrapped a towel around it.

When they arrived at Burnet Medical Center's emergency room, they took their seats in the waiting room, Lanie holding one side of the clipboard so Mamie could fill out the forms. Thankfully she was righthanded, and it was her left hand that had been injured. A nurse called for her soon after she had returned the forms to the receptionist window. Lanie went with her.

The nurse practitioner ordered an x-ray and had the results in less than an hour. No bones were broken, so she diagnosed a severe sprain and had the nurse wrap it tightly while giving instructions to rest it, elevate it, and ice it every couple of hours. She also recommended an anti-inflammatory. Relieved it wasn't broken, Mamie agreed with everything the NP told her and promised to take care of the wrist.

As she and Lanie left the ER, her stomach gnawed at her, making her realize that she hadn't had anything to eat that day. She hadn't had any coffee, either, which explained the dull headache that had added itself to her physical ailments.

"Hey, Lanie, I didn't have any coffee or breakfast this morning. Do you think we could find a drive-through and grab something?"

"Sure thing. It's almost 11:00, so maybe we should just find a restaurant and dine in for lunch. What do you think?"

"As long as they have coffee, that works for me," Mamie said.

"How does the Silver Spoon sound? I know we ate there yesterday, but there were other things on the menu that sounded good, too."

"Wonderful." She dug in her purse for some ibuprofen. Had she brought any with her on this trip? She would ask Lanie to stop at a store as well. She would need to pay for Lanie's lunch after all this trouble.

The popular diner bustled with people on their lunch breaks, the servers scurrying around trying to get orders taken and delivered in a timely manner. Mamie recalled the summer she had been a waitress while in high school. She knew how demanding the job could be, but the regulars made it fun. She even missed them when school resumed. She had certainly missed the tips.

She and Lanie were enjoying their pre-meal basket of cheese fries when Mamie, who was also enjoying a long-overdue cup of coffee, overheard a conversation that perked up her ears.

"I think she got what was coming to her," said one of the two women sitting at a table catty-cornered from theirs. Mamie's back was to them, but Lanie was facing them. Her eyes widened. She had heard it, too.

"You do? Why do you say that?" said the other.

"I heard she was embezzling funds from work because she had gotten involved in some pyramid scheme and owed the company a lot of money. Ten years isn't long enough, in my opinion."

"Yes, but she still has kids at home," the other woman said.

"It will be a lesson for all of them."

Mamie and Lanie stared at each other when they realized the subject of the gossip at the other table was not Sarah. Whoever the victim in that conversation was, she had gone to prison. Whether she was guilty of a crime or not, at least she was alive. Sarah was not. Lanie grabbed a gloppy cheese-covered fry and asked Mamie about her family.

Always happy to talk about her kids and grandson, Mamie told Lanie all about them and how she enjoyed being a grandmother. Lanie nodded while listening intently as she ate.

After a hearty lunch of patty melts, cheese fries, and chocolate pie, the two ladies piled into Lanie's SUV.

"My word, that was good. I'm stuffed. Do you think we could stop at the pharmacy for some pain reliever?" Mamie asked Lanie.

"Sure! I'm stuffed, too, but it was delicious," Lanie agreed. "I just love small-town diners."

After a quick stop at the town pharmacy, Lanie drove to the campground and dropped Mamie off at her camper. "I think I'll take a nap," she said.

"That's a great idea. Thank you again, Lanie."

Mamie would welcome some rest after such an eventful morning. But first she needed to go to the campground office and buy ice for her cooler so she could keep some ice on her wrist. Even though she had a small refrigerator in her camper, it didn't make ice and she liked to ice down her bottled water and canned sodas, not to mention having ice for her mug.

Mamie managed to wrangle the leash onto Babs without hurting her wrist. Then she shoved a five-dollar bill in her pocket before walking to the campground office. Babs trotted next to Mamie, seeming to have experienced no ill effects from being knocked down earlier. There were no hard feelings, either. The dog was remarkably forgiving, given she had to be locked up for hours at a time and only allowed outside on a leash. When they reached the low porch to the office, Mamie wondered if it was okay for Babs to enter. There were no signs indicating otherwise. She decided to try it and see.

She stopped short when she saw Office Man sitting at the counter. It hadn't occurred to her that he would be there. Seeing her didn't seem to bother him at all, though.

"Good afternoon, ma'am. What can I do for you? Help you find anything?"

"I'd like a bag of ice, please," Mamie said.

"Sure thing. That'll be $3.50." He got up from where he had been watching TV and stood at the counter facing her. "Who've you got there?" Mamie had to admit he had a friendly face with kind eyes. He seemed to have a touch of rosacea on his cheeks underneath a receding hairline where dark hair had given over to gray. Mingled gray and white chest hair peeked from the neck of an old golf shirt that had seen better days, reminding her of her late father-in-law. Funny she hadn't noticed the resemblance before. She laid the five on the counter.

"This is Babs."

"Pretty dog. Wife and I used to have a Boston. We loved that dog to pieces. Best dog we ever had." He handed her a dollar and two quarters in change. "What happened to your wrist?"

A notepad on the counter next to the register caught her eye. It looked familiar. "I got tangled up in the leash and fell. I'm a little clumsy. No biggie, though. It's just sprained."

"Ouch. Hope it feels better soon. Ice is on the porch. Self-service."

"Did you find the key to the bath house?" She couldn't help herself. Where had she seen that notepad before?

"Beg pardon?"

"You thought you might find it in Sarah's trailer."

Confusion contorted his face for a moment before he remembered. "Oh, yeah. No, she didn't have it. I found it. I had just misplaced it."

"That's good," Mamie remarked. "What's your name again?"

"Howard Story. And you are?"

"Mamie West. Thanks for the ice."

"Hey, need some help?" He seemed to realize that she might struggle with her injured wrist to wrestle a dog and a bag of ice.

"I think I can manage but thank you." Mamie left the office with a strange vibe from the man. She didn't think he was telling the truth. There had to be another reason he had been in Sarah's trailer that evening. And she recalled where she had seen the notepad. The note she had found in the trailer had been torn from that notepad, or one just like it. Had he been the one to write that cryptic message?

Chapter Ten

THE CAMPOUT AGENDA had mentioned a resort-wide bingo tournament in the clubhouse that afternoon and the Three Gees were invited. Mamie had never played bingo outside of school, but she figured it might be a good way to meet people, especially other campers who weren't part of their group. She might stumble upon a clue as well. Either way, it was a good way to pass the time and forget about her injured wrist. The ibuprofen seemed to be keeping the pain at bay.

She locked Babs in the camper with the a/c fan going and the jalousie windows open for circulation. The breeze off the lake should keep the camper comfortable, and for now, it was in the shade. She wouldn't stay very long, anyway. She wondered if there were cash prizes. Between LCR and bingo, she had become a regular gambler. *Sorry, Lord*, she prayed.

The clubhouse was packed full of people, many of whom Mamie did not recognize. Even children sat by their parents, ready to fill their bingo cards and win prizes. She spotted Marlene, Sissy, and Bertie at a table near the back and made her way there. A couple of empty seats were there for the taking, or so she thought. She noticed for the first time that the building seemed to have been there a while, built with natural pine walls and ceiling, giving it a rustic, lodgy look. Modern farmhouse décor lent a homey feeling.

"Hey, ladies," she greeted them, pulling out an empty plastic and metal folding chair next to Marlene.

"That seat is saved," said Marlene with a sniff.

"Oh." The cool attitude knocked Mamie back. She released the chair and turned to find another place to sit.

"No, it isn't," Sissy said. "Go ahead and sit there."

"I thought Darla was coming," Bertie said. Marlene nodded, then shook her head at Sissy.

"There's another chair, or she can pull up one if she comes. Please join us, Mamie." Sissy pulled the chair out farther so Mamie could slide into it.

"If you're sure," she said, suddenly doubting her standing in the group. It suddenly seemed like high school all over again.

"Yes, we're sure, aren't we?" Sissy frowned at the other two.

"Yes, please sit here," Bertie agreed. Marlene remained silent.

What's got a bee in her bonnet? Mamie wondered.

"You'll have to forgive Marlene," Sissy said. "She's a little upset."

"The police think one of us killed Sarah," Bertie said.

"One of us?"

"Yes, one of the Gals Gone Glamping."

"Really?" Mamie recalled Howard Story entering Sarah's camper. What about him? But then she remembered seeing Carly come out of the camper the night before. And what had she been doing there?

"An investigator named Sovern is questioning everyone. He'll be at dinner tonight to meet with those he hasn't talked to. Just want you to be cognizant of that and ready."

"I have nothing to hide," Mamie said. "I don't mind talking to him." Unless he wanted to know if she'd seen anything. There was that note, and Howard Story and then Carly in Sarah's camper. She would have to tell him about those things. Her stomach clenched, even though she had nothing to be afraid of, except maybe explaining why she hadn't already told the police what she had seen.

"What happened?" Bertie pointed to the bandage around Mamie's left wrist.

"I tripped over my dog's leash this morning. It's just a sprain."

Sissy raised her eyebrows. "Yikes, I bet that didn't feel good," she said through clenched teeth.

"They're going to be starting in about ten minutes. Did you buy your cards?" Marlene said to Mamie.

"Buy my cards?"

"Have you never played bingo?" The exasperated tone made Mamie feel like she was being scolded. "Go up to the front and buy your cards. They sell for one dollar each. I usually buy five. A lady will bring game pieces around before we start."

Glad she had stuffed more bills in her jeans pocket and trying not to take offense at Marlene's rudeness, Mamie did as she was told and returned with five bingo cards. Just as Marlene had said, a friendly older woman walked past their seats and dropped several chips at each spot.

The place grew noisier with each game, and after five non-winning games among the four ladies, they left the clubhouse.

"That was a bust," Bertie announced as they stood on the sidewalk outside the building.

"It was fun, though," Mamie said, the corners of her mouth forming a smile. "Thanks for letting me join you. I guess Darla decided to do something else."

"Yeah, there weren't many of us there," Marlene said. "I think I saw a few from our group but everyone else is probably shopping or sightseeing." She frowned slightly, then added, "Although I went to every retail store and business yesterday and discovered there really isn't much shopping in Magnolia Bluff."

"Maybe Marble Falls is better. We could check it out tomorrow if you guys want to. It's only about ten minutes away," Sissy said.

Mamie smiled. It felt good to be included. "Maybe so," she said. "What are you all going to do now? It's still a couple of hours before dinner."

"What's the agenda tonight?" Bertie asked.

"It's pizza night, remember? They're ordering pizza from Olivia's downtown," Marlene said.

"Do we dress up tonight or tomorrow night?" Bertie asked.

"Come as you are tonight. Tomorrow night it's petticoats with a western theme."

Mamie groaned and scrunched her face. "I knew I forgot something."

"What's that?" Sissy said.

"I forgot to find a petticoat and pack western

wear."

"No worries," Sissy said, offering a smile. "I have extra petticoats in my camper, and maybe we can find you some stuff in town tomorrow when we go shopping. I think I may have an extra pair of boots and a hat you can wear. If you want to follow me to my trailer, you can try them on."

"And if you don't like her petticoats, I have extras in my camper, too," Marlene said, apparently trying to make up for her rudeness earlier.

"Sorry. I don't wear petticoats," Bertie said with her palms outstretched.

"Bertie doesn't dress up," Marlene said.

"Really? Why?" Mamie asked.

"I don't know. I'm just not into that. But you gals have fun with it. I like to watch and take pictures. I am going to wear a cowboy hat and boots, though. Right now I'm going to relax and maybe take a short nap before dinner. See you guys later." Bertie headed toward her campsite.

"Me too," Marlene said. "Just knock on my door if you need to look at what I have."

"Will do." Mamie followed Sissy to her camper, which was parked next to Marlene's and Bertie's.

Sissy had a vintage Shasta trailer that was a couple feet longer than Mamie's, with the iconic wings on the back. Painted pink and white, the exterior matched the interior, which was piled full of fluffy pillows, plush shag rugs, and fur throws. All the appliances and cabinet doors had been painted pink as well. Even the curtains were pink with little white retro starbursts outlined in gold scattered in the fabric. It felt like a dollhouse.

"Your camper is adorable." Mamie watched as Sissy pulled petticoats out of an overstuffed pillow on her bed. "You keep your petticoats in a pillow?"

"Thank you. Yes, it's a tip I read somewhere. Makes your pillow do double duty. Here." She tossed a petticoat at Mamie. "Just pull it on over your pants."

She did as instructed, the fluffy green crinoline standing out stiffly around her and making her feel like a ballerina. And more than a little silly.

"Perfect! Now let me see if I can find that hat." Sissy glanced around her trailer and, after a minute or two, grabbed a cowboy hat from a corner on the floor next to the bed. "Here you go."

Mamie donned the natural straw hat and stepped a few feet from where she had been standing to look in the mirror on the closet door. "What do you think?"

"I think you look darling. Does it fit?"

She ran her fingers along the brim. "Yes, it seems to."

"You can draw the string up to your chin if you're worried about losing it. Let's see about those boots. What size do you wear?"

"Usually an eight."

"Same size as me." Sissy pulled a pair of black cowboy boots from under the bed. "I bet these will fit. Try them on."

"I'm not wearing socks."

"I don't care. I'll help you get them off."

Mamie kicked off her slip-on sneakers and pulled the boots easily over her bare feet. She stood to check the mirror. She looked western except for her tee shirt, which was burnt orange and sported the words "University of Texas."

"I just need a different shirt," she said.

"Or a different color petticoat."

"What other colors do you have?"

Sissy grabbed a black one, stuffed it back inside the pillowcase, and pulled out another. "You don't want to look like Halloween. Here, try this brown one."

Mamie wriggled out of the green one and pulled on the brown one, which also fit.

"There you go. You're ready for western night."

"Thank you so much, Sissy. I had no idea where to even look for a petticoat and here you have several. I'd better take off this shirt so I don't get it dirty before tomorrow night."

"Good idea," Sissy said, pulling the boots off Mamie's feet. "But I'd wait until you get to your camper." She laughed at her own joke as she opened a cabinet, grabbed a grocery tote, and stuffed the petticoat and boots inside. "I've picked my petticoats up over the years from other ladies who were selling theirs, or from thrift stores. I'm glad I had extras. We can't have you going to your first dress-up night without a costume."

"I'll get everything back to you after it's over, I promise," Mamie said.

"I have no doubt. Now go let that wrist rest before dinner."

"Good idea," Mamie said as she stepped out of the camper. She needed to ice it for a while. But first, Babs.

As she approached her camper, which was on the other end of the drive past the clubhouse, she noticed a man taking notes and talking with several of the ladies in the group who were gathered at Lou's camper. Must be the detective. She retrieved Babs, who growled as they walked by.

"Mamie, come on over," called Lou.

Great. Mamie fixed a smile on her face and led Babs toward the group. "What's going on?" She nodded at the man as Babs pulled on her leash trying to get close enough to sniff his legs.

"This is Mamie. She was on the scene soon after Sarah was killed, too."

Thanks ever so, Lou. Mamie looped the end of the leash over her good wrist and stuck her hand out. "Hello."

"Does your dog bite?" the man asked, shaking Mamie's hand with an iron grip.

Ouch. Too much of a grip. "Not usually," she said, feeling his eyes sizing her up.

"I'm Sergeant Reece Sovern, police investigator. Would you mind answering a few questions?"

"Not at all." She glanced at the women sitting in Lou's campsite. There were no empty chairs. "We could go to my campsite where there are a couple of chairs, and I can put my dog in the camper if you like."

The fact that the other ladies exchanged glances did not escape her, but Sovern didn't seem to notice. "Good idea," he said. "Lead the way."

Chapter Eleven

BABS BARKED ANGRILY when Mamie put her inside the camper and shut the door. As Sergeant Sovern settled his heavy-set frame into one of the two chairs on the patio mat, the dog whined unhappily and lay in front of the screen, her head on her front paws.

"It's okay, Babs." Mamie turned toward Sovern. "I should have asked you if you'd like anything to drink."

"No, thank you," Sovern said, an unlit cigar dangling from his lips.

Mamie sat in the chair opposite him and crossed her legs, trying not to appear nervous. She didn't have anything to be nervous about, right? Except…

"I understand you were on the scene shortly after Sarah Trenton was murdered. Can you describe what you saw? Did you know the victim?" Piercing blue eyes stared into her hazel ones.

"No, I didn't know her. I was visiting with some other ladies at another campsite when we heard a shot and ran to see what happened."

"So you arrived at Sarah's campsite right after she was shot?"

"Yes, I think so. She was lying on the ground, already dead." Mamie shivered, remembering the woman's lifeless body.

"You weren't afraid of being shot yourself?"

"I suppose none of us thought about that. We just wanted to know what had happened, and if we could help. We were too late for that, though."

"Did you see anything suspicious? A vehicle driving away? Someone running or hiding?"

"No, I didn't, and I would have reported it if I had. But there is something you should know." Mamie decided to come clean with what she had discovered in Sarah's trailer, even if it meant she might be in trouble herself.

Sovern's brow furrowed under receding, thinning brown hair as he looked up from his notepad. "What is that?"

"I was walking by Sarah's camper the next day and noticed the door was open, so I went to close it. Naturally I wanted to glance inside to see the décor, and when I did, I noticed a book on the dinette table. It was the same one I had been reading. I stepped inside to pick it up—I really don't know why—and a piece of paper Sarah had been using as a bookmark fell out. It had a creepy message on it. If you'll excuse me, I'll get it for you."

Sovern nodded. Mamie hopped up and reached inside her camper for the note that she had tucked inside her purse, which was resting on her dinette table. She was glad she had snapped a photo of it before she stuck it inside her bag. Babs stood and wiggled her bottom, hoping to be let out, but Mamie closed the screen again before the dog could escape. Babs yelped with indignance as Mamie handed the note to the officer.

Sovern examined it—read it and turned it over a couple of times—before pulling a clear plastic zipper bag from his shirt pocket. "Be careful what you wish for, honey. You may get more than you bargained for," he quoted. "Why didn't you turn this in earlier? You know you could be charged with tampering with evidence or obstruction of justice." With arched eyebrows, he inserted the note into the zipper bag.

"I was afraid of that. That's why I hadn't turned it in yet. But there's something else."

"And what is that?"

"The man who works in the office, Howard Story, came into Sarah's trailer while I was there. He said he was looking for a key to the bathhouse, but I got the feeling he might be after something else. I left him there."

Sovern jotted something on his notepad. "Is that all?"

"No, last night there was a light moving around inside the trailer and then one of our camping group ladies came out. She was very distraught when Sarah was found that day."

"What is her name?"

"Carly is all I know."

"Anything else?"

"I don't think so." Mamie squirmed in the chair. Would he arrest her for tampering with evidence or obstruction of justice? Would he take her to the police station? What would she do with the dog? She didn't know anyone in the group well enough to ask them to watch Babs. She didn't want to call her daughter. Yes, indeed, this was turning into one giant pickle.

The investigator stood and slid his notepad into his shirt pocket. "Thank you for the information. I wish you had contacted us the moment you found the note, but at least you've reported it. Let me know if anything else happens, or if you find anything else." He handed her a business card. "I'll be in touch."

As he walked away, Mamie was so relieved she felt weak in the knees. She sat a moment wondering if she had done the right thing. Babs barked to remind her owner that she was still inside the trailer. As Mamie got up to clip the leash on her pet, Lou, Sissy, Bertie, Florence, and Marlene flocked to her campsite.

"What did you tell him?" Lou demanded.

Mamie gripped Babs's leash, not wanting her to jump up on them. She didn't want to tell them about the note or about seeing Mr. Story or Carly in the trailer.

"I just told him what I saw when Sarah's body was found."

Lou's eyes narrowed. "I think you told him more than that. Do you know something we don't?"

Mamie flinched. Were they all turning on each other, suspecting each other?

"Leave her alone, Lou," Florence said. "She doesn't know any more than the rest of us. We all have our suspicions about Sarah's ex, but none of us know a thing."

Thank you, Florence, Mamie thought as she stared at Lou, hoping she would drop the subject.

"That's right, Lou. Mamie is brand new to this group, so she couldn't know anything about it. If anyone had anything against Sarah, it would be one of us. Mamie didn't even know her," Bertie agreed.

"That doesn't mean she couldn't have shot her. Mamie could be a serial killer, for all we know," Lou argued.

Mamie's eyes widened. "Me?"

"I'm just saying. Any one of us could be the killer."

Sissy came to Mamie's rescue. "I think we're all going a little crazy here. Let's just try to enjoy the rest of our campout. The police will figure it out. We just need to pray for Sarah's family and let the law do their job." She hooked an arm through Mamie's. "We don't want to scare away our newest Three Gee, right, Lou?" Sissy gave her a pointed look.

"I suppose you're right," Lou grumbled. "I'm sorry, Mamie. I guess I'm just afraid and want to blame someone."

"That's better," Bertie said.

"Who wants to take a walk before dinner?" Marlene said.

"That sounds good," Sissy said. "Does the dog need a walk? We can all go together."

"She can always use a walk," Mamie chuckled.

"Good. We can all burn off some steam." Marlene took off toward the lake, the others traipsing along behind her. Glad for the distraction, Mamie followed with Babs.

***

Marlene's idea of walking didn't quite match up with Mamie's concept. Marlene's gait resembled a race walk, making Mamie and the other ladies work to keep up.

"Marlene! For heaven's sake, slow down!" Bertie said between huffs and puffs. Her short stocky legs seemed to be doing double time to Marlene's long-legged strides.

"I have slowed down," Marlene said.

"Not enough," Sissy grumbled. "Come on, Marlene, this isn't a triathlon."

"What happened to a leisurely walk?" Lou questioned.

"What a bunch of weenies! Okay, okay." Marlene stopped to allow them to catch up, and then she took a couple of deliberately slow, short steps. "Is this better?"

"Much." Bertie stopped and bent over to catch her breath. When she straightened, she pointed ahead. "There's a bench up there. I'm going to sit for a minute. If anyone wants to join me, feel free."

"I believe I will," Mamie said, following with the dog.

The other ladies went with her--Florence perched on the free end of the bench as Lou, Sissy, and Marlene did some stretching behind it.

Without warning, the dog erupted in a fit of barking and growling, startling them all. As Babs pulled on the leash, Mamie noticed something pale and in stark contrast to its surroundings floating just off the shore, partially obscured by cattails, lily pads, and tall grasses. She followed Babs to the water's edge to see why she was barking. She clapped a hand over her mouth as bile rose in her throat. The floating object was a dead body.

"Oh, my Lord!" Bertie cried as Florence screamed. The other ladies had gathered next to Mamie.

"What do we do?" Marlene said through the fingers

that covered her mouth.

"Call 911?" Sissy said.

Lou turned away and vomited.

"I left my phone in my trailer," Marlene said.

Bertie was already on hers. Mamie led the barking dog away from the shore, hoping to distract her with something else. She knew she shouldn't leave the scene, but the incessant and annoying barking would interfere with law enforcement doing their job.

"Where are you going?" Marlene asked.

"Just getting Babs away from the shore," Mamie said. "I'm not going anywhere."

"Better not. Everyone stays here."

"The police are on their way," Bertie said. "Who could that be?"

"No one in our camping group, I hope," Marlene replied. "Are you okay, Lou?" She patted her friend on the back, Lou's face as white as the cumulus clouds leisurely crossing overhead.

She shook her head while keeping her hand over her mouth, looking as if she might vomit again.

"Why don't you sit down?" Marlene gestured toward the bench.

Lou's eyes widened as she shook her head again.

"Too close to the body," Bertie said. She took Lou's arm and led her a few yards over to a tree. "Why don't you wait here, honey?"

Lou nodded, her eyes red, her skin pale. She

backed up against the tree and slid to the ground, her arms hugging her sides. Mamie's heart went out to her, surprised she herself wasn't sick from seeing such a horrendous sight.

When the authorities arrived, Bertie took charge and led them to the lake's edge where the body floated in the watery grasses. As officers investigated, Sergeant Sovern approached the ladies who were standing in a group near Lou.

"We meet again," he said, staring at Mamie, who held Babs's leash tight against her.

Mamie nodded, uncomfortable with his pointed gaze. Did he suspect that she had something to do with it? Or Sarah's murder?

"Can anyone describe for me the events leading up to discovery of the body?"

"Yes," Bertie said. "We were just taking a walk before dinner and sat down on that bench." She pointed to it. "Then the dog started barking and growling, and when we got up to investigate, we saw the body in the water."

"Any idea who it might be?"

"No, of course not," Marlene said. "The body is facedown. And it doesn't look natural." She shuddered.

"I thought you might recognize the clothing," Sovern said, jotting something down on his notepad.

"Which is kind of hard to recognize being in the lake," Marlene said.

Sovern gave her a look which said she was in danger of being insubordinate. Sissy grabbed her hand

and frowned at her.

"Anything else?" He stared at Mamie, who shook her head and looked at the ground. "All right, ladies, if you'll leave me your name and campsite number, you may go back to whatever you were doing. Please don't leave the campground, though."

"Our campout is over Sunday morning," Florence said. "Do you mean for us to stay here longer?"

"It's quite possible," Sovern said before walking toward the other officers. "Now move along. You won't want to be here when the body is pulled from the water, trust me."

The ladies glanced at one another, their eyes wide.

"Come on, Babs," Mamie murmured, pulling the reluctant dog toward her camper. The ladies followed, huddled together, whispering.

"I have to be home by Monday morning." Florence said. "I can't take off work another day."

"You'll have to if the police say so," Bertie said.

"Can they do that? Make us stay?" Sissy asked.

"I would imagine so," Lou said, apparently feeling stronger.

"My husband will love hearing that," Marlene said. "He can hardly stand me being away three nights as it is. You'd think he was completely helpless, even though he was a bachelor for ten years before marrying me."

The other ladies snickered and murmured their agreement.

"Maybe they'll figure it all out by Sunday," Mamie

said.

Everyone stared at her.

"It's already Friday," Marlene said. "Ever heard of a police investigation taking only two days?"

That stung, but Mamie clung to her belief that things could work out. She shot a prayer toward heaven. *Please God, let them figure out who is killing people around here, and let them do it fast so we can go home. Oh yes, and please keep us safe. No more killing, please.*

Chapter Twelve

WHEN MAMIE ARRIVED for dinner, the clubhouse buzzed with activity. She scanned the crowd for familiar faces and found the group she had spent time with that afternoon at a table in the back, their heads together, serious expressions clouding their faces. Were they discussing that afternoon's discovery? She took one of the empty chairs at the table and leaned in to hear.

"Have they released the name of the victim yet?" Mamie asked.

"That's what we were wondering," Bertie said. "No one has heard."

"I guess they're busy trying to contact next of kin," Marlene said. "You know they won't release the name until the family has been notified."

"I'd just like to know if it was a man or woman. You couldn't tell from what we could see," Sissy said.

Lou turned green and clapped her hand over her mouth.

"I'm sorry, Lou. Let's change the subject, y'all," Sissy said, patting Lou's arm.

They didn't have to because at that moment, a train of about five people entered the clubhouse carrying pizza totes emblazoned with the words "Olivia's Pizza" and the slogan "Olivia knows what you like." The campout hostesses showed them where to put the totes and then arranged similarly labeled pizza boxes on the two large rectangular tables provided at the front of the room. Mamie thought it looked like enough pizza to feed an army, and it was, an army of about forty women.

As soon as one of the hostesses finished asking a blessing on the food, Mamie joined the other ladies in a long line to get pizza.

"Does anyone else know?" Florence said in a loud whisper behind Mamie.

Mamie whirled around. "I don't know. Have you asked the others?"

Sissy spoke up from her place in line behind Florence. "I don't think anyone else knows. I haven't told anyone, and I don't think any of us have. Have you, Florence?"

"No, that's why I was asking," Florence said, indignation coloring the frown on her face.

"What are y'all mumbling about?" Bertie said from behind Sissy.

"I was just wondering if anyone else knew about what happened today," Florence said.

"We agreed not to tell anyone, right?" Marlene said, leaning toward her.

"I don't remember that," Florence said, obviously not intimidated by Marlene.

"We shouldn't have to voice it," Marlene said. "Has anyone told?" She glanced at each of the others, frowning like a schoolteacher daring students to disobey.

Everyone in their group shook their heads, as if afraid of being sent to the principal's office.

"Told what?" Minerva, another lady who had lined

up in front of Mamie, overheard and turned around.

"It's nothing," Mamie said, her mind racing to come up with something.

"We're just talking about our costumes for tomorrow night. Marlene has a special outfit that she doesn't want anyone to know about," Sissy said.

Good recovery, Sissy. Mamie picked up a paper plate and moved forward with the line. Her stomach rumbled. Pizza would taste good.

Minerva grinned and launched into a description of her own western outfit, explaining how she'd had to beg, borrow, and almost steal to find everything she wanted. Mamie smiled, politely listening but wishing the line would just move on so she could sit down.

"Mamie!" Sheila called to her from across the room. Mamie waved and then loaded her plate before heading over to a table where Sheila sat with Lanie and Tessa.

"Sit with us," Lanie said, patting the seat of the chair next to her.

Thinking it would be nice to take her mind off the day's discovery, Mamie grinned and sat down. "Thanks." But when she glanced over to where Marlene and the other ladies were sitting, Marlene glared at her. *Great,* Mamie thought. *I've already picked the wrong group to hang out with. Will we never grow up?*

Before she knew it, the women had Mamie laughing as they described their afternoon kayaking adventures.

"You should have gone with us," Lanie said. "It was a blast."

"She couldn't have kayaked with that wrist," Sheila said.

"True, but she would have been entertained just watching from the shore. I'm sure we were a comedy act, all of us trying to learn how to kayak," Lanie said.

"I know that's right," Tessa said, rolling her eyes. "You should have seen us. None of us has ever paddled a kayak in our lives, and the guy who was supposed to be our guide just put each of us in one and sent us off. I was afraid I would tip over and end upside down in the water."

"That would have been a sight," Sheila laughed.

"Yeah, and you two would have laughed while I drowned," Tessa said with a groan.

"Another thing checked off my bucket list," Lanie said.

"What? Watching me drown?" They laughed at Tessa's pitiful expression.

"What's on your agenda for tomorrow?" Mamie asked, biting into a gooey slice of Olivia's pepperoni pizza.

"We've talked about doing some sightseeing, maybe hiking. What do you have planned?" Lanie asked Mamie.

"She wants to hike. We want to sightsee," Sheila said, laughing.

"After this pizza, I'll need to do some hiking," Tessa said, starting on her second slice. "It's really good."

"I'm sure I could use some exercise as well," Mamie agreed. "I don't really have anything planned."

"Then you should spend the day with us," Sheila

said. "Whatever we do will be fun."

"I don't doubt that at all." Mamie laughed. Then she remembered. Sovern had told her and the other ladies who had found the dead body to stay at the campground. How would she explain that she couldn't go anywhere? She decided to go along with the plan today and then perhaps feign a headache tomorrow. Another lie. She hated having to be dishonest, but she certainly couldn't talk about finding a dead body until it was public knowledge.

Everyone had finished dinner and dessert and were moving tables and chairs for the games to begin when Sergeant Sovern, Officer Vandegan, Officer Combs, and a couple of other police officers entered the clubhouse. Mamie's heart jumped in her throat. Had they figured it out? Were they here to arrest someone?

Hostesses Marlene and Sissy hurried over to where the officers stood just inside the door to the clubhouse. "Is there a problem, officers?" Marlene asked. A hush fell over the entire room, everyone waiting to hear what they would say.

"We need to speak to the person in charge," Sovern said.

"That would be us," Marlene said. "Could we find a more private place to discuss whatever is you need to talk with us about?" She smiled as she gestured toward the back door of the clubhouse which opened onto a deck overlooking the lake.

"Lead the way," Sovern said, motioning for the others to follow him. The ladies in the room remained quiet as the officers followed Marlene and Sissy out to the deck. As soon as the door closed everyone started talking at once, creating a low roar.

"Wonder what's going on?" Sheila asked. "Do you know anything, Mamie?"

Mamie's face warmed. "I'm not sure I do," she said, which was partially true. Maybe they weren't talking about Sarah's murder or the dead body in the water. Odds were not good they weren't, though. "Let's play a game," she said, trying to divert the conversation. Out of the corner of her eye, she saw Bertie, Lou, and Florence huddled together, whispering furiously. How she wanted in on that conversation. She forced her attention onto the cards that Lanie shuffled and dealt. Mamie would know soon enough what they were talking about, and she hoped it wasn't as bad as she feared. Was the murderer in this room?

Chapter Thirteen

SEVERAL MINUTES PASSED, maybe even half an hour, before Marlene and Sissy re-entered the clubhouse with the police. The room fell silent as the door swung open. The few women who had not been watching the door hushed as everyone else in the room stopped talking and laughing. The five uniformed officers strode through the room, led by Sovern, their faces expressionless. Only Officer Vandegan nodded as he caught Mamie's eye. She blushed, realizing that she had been staring at him wondering if he would recognize her. He did.

With one or possibly two murders during her first campout, the discovery of a body, and so many other things she should be concerned about now, she was most worried this man wouldn't notice her. Shameful. She gave him a half smile and averted her gaze, hoping no one else noticed the exchange between them.

Someone did.

Sheila nudged her, grinning. Mamie's face warmed as she nudged back.

Before Mamie could respond, Detective Sovern addressed the group of ladies.

"I know you're all curious as to what was happening out on the deck, what we were discussing. Please don't question these ladies." He indicated Marlene and Sissy, who were standing off to the side. "Just know that we are working on this case, and our meeting is confidential at this time. We appreciate your cooperation, and thank you, ladies, for talking with us."

Marlene and Sissy nodded, looking sternly at the group of ladies. Mamie knew she wouldn't be asking them any questions and would be surprised if anyone else dared to.

As the law exited the building, conversation and table games resumed.

Mamie turned to Sheila. "What was that nudge for earlier?"

"What's going on with you and that cop?" She said in a voice low enough the others couldn't hear.

"What do you mean?" By now Mamie's face must have turned fifty shades of red because it felt like it was on fire. Her antiperspirant had failed, too.

"I saw the way you looked at each other. I think I saw a spark there."

"Nonsense. I just ran into him earlier at Sarah's trailer. He helped me when I fell. He's a nice guy is all."

"I think there's more to it than that. He seems interested in you."

"Again I say, 'Nonsense.' He's just friendly." Mamie fanned herself with the napkin she had kept from dinner to use as a coaster.

To Mamie's utter mortification, Sheila turned to Tessa and Lanie, who were discussing what game to play next. "Did y'all see how that police officer looked at our friend Mamie here?"

Both women frowned and stared at Mamie, whose skin had cooled to only about thirty shades of red. Lanie glanced at Tessa. "Did you see anything?"

"I wasn't paying attention," Tessa said. "I was too busy wondering why so many officers had to show up here in the first place. It was almost like a raid, if you ask me. I felt like I was back in college at a frat party." She giggled.

Sheila snickered. "Hardly a raid. Can you see all of us old ladies rushing around trying to get away if someone had yelled, 'Raid'?"

Everyone laughed, even Mamie, relieved at the change of subject. "Old? Speak for yourself!" She winked at her new friend. "Let's play something. Have y'all come up with another game yet?"

"Yes, remember Spades?" Lanie shuffled the cards.

"I think I can remember, yes. Let's play," Mamie said, happy to divert their attention to something more benign. Was Officer Vandegan interested in her, or was she reading too much into that nod? Of course she was. He was much too young and attractive to be interested in her. He was only doing his job. Besides, he probably had a wife and a passel of kids to boot.

Mamie was studying her hand, trying to decide which cards to play when someone stumbled into her, almost knocking her out of her chair. Her cards scattered on the floor.

Lanie reached over to steady Mamie as the clumsy person recovered. It was Carly, and it was obvious she'd had one too many glasses of wine. Many of the ladies had brought wine or something stronger as their beverage of choice for dinner.

"Watch it, new girl," Carly said.

Mamie looked up at her, bewildered. "Maybe you should be more careful," she said, emphasizing the word *you*.

"Me be more careful? I think you should be careful. Be careful what you wish for, honey. You may get more than you bargained for," Carly said.

Mamie's stomach clinched as the blood drained from her face. How did Carly know those words? Was it just a coincidence that she would say them? Had she written that note and given it to Sarah? Had she had something to do with Sarah's murder? What about the body in the lake? Carly's eyes bore into Mamie's, challenging her to say something. Carly was drunk. Did she even realize what she'd just said?

"Carly, it's time for you to leave," Sheila said. "You've had a little too much to drink, and you are being rude." Sheila patted Mamie on the arm. "She doesn't mean it."

"Who are you to say I've had too much to drink? I haven't. Not me." Carly laughed, reminding Mamie of the cackling witch from *The Wizard of Oz*. "I'm about to get this party started," she said, wiggling her hips from side to side.

"Oh no, you're not." Sissy appeared behind her. "Come on, Carly. We need to talk. Why don't we take a walk outside?"

Carly frowned, seemed about to say something, and then rolled her eyes and followed Sissy toward the door. "We aren't finished," she said, pointing to Mamie.

"What's her problem?" Tessa said as everyone turned back to their games.

"She's probably trying to deal with finding Sarah's body. Some people get angry when they drink and take it out on innocent people," Sheila said. "Are you okay, Mamie?"

Mamie's heart pounded. What if Carly was the killer? What if she had written that note? Did she know that Mamie had given it to the police? Would she kill again? Had she already killed again? Who was that person they found today? Why hadn't the police told them who it was? She gripped the edges of her chair to keep her hands from shaking.

"Mamie, are you okay?" Sheila said again.

Mamie stared at her, willing herself to calm down. There was no need to get all worked up. At least not yet. Still, how did Carly know those words? Why did she say the exact words that were found on the paper? "Yes, I'm fine," she lied. Again.

"It's your turn to shuffle." Lanie, who had retrieved the scattered cards from the floor, set the deck on the table in front of Mamie. "Unless you want one of us to do it for you, with your wrist and all."

"Oh, okay. Sorry. No, I think I can do it." Mamie picked up the cards and managed to shuffle them, although she had to do it several times because some kept slipping out of the deck. Thankfully no one was paying attention. They were all talking about Carly and how devastated she was about Sarah's death. Hadn't they been best friends? Best camping buddies?

Mamie dealt the cards, and the game began. It was

difficult to keep her mind on what she was doing and when the round was over, she told them she was tired and wanted to turn in for the night.

"But the night is young! And there'll be a fire. Don't you want to sit around the fire?" Tessa asked. "I brought my guitar and some new songs I just wrote."

Mamie smiled. "I'm sure they are wonderful. Maybe another time? I'm really beat, and I'm sure Babs needs a walk. I'll see you ladies tomorrow."

The night was pitch black, cloud coverage preventing the moon from peeking. With everything that had happened around the campground, it was probably not a good idea to be wandering around by herself at night, but she desperately needed to be alone. She needed to think. At least there were tall security lights scattered around, and each campsite had its own nightlight attached to the power pole. Still, shadows lurked around every corner, hiding who knew what in their darkness. Mamie shivered, wishing she had stuck her .38 in her waistband. She hadn't even thought of it when she'd left her trailer earlier.

As she approached her campsite, she noticed she'd also forgotten to turn on the exterior light by her camper door. She hadn't even remembered to leave a light on for Babs. What a good dog mommy she was. That poor baby was alone in the dark, even though she was probably asleep.

As she unlocked the door, she noticed a piece of paper wedged underneath. As the door opened, the paper fluttered to the ground and was caught in a breeze that blew it under the trailer. Instinctively, Mamie reached for it just as Babs jumped up on her, knocking her off balance. She fell off the aluminum step with Babs all over her, licking her and pinning her to the ground. As she struggled with the dog while trying not to reinjure her wrist, she peered under the trailer looking for the slip of paper. It was just within reach.

Mamie was finally able to shove the dog off her body. She reached for the paper, but just as her fingers touched it, another breeze caught it.

That's as good as gone, she thought as she scrambled to her feet, brushing herself off. Had anyone seen her fall? What a klutz. If anyone had, they had probably gotten quite a show. That dang dog. Speaking of dog, where had Babs gone?

Mamie retrieved her bag from where it had landed on the ground and set the overturned step in place as panic squeezed her chest. "Babs?" she said. "Babs?" Louder this time. "Babs, come here, baby." Forgetting about the slip of paper, she peered into the darkness looking for her little companion. Where could she have gone?

Don't panic. She couldn't have gone far. Yes, she could have. The little dog could run like nobody's business. But in a strange place she might be too afraid to wander off. Mamie stepped onto the road, hoping to catch a glimpse of her dog. Tears sprang to her eyes. What would she do if she couldn't find her? She refused to panic. Babs had to be somewhere close. She had to be.

"Babs, where did you go, silly? Mama's looking for you. Come on back." She walked toward the clubhouse, thinking maybe the dog was looking for a place to relieve herself. There was a grassy spot at the end of the row of campsites that she had used before. But as Mamie neared that area, there was no sign of the dog.

Panic seized her as she fought to keep her fear in check. She could not lose this dog. She *would not* lose this dog. The little four-legged creature had saved her sanity when West had been so sick. When she had trouble coping with his declining health and mental faculties, Babs had been there to keep her from giving up. It was Babs she had snuggled with in the guest bedroom at night because she couldn't share the bedroom with West—he had become too restless and violent. It was Babs who gave her comfort when no one else saw the tears.

"Babs! Where are you?" she cried, tears spilling down her cheeks.

"Looking for somebody?"

Mamie whirled around to see her beloved pet in the arms of Brady Hayden. She had never been so happy to see a campground maintenance worker. A broad smile spread across the young man's face as he deposited the wiggly dog into Mamie's arms.

"You found her! Where was she?" Mamie pressed her face into the back of the dog's neck, hoping her fur would wipe away the tears so Brady couldn't tell she had been crying.

"She wasn't far. I was making my evening rounds and saw her trotting around the park. I'm just glad I found her before she got hit by a car or attacked by a coyote or something."

Mamie hadn't thought of that. Her knees suddenly felt weak, but she dared not let go of the dog. Not without her harness and leash.

"How did she get loose?"

"I…uh…I forgot to leave the outside light on, or a light on in the camper, and when I opened the door, she jumped up on me, knocked me down, and took off. I guess she needed to go to the bathroom." Mamie was glad Brady couldn't see the color that crept into her warming face.

"Are you hurt?" Brady's brow furrowed with concern as he touched her shoulder.

"I'm fine, just embarrassed. Thank you so much for finding her. I just can't imagine my life without this little stinker."

"No problem. We do get attached, don't we? Why don't I give you a ride to your camper?" he said, gesturing to the golf cart behind him.

Mamie almost declined the offer, but it was dark, she was tired, and the twenty-five-pound dog was heavy, so she agreed and climbed in, sitting on the bench seat with the dog in her lap.

"Thank you again," she said as Brady pulled into her campsite a couple of minutes later. They hadn't even had time for conversation. She noticed he waited until she and Babs were safely inside before he left. Then she remembered the note. Could it still be under the trailer?

She settled Babs on the bed, covered her with a throw, grabbed a flashlight, and flipped on the exterior light before stepping carefully outdoors. The cool night air made Mamie wish she had thrown on West's shirt. She knelt next to her camper and peered underneath, shining the light around but seeing nothing that resembled paper. She stood and walked around the back, scanning the ground with her flashlight. Just as she gave up, something white fluttered at the base of the pole under the water faucet. She bent to see what it was. The piece of paper. She could hardly believe it hadn't gotten away.

She grabbed it and went back inside the camper where she laid the note on the countertop, and then changed into her pajamas. It had been a long day. As curious as she was to see if there was anything written on the paper, she wanted to get comfortable and climb into bed.

It was nearing 9:00 when she finally settled into bed in her comfy pajamas, her pillows arranged just so, her teeth brushed, her face scrubbed, her whiskey and sparkling water made and sitting next to her on the counter. She lifted the paper and uncrumpled it. There were indeed words scrawled on it, almost unintelligible, but her teacher's background had made her an expert at deciphering bad handwriting.

Be careful what you wish for, honey. You may get more than you bargained for.

The same words as the note she had found in the book in Sarah's trailer. But this was a different piece of paper, not like the other, which had been torn out of the notepad on the counter in the RV park office. This note was written on a white sticky note, and the sticky part had dirt, leaf particles, and grass stuck to it. It must have been stuck to her door and fallen off.

Another clue for Sergeant Sovern. Another clue for herself. She used her phone to snap a photo of the note before stuffing it into the side pocket of her purse. Even after the warming, relaxing effect of the cocktail, she had a hard time going to sleep. The faces of Howard

Story, Brady, Sarah, Carly, and the other ladies she had met kept running through her mind with questions, not to mention the image of that body floating in the water. There was only one day left on the campout, and a solution needed to be found. As much as she liked Magnolia Bluff, she didn't want to have to stay longer than she had planned.

Chapter Fourteen

SATURDAY. ALREADY. MAMIE woke up just as tired as she had been when she went to bed the night before. Babs, realizing that her owner was awake, pounced on her, no doubt needing to go outside.

"Give me a minute, crazy dog," Mamie muttered. It sure would be nice to get a cup of coffee first, but that wouldn't happen. She swung her legs off the bed and put her bare feet on the cool camper floor. Babs jumped down and stood at the door waiting. Mamie donned her slip-on sneakers and West's old shirt before wrestling with Babs to get her harness and leash on.

The pleasant morning promised a beautiful day—sunny and cloudless with the birds chirping happily in the trees. In the distance Mamie could see swans and ducks waddling along the shore as she and Babs headed toward the lake, passing other campers.

She heard talking and spotted several ladies gathered in one campsite, including Marlene, Sissy, Bertie, and Carly. Carly sat bent over with her hands cupping her face. The other ladies stood around her talking, but as soon as they saw Mamie, they hushed.

"What is it?" Carly sat up and turned to see Mamie. "Oh, it's you."

Mamie ignored the rudeness. "Good morning, ladies. Sorry if I interrupted. We're just headed to the lake on our morning walk. Care to join us?" Mamie forced herself to be chipper, dying to know what they had been talking about.

"No, we do not," Carly said.

"There's no need to be rude," Sissy said. "Good morning to you, too, Mamie. Thank you but I think we will pass."

"Okay, maybe I'll see you around later."

Carly kept her sullen expression as she turned away. The other ladies smiled and waved before Mamie continued her walk. They then started talking to Carly in low voices that Mamie could not make out. What was going on? Did they know something about Sarah's murder? Or about the body found in the lake?

After walking Babs, Mamie decided to go to the clubhouse to see if any ladies were gathered there and if she might hear anything. But coffee first. After starting her coffee maker, she dug in her vintage suitcase and pulled out a pair of Bermuda shorts and a T-shirt. Then she ran a wet wipe over her face and body and brushed her hair and teeth. When the coffee had finished dripping, she filled her mug, cranked open a couple of windows, turned on the fan for Babs, locked the camper, and headed to the clubhouse. Would the same ladies be there? Would they have heard anything about the murders? Mamie hustled, hoping her curiosity would be satisfied.

Lanie, Sheila, and Tessa sat at a table working a jigsaw puzzle. A few other ladies, including Lou and Florence, sat at another table playing cards. Coffee and tea were ready on the counter that opened into the kitchen, along with breakfast pastries and fruit. Mamie's tummy rumbled.

"Hey, Mamie! Help us put this puzzle together,"

Lanie said, waving Mamie over to their table.

"Good morning," Mamie said as she joined them.

"What's up, our new friend?" Tessa said.

Should she tell them? Surely they'd already heard. "You've heard about the body I spotted floating in the lake yesterday, right?"

"You found the body? I thought Marlene did," Sheila said. "So creepy!"

"Yes, I did—well, Babs alerted me to it—but Marlene and several others were with me. And yes, it was creepy. Any news on who it may have been?"

"I heard it was a woman who lives across the lake," Lou piped up from the other table. "I don't think it was one of us."

"Well, that's a relief," Sheila said. "I mean, not to say it isn't horrible. It certainly is a coincidence that there have been two bodies found this weekend in this campground. Wonder if one has anything to do with the other?"

That's what I would like to know, Mamie thought.

"Maybe there's a serial killer out there," Florence said. She shuddered. "Deal the cards, Lou. I don't want to think about that."

"Sergeant Sovern did tell us to watch our backs," Lou said. "We just need to be careful."

"I'm thinking about leaving early," Florence said.

"We can't, remember?" Lou said. "The police told us to stay here. Besides, I've been looking forward to this campout for months, and I'm not going to let any killer run me off."

Sheila laughed. "No, we'll run him off."

Lanie shook her head. "You guys are crazy. This is serious, you know. We need to stay together and not venture anywhere alone. I doubt if anyone is going to get to leave until they figure out who the killer or killers are."

"I'm terrified of going anywhere by myself," Tessa said. "Even to the bathroom."

Mamie smiled at the young woman. Maybe she shouldn't be walking Babs alone anymore. She had seen another lady with a dog. Maybe they could walk their dogs together.

"My family isn't going to be happy if I can't go home Sunday," Sheila said. "My husband especially."

"Mine, either," Lanie agreed. The other ladies nodded.

The door to the clubhouse swung open and two officers strode in: Investigator Sovern and Officer Vandegan. Mamie almost dropped her coffee mug.

"Good morning, Officers," Sheila said, ever cheerful and outgoing. "We have breakfast if you like." She gestured toward the spread of pastries on the counter.

"Thanks. I will take some coffee if you have it," Sovern said.

"Coffee sounds good," Vandegan said. "How are you ladies doing this morning?" A hint of a smile curved his mouth, a handsome mouth, Mamie decided. She blushed as Vandegan's gaze rested on her. Thank goodness she'd brushed her hair and put on eyeliner, blush, and lipstick. She hadn't worn makeup since she'd left home. She must have known on some level that she would see Vandegan that day.

Sheila hopped up to fetch coffee for the men as Lanie pointed to a chair. "Please join us."

"Thanks, but we have work to do. I hope you ladies are being cautious," Sovern said.

"We were just talking about that," Lou said. "We're all supposed to go home tomorrow. Will that be happening?"

Vandegan glanced at Sovern. "We're in the process of taking statements from everyone. As soon as we sift through those, we'll decide who needs to stay, if anyone, but it may be a couple more days before we get to everyone."

The ladies glanced at each other and sighed.

"I'm afraid it's just the nature of investigations. Thank you, ma'am," Vandegan said as Sheila handed him a steaming Styrofoam cup.

"Thank you," Sovern said as he received his.

The door to the clubhouse swung open as two women stormed in, huffing and puffing.

"We heard who the person in the lake was!" one of them said.

Mamie and the other ladies turned toward the officers.

"There's nothing official, yet, ladies," Sovern said. "What you may have heard is just hearsay. The investigation is still underway."

The ladies who'd burst into the clubhouse seemed to deflate. "Oh," one said.

Sovern tipped his coffee cup, finishing the last drop of the stimulating liquid. Vandegan did the same.

"Ladies, thanks for the coffee. If you haven't given your statement yet, someone will be in touch. Stay here at the campground, if you would, to make it easier for us to find you," Vandegan said, even though they had already been told to do just that. The two men tossed their cups into the trash can near the door and exited the room.

As soon as the door shut, all eyes riveted to the two women who had entered.

"So, who was it? Do tell," Sheila said.

"We didn't know her, but she was a new member of Gals Gone Glamping and wasn't supposed to be here until yesterday. She didn't have a camper, so she was staying in a cabin. No one really knew her, so no one noticed she was missing. I guess her family must have called here to check on her after she wouldn't answer her phone."

"How do you know all this?" Lou said.

"We were buying firewood from the guy in the office and happened to mention it and he told us."

Happened to mention it? Mamie thought. "Did he give you any other details?"

"Only that he found a strange note in her cabin that was written on paper from a note pad he keeps on the counter in the office."

Mamie's stomach clenched. "What did it say?"

"Something like, *Be careful what you wish for. It*

might be more than you bargained for."

Chapter Fifteen

"THAT NOTE IS cropping up too often for my comfort," Mamie said.

"What do you mean?" Sheila said.

"I found a note with that message in Sarah's trailer, and then the same message was left at my camper door. Now one has been found in the dead woman's cabin." Mamie shuddered.

"Did you tell the investigators?" Lanie said.

"Yes, I did, at least about the first note. It was written on paper from a notepad on the office counter."

"Are you sure?" Sheila said.

"Yes, I'm sure of it. Unless the killer got hold of another notepad just like it."

"That's unlikely," Tessa said.

"I know."

"What worries me is that you found a note at your camper door," Sheila said. "Aren't you afraid you're being targeted?"

"I wasn't, really. Besides, I have that ferocious watchdog, you know." Mamie smirked.

"Shouldn't you give that note to the officers?"

"I should, I suppose. I left it in my camper," Mamie said.

"Mamie, why don't I go with you to get the note, and Lanie can call the detective and have him meet us here. He should still be in the campground taking statements." Sheila stood.

Mamie nodded and followed her new friend out of the clubhouse. "So much for going shopping," Sheila said.

Officer Vandegan came out of the motorhome parked next to Mamie's camper when she and Sheila got to her campsite. Sheila nudged her and smiled. "Look who's here," she whispered.

Mamie rolled her eyes and unlocked her camper door. She heard a thump inside as Babs landed on the floor, probably napping on the bed again.

"We meet again, ladies. Ms. West? I'm ready to take your statement. Would you excuse us for a few minutes, ma'am?" Vandegan said.

"I'm Sheila Webb. Will you be needing mine soon?"

"Yes, as a matter of fact. I can take yours as soon as we're done here."

"I'll be at my camper," Sheila said. "Site 82. Don't forget what we came for," she told Mamie, who nodded and gestured to a chair for Vandegan.

"Thanks, Ms. Webb. I'll see you in a bit. Now, Ms. West, I need you to tell me everything you know about the discoveries of the two bodies at this campground." He pulled a recorder from his shirt pocket and motioned for Mamie to begin.

It only took a few minutes for Mamie to describe her involvement as Babs whined from behind the camper door. "I have something to give you," she said.

Vandegan nodded, his eyebrows raised. She opened the camper door, blocking Babs from getting out while she retrieved the note she had found under her door the previous night.

He took it from her, read it, and frowned. As he placed it in a plastic bag from his other shirt pocket, he said, "Someone obviously considers you a threat. We're having a patrol unit stay here at the campground. Don't go anywhere alone. If you can, have someone stay with you in your camper."

"Have you seen how small my camper is? There isn't room for anyone else. Besides, Babs is a good watchdog. She'll protect me, or at least alert me if someone comes around."

His expression softened, giving her goosebumps. Why was he affecting her this way? She glanced at his left hand, hoping to see a wedding band, but there was nothing. Could he possibly be single? Probably divorced, with a minivan full of kids. *Run away.*

"I'm concerned for your safety, even if you aren't," he said. "I wish you would consider what I've recommended."

Mamie threw all caution to the wind as she reached forward from the chair she occupied opposite him and touched his knee. "Thank you, Officer. I've gotten used to taking care of myself. I'm not afraid. I'm sure I will be fine."

He stared at the female hand resting delicately on his knee before she suddenly removed it as if she'd been bitten. He grabbed it before she pulled it out of reach. She gasped.

"Ms. West."

"Please call me Mamie."

"Mamie, I—"

"Officer, are you going to get my statement now?" Sheila had returned to Mamie's campsite. Vandegan dropped her hand. Her face burned.

"Yes, I'll be right there. We're just finishing up."

"I can see that," Sheila said. "I have coffee ready if you'd like a cup."

Vandegan stood. "Thank you, Ms. West. We'll be in touch. In the meantime, please do not leave the campground." In a softer voice, he added, "And please be careful."

Warmth suffused her body as she nodded, at a loss for words. He had a personal interest in her safety, or at least it seemed he did. She caught a wink from Sheila as the police officer followed her to her campsite. Mamie rolled her eyes. She felt like a teenager again. It had been a long time since a man had made her skin tingle. She glanced at the hand he had held for a moment. It looked the same as it always had, but it sure felt different.

She fastened the harness and leash on Babs and walked toward the lake, careful to keep an eye on Sheila's campsite. Vandegan was sitting outside opposite Sheila, probably asking some of the same questions he had asked Mamie. In a few minutes, he left Sheila's campsite and walked to the next one, knocking on the camper door. Lanie opened the door and then joined him outside. One by one, he would be talking to every woman in the camping group. Mamie didn't envy his job, and it seemed much too slow, when the clues were there. Why weren't the police tracking down fingerprints, note paper, and handwriting samples? Why hadn't he asked her and

Sheila for samples of their handwriting? It didn't make sense.

Maybe she should do some investigating on her own. She would start with handwriting samples. It was good she had taken photos of those two notes she had found. She hadn't seen the note found in the cabin, though, but it had to have been written by the same person.

Now to figure out how to get those samples without stirring suspicion. *Wait.* Hadn't everyone had to sign in when they picked up their nametags and goodie bags in the clubhouse? Maybe the sign-in sheet was still there.

Mamie hurried Babs back to her camper, locked the dog inside, and dashed to the clubhouse. *Good.* No one was inside. She went to the table that held the remaining nametags and goodie bags, thankful that Marlene and Sissy hadn't put them away yet. The sign-in sheet was still there. *What luck.* Mamie glanced around to make sure no one had come in from the kitchen or restrooms, pulled her phone out of her pocket, and snapped a couple of photos of the signature-filled sheet. She couldn't wait to get back to her camper to start the comparisons.

But as she neared her campsite, she saw that two ladies were there waiting for her. They had introduced themselves at the LCR game, but she couldn't remember their names.

"Hey, Mamie," one of the ladies with flaming red hair said, "we were wondering if we could take a look inside your camper."

"It's so cute. We wondered who it belonged to," said

the other lady, whose gray curls escaped a ball cap.

Darn. Her job would have to wait. "Sure!" Trying for a cheerful rather than disappointed tone, Mamie unlocked the door and grabbed Babs before she could escape. "Let me get her leash on her and then feel free to go inside."

As soon as Mamie had leashed the dog, she stepped aside so the ladies could peek inside. They used the step to enter one at a time, their *oohs* and *ahs* bringing a smile to Mamie's face.

"You've decorated it so cute!"

"Where did you find your bedding?"

"I love the colors."

"I envy you ladies with these vintage campers. I could never give up my modern conveniences, though. Does it even have a bathroom?"

Mamie laughed and pointed to a lower cabinet door. "I have a port-a-potty in there."

One of them opened the door, and then they glanced at each other, their eyes wide. "A bucket?"

"Yes, with a toilet seat I ordered online. I line it with a trash bag and an adult diaper or kitty litter. It works great."

"Ew," the lady with the red hair said.

"Beats hooking up to the sewer and flushing lines," Mamie countered.

"To each his own," the lady with the ball cap said.

"Exactly," Mamie agreed. "By the way, what are your names again? I've forgotten."

Ball cap lady stuck out her hand. "I'm Greta, and this is Ruthie."

"Thank you so much for letting us look," Ruthie said. "It's darling, bucket and all."

"Thank you. I'm enjoying her. It's Miss Maisie's and my first trip together, and it's like having a playhouse. Babs seems to like it, too."

"Miss Maisie. Great name. We'll see you at dinner." And off they went.

Much to Babs's dismay, Mamie entered the camper with her and closed and locked the door. It was time to compare notes. Literally.

Chapter Sixteen

ALTHOUGH THERE WERE only forty-two signatures, it was tedious switching from the photos of the notes to the photos of the signatures. What if the writer of the notes wasn't a woman, or even the killer? Why would the killer shoot a woman from a car the first time and then drown someone the next time? Maybe it wasn't a drowning. Maybe the victim had been murdered and then thrown in the lake.

None of the signatures seemed to match the notes, but there was another problem. The handwriting was a little different on each note. She was no handwriting expert, but there was no time or money to hire one.

Banging on her camper door elicited fierce barking from Babs, who had been balled up on the bed while Mamie sat at the dinette going through signatures.

"Wait a sec," Mamie said as she got up to open the door. "Quiet, Babs, it's okay." At least she hoped it was. She hesitated before unlocking the door. Surely the killer wouldn't bang on the door in broad daylight with the police nearby. Besides, the killer would probably just try to come in without knocking, and she had locked it. When she finally opened it, the person standing on her step wasn't who she expected, though she couldn't be sure who she did expect. It was Carly, but this time she wasn't mad as a wet hen. She seemed contrite.

"Hey, I just wanted to apologize for my behavior at the clubhouse last night. I had a little too much wine."

You think? Mamie thought as she stared at her,

waiting for her to continue. There wasn't enough room in her camper—or her heart, for that matter—to invite her inside. She decided to give her the benefit of the doubt, anyway.

Carly shifted from one foot to the other. "I don't really remember what I said, but I know I upset you, and I'm sorry. It's just so messed up, what happened to Sarah. If I could, I would go back home, but the cops won't let me leave."

"Are you a suspect?"

"What? Me? No, but I was on the scene when her body was found. And we were good friends, Sarah and me."

"I just wondered. Do you know anything about the notes that have been found?"

"Notes?"

"Yes, the ones that say 'be careful what you wish for, honey. You may get more than you bargained for.' Those are the words you spoke to me last night."

Carly's face paled. She backed off the step and plopped in one of the chairs sitting outside the trailer. Mamie stepped outside, careful to close the screen so Babs wouldn't escape.

"It was you, wasn't it? You wrote those notes."

"No, I didn't. I don't know anything about any notes."

"I don't believe you. You either wrote them, or you know who did. Otherwise, you wouldn't have almost fainted just now, and you wouldn't have quoted the same words to me."

"I haven't eaten anything all day," Carly said.

Mamie rolled her eyes and frowned, her hands on her hips. "Carly, tell the truth. You knew about those notes."

"Okay, I saw the note that Sarah had. Somebody had tucked it into the book she was reading without anyone seeing who did it. I don't know who wrote it, and neither did she."

"Why do you think someone would write that to her?" Mamie sat in the chair opposite Carly.

"I don't know why I should tell you anything. It's really none of your business, is it?"

"Any information you share might help the investigation and help us go home that much sooner," Mamie said.

"All right. I guess you heard Sarah had a troubled marriage. She had told me and probably others that she wished she had never met that husband of hers. He had caused her nothing but grief."

"No, I hadn't heard that at all. I heard they had been married thirty years, and that their daughter Dannie is about to get married. The husband's name is Hunter, right?"

"Yes, that's right. He has a drug problem and has been in and out of rehab so many times I lost count. I think Sarah even lost count. Before this campout, he fell off the wagon again and threatened to kill her if she sent him to rehab again. She was at her wits' end with him and had told him she wanted a divorce. She told me all this Thursday afternoon while she was setting up her campsite. It wasn't two hours after that when she was killed."

"You think he shot her?"

"If he did, he was driving a different vehicle. People who saw it said it was a brown nineties model Chevy pickup. Hunter drives a new Toyota Tundra."

"Have you shared this information with Sergeant Sovern?"

"Not all of it. He knows about the pickup, though. He was tracking down the plate number. One of the other campers—not in our group—had gotten the license plate number."

"Carly, you should tell Sovern everything. Do you think Hunter wrote the note, then?"

"If he did, he had someone else put it in her book. Someone who is camping with us."

Mamie shivered. Had one of the ladies helped set Sarah up?

"So how and when did she discover the note in her book?"

"She had left her book outside on the picnic table while she was inside her trailer. The next time she picked up the book she saw the note."

"When did she show it to you?"

"I was actually there with her, you know, when she was setting up her camper. She showed it to me a minute after she found it."

"And she had no idea who wrote it?"

"She figured Hunter did. She figured someone

must have told him what she had said about wishing she had never met him."

"But you weren't there when she was shot."

"No, I had gone back to my camper to see if I had any extra paper towels. Sarah had forgotten to bring any. I was on my way back when I heard the shot."

"But you didn't see the vehicle or the shooter?"

"No. What are you, anyway, a private investigator?"

Mamie laughed at the thought. "Nowhere near. My late husband was a police officer and we used to watch murder mysteries on TV. I guess I am just curious. Plus, I'd like to be able to go home. Tomorrow is Sunday. It looks like we will be here a lot longer than that."

"You said there were notes. Did you see them, too?"

"I didn't see the one that was found in the other victim's cabin, but there was a note left here at my camper."

Carly looked surprised. "Did it say the same thing?"

"Yes, but it was written on different paper. The first one was written on the same paper that I saw on a notepad on the campground office counter. This one was on a white sticky note, but the handwriting is similar."

"A notepad in the office? Maybe the guy in the office wrote it, then. Maybe Hunter had him write it and put it in Sarah's book."

"I don't know. I haven't seen his handwriting. Maybe I should try to get a sample, although Hunter having Howard Story write a threatening note and leave it in Sarah's book is pretty farfetched, don't you think?"

Carly stood. "Yeah, I guess you're right. It had to be someone Hunter would trust to do his dirty work, someone who would know how and where to leave the note. I can't imagine who that might be, but if I can help you in any way, let me know. The police haven't done anything, and I'd like to get home. I have a job to get to."

She doesn't understand police work, Mamie thought. "I'm sure they're working as hard as they can behind the scenes to find the killer. Thank you, Carly. I appreciate your help."

Mamie watched Carly walk away, then entered her camper, where Babs greeted her by jumping up on her legs, which were exposed below the hem of her Bermudas.

"Ouch, girl!" More scratches on her legs. She bent and let the dog lick her face before turning her attention back to the photos on her phone. Who could have written those notes? And why would Sarah's husband have something against the other dead woman? Was she getting too close? Is that why she got a note, too?

Chapter Seventeen

THE DAY WAS still young, and Mamie felt an urgent need to get a sample of Howard Story's handwriting. How would she do that? She checked the ice in her cooler, and much of it had melted. Vintage ice chests had nothing on the newer thick-walled ones. She'd have to invest in a newer one soon.

Leaving Babs in the camper, she trekked up the hill to the office, hoping to find Mr. Story working the counter. But instead of Office Man, it was Brady. As easy as he was on the eyes, Mamie's heart sank.

"Good morning, Mrs. West, I mean, Mamie. How can I help you?"

Sweet young man remembered her name.

"I was hoping to speak to Mr. Story," she said, trying to come up with something that would make sense. She couldn't say she was there for ice and wanted to purchase only from Mr. Story. It wouldn't pay to hurt Brady's feelings, either. He had been so helpful.

"He's off this afternoon, but I can help you. What do you need?"

That was it, then.

"I wanted to speak with him about something, but I'll have to catch him another time. While I'm here, though, you can sell me a small bag of ice."

"I can certainly do that. It'll be $3.50. Howard will be back in the morning. Want to leave him a message?" Brady picked up a pen and prepared to write on the notepad she wanted Howard to write on. Maybe she should look at Brady's handwriting as well. Her mind scrambled for something to say.

"Yes, please ask him to let me know when he's back." She watched Brady write the note as she laid a ten-dollar bill on the counter. How could she distract him so she could steal the note? "Do you think you could take the ice down to my camper for me? My knee has been giving me a bit of trouble and I don't want to aggravate it, plus my wrist still hurts." Which was not a total lie.

"Could you watch the office while I do that?" Brady placed the money in a drawer under the counter and counted out her change.

She waved it away. "Sure, and keep the change. Just put the bag of ice on the cooler outside my camper. Thank you so much, Brady."

"You don't want me to put it in your cooler?" He shoved the money into his pants pocket.

"I need to empty the water out first."

"I'll take care of it. I'll be back in a bit."

"You're the best, Brady. Thank you." Good, that would give her more time. She made sure he had driven away in the golf cart with the ice before ripping the top sheet off the notepad. She studied the handwriting, trying to decide if it was similar to the writing on the notes.

She whirled around, shoving the slip of paper in her pocket as the old door creaked open and the screen door slammed shut.

"Well, hello, there, Missy," Howard Story said as he

lumbered toward her.

"Hello, Mr. Story. I didn't expect you. Brady said you were off this afternoon." Now she could tell Brady that she had torn up the note because Mr. Story had come in after all.

"The wife took off to visit her parents so I thought I would come on in. Young man like Brady needs more time off to spend with his girl and have fun while he can." Story chuckled. "I remember them days. Where is he, anyway? He's supposed to be minding the store."

"He is taking a bag of ice to my camper for me." Now to get Story to write something. She picked up the notepad and handed it to him. "I need to go. Could you leave a note for him from me?"

"I could, but your handwriting has got to be nicer than mine. Why don't you write it? Or I can just tell him. My mind's not that far gone yet." He chuckled as he passed the notepad back to her and pointed to the pen on the counter.

Rats. Another idea popped into her mind. "Mr. Story, I'm thinking of going into town to find the hardware store. Could you jot down directions for me?" She laid the notepad on the counter.

By this time, Mr. Story had made his way behind the counter. "Sure thing. I'd rather just tell you, but you want me to write it down, huh? Why don't you write it down while I tell you?"

"No, I'll get it wrong. I'd rather you do it. Plus, my wrist is still bothering me." He didn't need to know that she was right-handed and could write just fine. He also didn't know that she wasn't supposed to leave the campground.

"Well, all right. I warned you. I hope you can read my hen scratch."

"I was a teacher. I can read anyone's handwriting." Mamie laughed.

"I bet you can." Story proceeded to scrawl directions onto the paper as she waited. When he was finished, he tore off the sheet of paper and handed it to her. "See if it makes sense to you."

She glanced at it, barely reading it at all. The handwriting was what she needed, not directions to the hardware store. If she needed to go there, her phone's GPS worked just fine. *I'm glad he didn't think of that,* she thought with a smile.

"Thank you so much, Mr. Story. These directions are easy to read and understand."

Just then Brady burst into the office. "I thought you were taking the afternoon off, Mr. Story."

"I was, but then my wife left, so I figured I'd come and let you have some time off, son."

"Really? Thanks!" The grin on his face was as big as Texas. He flung the key to the golf cart onto the counter. "Your ice is in your cooler, Mrs. West. If you're not here when I come to work tomorrow, it's been a pleasure. Oh, Mr. Story, there's a note for you on the counter, but I guess she has already spoken to you. Thanks again, sir." With that, the young man was out the door and starting his classic pickup truck.

"Was there a note for me?" the office manager asked Mamie. "Did you need to tell me something?"

"It was nothing. I tore it off. I just wanted to tell you what an absolute gem you have in Brady. He is just the best."

"That he is, that he is," Story agreed. "In spite of his Aunt Scarlett. His parents are nothing like her, believe me. But she was nice enough to let him work here. I can say that for her. Anyway, that's neither here nor there. Did he take your payment for the ice?"

"Yes, he did. Thank you, Mr. Story. I will see you later. I'm supposed to check out tomorrow, but we'll see. I'm waiting for a release from the investigator."

"I hope they arrest a suspect soon. Having a murderer on the loose around here is unsettling. You be safe, you hear? And let me know if you need anything."

It was unsettling. She tried not to think about it, but even walking back to her trailer by herself she was on edge. She couldn't wait to compare the handwriting samples to the notes on her phone in private. Babs would just have to wait to go for a walk. It hadn't been that long since her last one anyway.

"Hello, Babsy," Mamie said as she stepped into the camper. The dog jumped off the bench seat of the dinette, her bobbed tail wagging furiously. Mamie allowed her to cover her face with wet kisses before she sat on the bench to compare notes. The blood drained from her face. It couldn't be, but there was no doubt. The handwriting on the notes belonged to Brady.

Brady? No!

***

Mamie clipped the leash to Babs's harness and

stepped out of the camper in a daze. It would take a minute to wrap her head around the fact that Brady was the killer. Or was he? Just because he wrote the notes didn't mean he was the actual killer. He could have been coerced or bribed to write those notes. What was his connection to the women who had died? Did he know Sarah's husband? Did he know the new Three Gees member who had rented the cabin and been found in the lake? He hadn't been driving the vehicle from which the shots had been fired. Had he? Hadn't he been at the campground during the shooting?

Then she remembered that she had seen Carly leaving Sarah's trailer after she had found the book with the note. What had Carly been doing in the trailer? Was she connected to Brady somehow? Did she know him before this campout? So. Many. Questions.

Carly was outside her camper when Mamie walked by with Babs. "I wonder if I should ask her why she was in Sarah's camper," she said to her dog. Babs looked up at her and then continued to sniff along their path.

"Hey, Mamie, any new developments?" Carly asked as they met in the roadway. "I mean, I know it's only been a little while since we talked, but I saw you walk up to the office. Did you find out anything?"

Mamie looked at her. "Can we sit and talk somewhere?"

Carly frowned. "Sure, let's go inside my camper."

"You don't mind if Babs comes in?"

"Not at all. I have dogs at home. They go camping with me and my husband sometimes."

Carly opened the camper door and motioned for Mamie and Babs to enter. Mamie glanced around, taking in the modern and roomy interior of the new RV. It didn't quite have the charm of her little vintage camper, but it did have its perks, including a bathroom and a full-size refrigerator.

"This is nice and roomy," she said.

"Much bigger than yours, yes. I used to have a vintage trailer, but I'm enjoying all the modern amenities this one has. What do you need to tell me? Would you like a glass of wine? I was about to pour myself a pinot grigio."

"Sure," Mamie said as she sat at the dinette. Babs curled up on the floor next to her. "First, I'd like to ask you a question."

Carly poured two glasses of wine and set them on the table. "Shoot away." She slid onto the bench opposite Mamie.

"The night after Sarah's murder I saw you come out of her trailer. Why were you in there? I saw a light inside and then you came out."

Carly swallowed her first sip of wine and looked at Mamie. "I was looking for the book and the note."

"The book and note I had already found. Why were you looking for it? You know who wrote it, don't you? Why don't you tell me the truth, Carly?"

"I wanted to find it and turn it over to the authorities. No, I do not know who wrote it, and that is the truth. I've already told you that." She took another sip of wine.

"I'm still not sure I believe you. That seems like a

flimsy excuse for you to be sneaking around inside the trailer at night." Mamie's wine sat untouched.

The familiar hardened expression came over Carly's face. "You can believe me or not, but it's the truth. I had no idea you had already found it. Have you found out anything else or not?"

Mamie swallowed. Should she tell Carly her suspicions about Brady? What if Carly went to him and he fled before the investigators could question him? She decided to keep her thoughts to herself.

"Nothing that I can share," Mamie said, scooting out of the dinette.

"Are you leaving? You haven't even tasted your wine. It's a local wine. You should try it."

Mamie picked up the glass and brought it to her lips. She preferred sweet red wine, but this was pretty good.

"What do you think?"

"I'm not exactly a wine aficionado, but it's good, I must admit. Thank you for sharing a glass with me." Mamie stood, Babs hopping to her feet as well. "I better get this dog walked and get some rest before dinnertime. I apologize for accusing you." It might pay to keep Carly in her good graces.

Carly smiled. The way to her heart was to enjoy her wine, apparently. "So you believe me. Good. I forgive you. Please keep me in the loop about what you find out. I'd like to help if I can."

Mamie nodded before taking a couple more sips. She opened the camper door, led Babs out and closed the door behind her. Even if she didn't fully believe Carly, it didn't hurt for Carly to think she did. Now to find out more about Brady.

***

A Magnolia Bluff patrol car was parked outside the clubhouse. Curious, Mamie walked Babs over, hoping an officer would emerge. She let Babs sniff around the bushes near the door and tried to gather her thoughts. If Brady was the killer, what was his motive? Why would he have anything against Sarah or the other woman? Was he in cahoots with Hunter? Were the two murders related? Was he just a serial killer looking for random victims?

Her skin crawled at the thought.

Nick Vandegan stepped out of the clubhouse and her heartbeat quickened. She stared at him, wondering how long it would take him to realize she was there. Not long, to her great satisfaction.

"Hello, Mamie."

She pulled on the leash to keep Babs, who had headed his way with full-on wigglebottom, from jumping up on him.

"Do you think she would let me pet her?" He stepped toward the dog.

"Probably, but she might take a nip at you. You never know, and I can't tell if she does it because she wants to play or if she really wants to bite."

He reached down to allow the dog to sniff his hand. "My family had Boston terriers when I was growing up. I miss them." He rubbed Babs's back before straightening.

"Are you still interviewing ladies from our group?"

Mamie asked.

"I think I may be finished. I just wanted to see if anyone was in the meeting room in case I missed someone. I need to go back over the list Marlene gave me and make sure I've gotten to everyone."

She nodded. "I guess no one is getting to go home tomorrow, then."

"I'm fairly positive most of your group will be released tomorrow, but I want to go over my notes one more time tonight. I'll be back in the morning to let everyone know."

"I found out something else a little while ago that I think you should know."

"Could we discuss it over coffee? I'm having an afternoon slump and I could really use a good cup. Would you like to ride into town with me?"

Her eyes widened as a long-forgotten kind of shiver ran up her spine. No, she wouldn't take this as anything other than a meeting with the officer to share evidence. But the butterflies in her stomach were not paying attention.

Chapter Eighteen

THE REALLY GOOD Wood-Fired Coffee Shop and Ice Cream Emporium bustled with Saturday afternoon customers. Several greeted Officer Vandegan, speaking his name or shaking his hand or both. Mamie felt curious eyes on her as she slid into a booth opposite him.

"Everyone seems to know you, and everyone is really friendly," she said.

"Yes, it's a small town. Everyone knows one another. They'll be asking all kinds of questions about you." He chuckled. "Fuel for the gossipmongers."

A blond medium-built man wearing nice slacks and a polo shirt approached their table. "Good afternoon, Officer, and. . ." he paused, waiting for an introduction.

"This is Mamie West. She's camping out at the reservoir this weekend with a group of ladies. Mamie, this is Harry Thurgood, owner of the coffee shop."

"Hayden's Resort?" Harry extended his hand in a warm handshake, which reminded her of those of the men in her church back home.

"Yes," she replied. "Pleasure."

"What can I get for you?"

"I'd like my usual cup of strong black, and maybe half a bagel with cream cheese. He has specialty coffees and other pastries, if you'd like to see a menu, Mamie."

"Just a small cup of decaf for me, please."

"Nothing to eat?" Harry asked.

She shook her head.

"Coming right up."

"All right," Vandegan said when Harry was out of earshot. "What is it you have to tell me?"

Mamie pulled her phone and the slip of paper with Brady's handwriting out of her bag. "I took it upon myself to see if any of the ladies' signatures matched the handwriting on the notes I found. I also compared the handwriting of a couple of campground staff. Look at this." She showed him the photos of the found notes and the note she had gotten from the office counter notepad.

Vandegan frowned as he looked at her. "Looks like a match to me. Whose handwriting is it?"

Mamie shifted in her seat and bit her bottom lip. She hated to say it aloud. "Brady Hayden," she whispered.

Vandegan's eyes widened but he remained silent as Harry and a server set two cups of coffee, a saucer with a bagel and cream cheese, and another plate with biscotti on the table. Mamie covered the note with her phone.

"Anything else we can get you?" he asked.

"Looks great," Vandegan said.

"Creamer, please?" Mamie asked.

"Of course. Be right back with that."

Vandegan stared at Mamie. "Let me see that again."

She shoved her phone with the note underneath towards him. He picked it up and examined it without saying anything. "I'm going to have to show this to Detective Sovern. Do you mind if I send your photos to my phone?"

"No, not at all," she replied.

"I'll need to keep the note as well."

"May I take a photo of it first?" Mamie asked, kicking herself for not doing it earlier.

"I guess that would be all right," he said as he put his phone number in her phone. She smiled. Now she had his number.

When he handed her phone and the note back, she made quick work of snapping a photo before returning the note to him.

"I'm going to call Sovern and ask him to meet us here if you don't mind. Unless you want to go to the station."

"I don't mind either way. Whatever is best for you."

West's words came to her as clearly as if he were right next to her. *Don't say anything that could incriminate you. You could be a suspect and not even know it. Call Dave before giving the police any information.* Dave. Their attorney and Starla's husband. It was too late for that. She had already given the police the notes and the photos on her phone. Still, Dave might have some advice.

As Vandegan made his phone call, Mamie had the uneasy feeling that someone was watching her. Trying not to be obvious, she glanced around the small coffee shop and noticed a man with a long salt and pepper beard frowning at them as he sipped from a mug. From under bushy eyebrows, his eyes dropped to the phone he was holding as she caught him staring. Like others in the shop, maybe he was wondering who Officer Vandegan had with him. Unlike the rest of them, though, his staring left her feeling uncomfortable.

She watched Vandegan as he finished his phone conversation and downed the last of his coffee. "I'm going to have to go to the station. You can wait here or come with me."

She took a large gulp of her decaf before replying. *Leave me here for the vultures? No thanks.* "I would rather go with you."

He stood and pulled a bill from his wallet. Mamie laid a five-dollar bill on the table with his. "I've got this, Mamie."

"No, I won't let you pay for mine."

Harry met them as they turned toward the exit. "Leaving so soon? Let me get you a to-go box and cups of coffee."

"That's nice, Harry, but I'm kind of in a rush."

"Nonsense." He waved to the server. "Estrelita, two coffees to go--one decaf, two biscottis, and wrap up that bagel with some cream cheese."

"Thank you," Mamie said.

"And keep your money," Harry added, returning Vandegan's cash. "I support our men in blue. And their guests."

"Now you're just showing off, Harry," Vandegan protested.

"Maybe so, but I mean it. It's on me today. You go and do your job. Pleased to meet you, Ms. West. I hope to see you again sometime."

As Harry headed toward another booth, Vandegan

returned Mamie's five-dollar bill. "You heard the man."

She smiled and shoved the bill into her bag. She'd decided not to mention the guy who'd been watching them.

***

The police station was much smaller than Mamie expected, just a desk in the front for the receptionist and dispatcher and a couple of offices down a hallway. Detective Sovern strode out of one of the offices and motioned for Vandegan to enter.

"I'll just wait out here," Mamie said, looking around for a chair. There were only three in the waiting area and they were occupied.

"Aw, honey, here you go. I have to leave anyway. I have a nail appointment to get to. Can you get the phones, please?" the receptionist asked the dispatcher. "I'm out of here." The receptionist pushed her rolling office chair to the waiting area and motioned for Mamie to take it before grabbing her purse and heading outside.

"I shouldn't be long," Vandegan said before disappearing behind Sovern's office door.

Mamie nodded. She took a sip of Harry's coffee and a bite of one of the biscottis from the bag he had handed her. Yum, it was really good. The name of the coffee shop didn't lie. She'd been too preoccupied to notice how tasty it was while they were at the shop.

She glanced at her phone to see if there were any new messages. When had Starla texted her? She hadn't heard the alert.

"*Hey, hadn't heard from you and was just wondering*

how it was going. You were supposed to let me know when you got there!"

"And it's taken you two days to check on me? I could be in a ditch somewhere!" Mamie typed furiously, smiling.

Three dots flashed, indicating that Starla was writing a reply. *"Yeah, I know, great friend I am. Having fun?"*

"You wouldn't believe the adventure I'm having," Mamie replied. *"I'll fill you in later."*

"Can't wait."

***

It was past dinnertime when Vandegan dropped her off at her camper. Small talk between them on the ride back to the campground had been awkward, to say the least, even though she was dying to know about his family and his background and how he wound up in Magnolia Bluff with a name like Vandegan. She had never been this shy, at least not since her teen years. Maybe it was the uniform. She did manage to ask him a few questions.

"Your name is unusual. Is your family originally from this area?"

"Vandegan is a variant of Vandeven, which is Dutch. My family settled here in the mid-1800's. I never listened when my grandparents talked about my ancestry. Typical kid with better things to do, I guess. Now I'd give anything to be able to ask them some questions."

"There are websites for that, you know. You could research it."

"In my spare time, I suppose. But I would rather work out, read, or watch sports."

"So you're a sports fan? What teams?"

"All the Texas teams, pro and college. I don't really have a favorite team. I enjoy them all."

"Did you go to college?"

"Just the police academy."

Mamie nodded. Dare she ask if he had a significant other? She dared.

"So, is there a girlfriend or wife in your life? Significant other?" She hoped he didn't notice her flushed cheeks.

He chuckled softly. "No, ma'am, there's not, and there hasn't been for a very long time." He glanced over at her. "What about you? Husband or boyfriend? Significant other?" He smiled.

She shook her head. "I lost my husband about a year and a half ago."

"I'm sorry to hear that."

"It's okay. Doesn't hurt to ask. I have two grown children, a boy and girl, and one grandson. Do you have kids?"

"None that I know of." He laughed. "Not that there would be," he added hastily.

She laughed. So that was established. They were both single. But was he in the market for a romantic companion? Was he attracted to her like she was to him? Did he think she was too old for him? She had admitted to being a grandmother, and he hadn't even flinched.

"I do have a nephew I'm close to," Vandegan said. "You know him. He works at the campground. Brady Hayden. The one whose handwriting matches the notes. His aunt is Scarlett Hayden, the owner of the resort."

Mamie's eyes widened. "So that's why you had that reaction when I showed you the photos of the handwriting and the note. Brady? Yes, he's been very helpful. So you're related to Scarlett as well."

"It's complicated. He's her brother-in-law's son, who is my cousin. I'm not sure if that makes him my nephew officially, but that is what I call him. I can't imagine him being involved in this murder case."

"I can't, either. He seems like such a nice young man. What will you do?"

"I will investigate just as I would any suspect, if we determine he is a suspect."

She reached over and touched his arm. "I can't imagine how difficult this may be for you, having to tell his aunt, and possibly having to arrest him."

He shrugged. "When you do the crime, you have to be ready to do the time. I just hate that it has to be a family member."

When they arrived at her campsite, it was still light enough to walk Babs before going to the clubhouse. He apologized for having her back so late.

"It's later than I realized. I hope I haven't caused you to miss anything," he said as he opened the cruiser's passenger door for her.

"It's fine, Officer. . ."

"Please call me Nick." He grinned as he took her

hand. Strong grip, yet gentle grasp, she noticed. She was glad he couldn't tell she was blushing in the lengthening shadows of the trees.

"It's okay, Nick. I'll be a little late to dinner, but it's not a big deal. I enjoyed our time together."

"Really? Even if it was about trying to solve murders and then leaving you alone in the station? I hope no one bothered you."

She laughed, recalling the squabbling couple who had been waiting to give statements and the homeless man who kept falling asleep and slipping out of his chair. Entertaining as they were, they did bring up old memories of stories West used to tell her about his days at the police station. Her smile faded.

"You are mad, I see."

"No, not at all. It's not that. It's nothing." She smiled again. "Thank you for bringing me back to camp. I'll look forward to hearing what you have to say tomorrow."

There was an awkward moment when he leaned toward her and she wondered if he was going to kiss her, but he didn't. There was only a short pause as he gazed into her eyes. *What would you have done if he had kissed you?* she asked herself. She had no idea. He let go of her hand and walked around the car to the driver's side.

"Let me know if anything else happens. In the meantime, promise me you'll be careful."

"I will," she said, thinking she heard a faint whine from inside the camper. Babs must need a break.

As she turned to unlock the camper door, she saw

out of the corner of her eye that Vandegan had pulled into another campsite. *None of my business*, she told herself. But still. Was that Carly's camper?

Chapter Nineteen

MAMIE DIDN'T HAVE time to see what Vandegan was doing outside Carly's camper. Babs needed out. Now.

The dog didn't give her a chance to clip the leash onto her harness. She jumped out of the camper door, skittered across the plastic patio rug, and squatted. Poor thing needed to go. Mamie bent to fasten the leash onto her harness while she was still. A few seconds later, the dog stood and looked up at her owner, as if to say, *Really?*

But Mamie's attention had strayed from Babs. Vandegan had stopped at Carly's camper because she had been standing on the steps waving to him. It was too far away for Mamie to hear what they were saying, but she could tell it was a serious conversation. Had he found out something else? Did Carly have a connection to the murders after all?

Babs pulled on the leash, wanting to walk in the opposite direction from Carly's camper, so Mamie relented and followed. She would talk to Carly later. Carly would be late to dinner as well, if she even planned on going.

By the time Babs had finished her aimless sniffing expedition, it was half an hour after dinnertime. She hated to do it, but she locked the dog in the camper again and headed to the clubhouse. It was supposed to be a catered meal, and everyone was supposed to dress up in their petticoats, but there was no time to fool with that. She hoped Sissy wouldn't be upset with her after going to all the trouble to help her with a costume.

As she stepped inside, she scanned the large room for her new friends. There was still a line at the buffet tables, so she hadn't missed much. She grinned and waved as she spotted Sheila waving at her from the back of the room. She picked up a plate at the end of the line, her tummy growling in anticipation of barbeque brisket, sausage, potato salad, and beans.

Someone fell in line behind her as she reached for a slice of white bread. There was someone even later than she was. In her peripheral vision she recognized Carly.

"Did you have a nice visit with Officer Vandegan?" Mamie said with a side glance. She heard Carly sniff as if she had been jabbed.

"What are you talking about?"

"I saw him stop at your camper after he dropped me off. We had coffee in town."

"You had a date with Nick?" Carly dropped the serving spoon she was holding and stared at Mamie.

Mamie suppressed a smile. "Not exactly a date. Just coffee. I wanted to talk to him about the notes."

"So he took you to the coffee shop when you could have talked to him here at the campground. I'm not buying it."

"He said he was having an afternoon slump and needed coffee, so he suggested going. No big deal, really. Besides, you didn't answer my question. And you're on first-name basis with him?"

"Not really. He asked me to call him that. I guess he is tired of hearing 'Officer Vandegan' all the time. What question?" Carly spooned potato salad onto her plate.

Mamie picked up the tongs on the edge of the pan holding sliced brisket and transferred some to her plate. Her mouth watered. She swallowed before replying to Carly. "Did you guys have a nice visit?"

"I wouldn't call it a visit, exactly. He questioned me about my relationship with Sarah."

"I see." That made sense. Mamie used tongs to add some slices of smoked sausage to her plate.

They had reached the end of the buffet table with loaded plates. Mamie laughed as she stared at hers. "I'll never be able to eat all of this," she said.

"I will. I may need to come back for seconds. I haven't eaten all day. Where are you sitting?"

Mamie glanced in the direction she had seen Sheila waving at her earlier. Tessa stood and waved.

"I'm going over there," Mamie indicated with a nod. "You're welcome to join us. I would like to finish our conversation later, though."

"After dinner," Carly said as she followed Mamie toward the table.

"Hey, you guys didn't dress up," Lanie observed as Mamie and Carly set their plates on the table. There were exactly two empty chairs.

"Sorry, I was in town this afternoon and didn't get back in time to dress up," Mamie said.

"I didn't feel like it tonight," Carly admitted. "But you girls look cute."

All three ladies—Sheila, Tessa, and Lanie—were wearing matching pink Three Gees T-shirts and bright pink petticoats with cowgirl boots. Matching pink bandanas used as headbands held their hair back.

"Adorable," Mamie agreed. "Did you have the T-shirts made?"

"We got them at one of our other campouts," Sheila said. "Sometimes Marlene has some made and sells them."

"I have one you can have," Carly said. "I never wear it."

Mamie's expression brightened. "That's so nice! I'd love that!"

"Just come by my camper. I know exactly where it is."

Mamie nodded with a smile. Carly just might turn out to be a friend, after all.

"How were you able to leave the campground, Mamie?" Lanie asked. "I thought we were told not to leave. We just hung out in the clubhouse and played cards. We wondered where you were."

"And took naps," Sheila added. "Not much else to do when you can't leave the campground. You left anyway?" she asked Mamie.

"Officer Vandegan needed coffee and asked me to go with him," Mamie said, her face warming.

"I just sat by the lake, soaked up the sun, and finished my novel," Carly said.

"Wait. You're a writer?" Mamie said. "I've always wanted to write a novel, and I figured retirement would offer me the time to do so, but I never seem to find the time to sit down and begin."

"No, no, I just meant I finished reading a novel. I could never write one. No way. I can barely write my name," Carly laughed.

"No fair, Mamie. You got to leave. At least you're not in jail, though," Lanie said with a chuckle.

"I had some evidence to show him, and, like I said, he wanted coffee, so he suggested we go to the Really Good."

Sheila laughed. "Was it?"

"Was it what?" Mamie frowned.

"Really good?" Sheila giggled as Tessa and Lanie rolled their eyes.

"I doubt she even noticed," Carly said.

"I did notice, and yes, it was good," Mamie said, her cheeks growing hotter by the second. No one seemed to catch her remark about having evidence to show Vandegan.

"Mamie's got a boyfriend," Lanie sang.

"Shhh! Please stop," Mamie begged, her face flaming.

To her relief, Sheila changed the subject. "I almost forgot. I brought my money for the tip jar. Where is it?" She glanced around the room.

"You'll have to ask. It was on the table by the kitchen but I don't see it now. I guess someone moved it."

"Tip jar?" Mamie managed, her face cooling a bit.

"Yeah, at every campout there is a tip jar for the

hostesses. It helps them with expenses," Tessa said.

"Oh, I guess I hadn't heard about that. Is tonight the last night, or will it be here in the morning?" Mamie said. She hadn't brought any money with her to dinner.

"Usually not."

"I'll have to run back to my camper to get some money," she said, wondering how much she should contribute.

"I usually put a twenty in the jar," Sheila said, seeming to read her mind. "The hostesses work hard and spend a lot of money on nametags, goodie bags, and decorations."

"Twenty?" Lanie said. "I feel bad. I've only been giving five to ten dollars."

"You cheapskate!" Sheila laughed. "Just whatever you want to give, Mamie," she said to the newest member of the group.

"Okay, I'll be back in a jiffy." Mamie gathered her trash and headed out.

Carly caught up with her before she reached the door. "Wait, Mamie."

"What is it?"

"Please don't tell Nick that I was questioning you about going into town with him. He wouldn't appreciate it."

Mamie nodded and opened the door. No way would she make any promises to Carly.

Chapter Twenty

THE NIGHT AIR was heavy with early summer humidity. Bullfrogs, crickets, and cicadas serenaded Mamie as she made her way through the darkness to her camper. Babs wouldn't be happy when she popped in and left again, but this was something she needed to do. It wouldn't be right to enjoy everything the hostesses had done and not give something in return. She thought she had a twenty-dollar bill in her wallet.

There was something eerie about the campground that night. No one was outside moving around. There were no campfires burning. The only activity seemed to be inside the clubhouse. Maybe it was too early for campfires. Maybe everyone not with the Three Gees was eating dinner inside their nice, large, air-conditioned RVs. Only the dim lanterns atop the power poles at each site illuminated the darkness. Even in the mild temperatures, Mamie felt a chill as goosebumps popped out on her arms.

She walked faster, wishing she had thought to bring a flashlight. It wasn't dark when she had gone to dinner. She also wished she had turned on the exterior light of her camper, which was only about thirty yards away at this point.

As she finally arrived at her camper and inserted the key in the door, she had the uneasy sense that she was being watched. *I wish I had packed my pistol before going to dinner,* she thought. She fought the desire to look around her as she opened the door. Weird. Even her dog didn't greet her. Something was definitely off.

"Babs?" She flipped on the lights and glanced at the

bed and then the bench, the only two places the dog ever slept. But she wasn't there. "Babs?" Where was she? She couldn't go underneath the bed or benches. There was no space. She opened the cabinet door where her bucket was. If she had been in there, she would have pushed the door open herself. Besides, there wasn't enough room there. Had she slipped out when Mamie left for dinner? No way. She would have noticed. Panic rose in her chest as tears sprang to her eyes. Where was her dog?

She grabbed her flashlight, turned on the exterior light, and went back out to search around the camper, even though she knew that if Babs had been nearby she would have made herself known. "Babs? Babs!" she called until her voice turned to sobs.

She stumbled back to the clubhouse, tears half blinding her, without bothering to lock the camper. If Babs was gone, it didn't matter. Someone could take the whole trailer and she wouldn't care.

Sheila, Tessa, and Lanie were leaving the building when Mamie ran up to them in desperation.

"Mamie! What is it? What happened?" Sheila cried when she saw her friend's tear-streaked face.

"Come back in, let's talk," Lanie said, grabbing Mamie's arm.

"No! It's Babs! She's missing! Someone has taken my dog!" Mamie cried, pulling away.

Tessa re-entered the meeting room and summoned the loudest voice she could muster. "Hey, everyone, Mamie's little dog is missing. We all need to help her look."

Bertie chimed in. "Her name is Babs. She's a black and white Boston terrier. Let's go."

Mamie stepped aside as the whole group of women stormed outside, whistling and calling the dog's name. Grateful tears poured down her cheeks. *God, thank you for these women. Please help us find my baby*, she prayed. *Please let my dog be okay.*

Everyone fanned out, taking all the roadways and paths through the campground. Lights came on at many of the campsites as other campers stepped out to see what was going on. Sheila urged Tessa and Lanie to join the search as she tried to get Mamie to sit on an iron bench outside the clubhouse.

"No, I want to look for Babs," Mamie protested.

"You need to stay here in case someone finds her so they can bring her back to you," Sheila said. "I'll stay with you. Tell me how you know she was taken from your camper."

"Because she wasn't there when I went inside."

"Had you locked the door?"

"Yes, of course, I had. I always do."

"Are you sure? Maybe you accidentally left it unlocked."

"No, Sheila. It has a deadbolt lock and it unlocked when I turned the key. I know it was locked." More tears trickled down her cheeks. "She just wasn't there."

"And there's nowhere inside she could hide?"

Mamie shook her head, tears rolling down her face.

"Does anyone else have a key to your camper?"

"No, the only other key is in my car console."

"Maybe someone got it. Maybe you left your car unlocked."

Mamie shuddered with an unexpected chill. What if whoever had gotten Babs had also gotten her pistol? It was lying in plain sight next to her bed unless her bedspread had somehow covered it. The only way they could have gotten inside her camper was with a key. Hadn't she locked her car? She never left it unlocked. Unless she had forgotten because she'd had to walk Babs as soon as they had arrived at the campground. Had she left her car unlocked then? Maybe someone did get the key from her car console. But at that time the pistol would have been in the console as well, and surely they would have stolen that, too.

"Maybe you're right," she said.

The two women listened as the voices calling for Babs and the whistling grew fainter. The ladies were searching every possible place, and apparently some of the other campers were too, because there were male voices mixed in.

Where are you, Babs? Mamie wondered miserably.

Headlights approached from the entrance to the campground, slowed, and stopped at the clubhouse. Mamie squinted as she watched the police cruiser's door open and a tall, uniformed officer appear. Who would have called the police about a missing dog?

"It's Officer Vandegan," Sheila whispered, squeezing Mamie's hand. "Hello, Officer," she said as he approached.

"Good evening, ladies. I have an announcement to make to the ladies and I wondered if everyone was still gathered inside." He stared at Mamie. "Is something wrong?"

Her face had to be a mess. She studied the ground, wishing he didn't have to see her like that.

"Mamie's dog has disappeared. Everyone is out looking for her," Sheila explained.

Vandegan's brow creased as he knelt in front of Mamie and looked into her eyes. "Babs is missing? Tell me what happened, everything you know."

Mamie turned to her friend. "Sheila, can you tell him? I'm not sure I can." Her voice cracked as fresh tears watered her face.

"Sure I can, honey. But this isn't really a police matter, is it? I mean, there's not much you all can do."

"If it's related in any way to the murders, it will be part of the investigation, so yes, there is much we can do. Just tell me what happened."

After listening to Sheila's retelling of Mamie's story, Vandegan stood and stepped a few feet away to make a phone call. Sheila patted Mamie's hand as she leaned her head on Sheila's shoulder. Why hadn't someone found her baby yet? She tried not to think of all the bad things that could have happened. Could Babs even swim? They had never been in the water together.

Vandegan was still on the phone when another set of headlights, smaller this time, rolled up to the clubhouse. Brady stepped out, holding a wiggling, furry package under one arm.

"Good, I found you. Isn't this your dog, Mrs. West?"

Mamie sprang to her feet and rushed to Brady. "Babs! Where have you been?" She took the dog from his arms and let the dog wash her face with her long pink tongue. "Where did you find her?" she asked the young man, Babs licking the happy tears from her cheeks.

"I was about to do my evening rounds and noticed something sniffing around the picnic table behind the office. When I shined my flashlight on her, she froze, and I recognized her as your dog. How did she get loose?"

"I have no idea. My camper was locked, so someone had to let her out. Thank you so much, Brady. I'm just glad nothing happened to her."

"My pleasure, but she might have a tummy ache. There were some food scraps around that table that we had left for the raccoons."

"I'm sure we can manage that. You silly dog," Mamie told Babs, hugging her tight.

"Is this the dog that got away?" Vandegan asked as he ended his phone call and rejoined the ladies.

"Yes, thanks to Brady here," Sheila said.

"Good work, son. I'll let the station know not to send anyone else out here. Now if we could get everyone back inside the clubhouse, that would be great."

"Several of the ladies saw me with the dog as I brought her back to the clubhouse. I'll drive around and let the others know," Brady offered.

"Sounds great, man. Thanks for your help." Vandegan patted him on the back as he climbed behind the wheel of the golf cart. "Ladies, want to wait inside where it's cooler?"

"I need to take Babs back to my camper," Mamie said.

"Are you going to leave her there?" Sheila asked.

"I guess that's not a good idea. That's what I had done when she disappeared. I'll just need to get her leash and bring her back with me."

"I'll walk with you. I'd like to take a look at the lock on your door," Vandegan said. "I'll be back in a few minutes to make my announcement to everyone," he told Sheila.

Mamie gratefully handed the dog to his outstretched arms. At twenty-five pounds, Babs grew heavy fast.

"I have some bad news for you, Mamie," Vandegan said as they walked toward her camper. "Forensics uncovered fingerprints from both murder scenes, and they belong to a couple of the staff members here at the campground. We'll be making arrests tonight."

Mamie stared at him. "Is Brady one of them?"

"Off the record?"

She nodded.

"You can't tell a single soul. No one."

She nodded again.

"I'm afraid so."

Her stomach clinched. *Not Brady.* She studied Vandegan's face in the dim light. He was a good cop. No emotions showing there.

Chapter Twenty-One

VANDEGAN EXAMINED THE door lock on Mamie's camper and determined that someone had either opened it with a key, or she had left it unlocked. There were no signs of tampering.

"Don't leave the dog here alone. I'll clear her to come inside the clubhouse with you. It will only be for a few minutes, anyway. My announcement won't take long."

He watched as Mamie clipped the leash onto Babs's harness and then they walked together to the clubhouse. It looked like every one of the Three Gees had gotten the message to gather there. The room was full and it seemed everyone was talking at once. Scarlett Hayden and Howard Story had even shown up.

Vandegan raised his hands and lowered them. A hush settled over the room.

"You can't have that dog in here," one lady told Mamie in a stage whisper.

"I believe you can excuse her this one time," Vandegan said, causing the woman to shrink back and glance at the others, some of whom shook their heads in reproof.

"First of all, I would like to thank you all for banding together to help find Babs. I'm impressed by the support you give each other, especially to a new member of your group. I know most of you, maybe all of you, are not from Magnolia Bluff, but you seem to have the same spirit that our town has, and that shows in how you take care of one another."

One woman raised her hand.

"Yes, go ahead," Vandegan said with the smile that Mamie found so captivating. It seemed to light up the room.

"Who found the dog?"

"Brady Hayden found her behind the office," Vandegan replied. "You all know him. He does maintenance for the campground, and he showed each of you to your campsite. But the dog isn't the reason I called you all together tonight," he continued. "I want you all to know that forensics was able to identify some fingerprints found at the murder scenes, and they do not implicate any of you ladies. You are all free to pack up and go home tomorrow."

Collective cheers and whoops rattled the rafters of the building as the Three Gees received the news.

"Hold on, the park staff would like to say something," Vandegan said with a laugh, after raising and lowering his hands again.

A pretty middle-aged woman with perfectly coifed hair, manicured hands, and designer jeans stepped in front of the officer and waited for their complete attention. As she waited, Mamie watched Vandegan move through the crowd until he found Carly. Then he pulled her aside to speak to her.

"Ladies, I'm Scarlett Hayden, owner of the resort. I would like to thank you for choosing Magnolia Bluff and Hayden's Resort and Campground to host your gathering. We hope you return soon, don't we, Howard?"

"We most certainly do," Howard said with a grin.

As the crowd of women dispersed, Scarlett sidled up to Vandegan and whispered something in his ear. Even though she knew it was none of her business, Mamie strained to hear, but Howard leaned toward her and spoke.

"So how's our little escape artist?" he grinned, leaning too close for her comfort.

She backed up, swallowed hard, and forced a smile. "Babs is fine. I just wish I knew how she got out of my camper in the first place."

"Heh, heh," he chuckled, reaching down to pet the dog. Babs rewarded him with a snarl and a flash of white canines. "Whoa! Not very friendly, is she?"

Mamie suppressed the urge to tell him that she was only that way with certain people. So Babs felt uneasy around Mr. Story, too. She pulled the dog away from him and turned to see if Vandegan was still talking with Scarlett Hayden.

"Howard is right here," the resort owner said, pointing to Story. Vandegan pulled his handcuffs from his belt and turned to the office manager.

"Mr. Story, you're under arrest for suspicion of the murders of Sarah Trenton and Holly Fuller. You have the right to remain silent. . ." He continued to recite the Miranda rights as he pulled Story's hands behind him and cuffed his wrists.

"Wait a minute," Story protested. "You've got the wrong person."

"Be quiet," Scarlett hissed. "You're already in

enough trouble as it is."

"I want a lawyer."

"You'll have the opportunity to call an attorney when I get you booked. Right now you're coming with me. Mrs. Hayden, I need to see Brady as well." Mamie noticed his Adam's apple bobbing as he swallowed hard.

"Brady? Brady's a suspect?" Scarlett's eyes grew wide.

"I'm afraid so. His fingerprints were found as well."

"That's just ridiculous. Besides, you can't arrest your own nephew."

"Careful, Mrs. Hayden. You don't want me to arrest you for obstruction of justice. And yes, I can."

"You wouldn't dare."

Vandegan gave her a warning look. "Oh, all right," she said as she pulled her cell phone from her jeans pocket. "Brady, I need you at the clubhouse. Yes, I know you just got off work. This cannot wait. See you in a minute."

Vandegan walked Story outside to his cruiser and placed him in the back seat. Mamie and Scarlett and some of the other ladies who had remained behind followed, their eyes wide in disbelief. Carly appeared beside Mamie. Scarlett was on the phone again.

Vandegan reached inside the car and radioed dispatch to send another officer. Then he turned to Mamie.

"I'm sorry you had to witness this," he said. "At least you have your dog. However, I am going to have to ask you to remain at the campground and not go home yet."

"Just me? Am I a suspect, too? What about Carly? Is she a suspect?"

"Gee, thanks, friend," Carly said sarcastically.

"No, neither of you are suspects, but you may have information we need. I need you to stay behind at least a day or two more, until we have our facts in order."

Mamie and Carly glanced at each other.

"I'm not believing this," Carly muttered, rolling her eyes.

The other squad car rolled up at the same time Brady arrived in his pickup. Brady hopped out and trotted over to his aunt.

"What's going on, Aunt Scarlett?" he asked. "I was about to head to Round Rock to pick up my date."

"I'm afraid you won't be going out tonight," Vandegan said. He motioned to the officer getting out of his cruiser. "You're under arrest."

"What? Me? No way! I didn't do anything!"

"Quiet, Brady. Just go with the police. We will figure it out later."

"But I haven't done anything! I have rights!"

The other officer yanked Brady's hands behind him and cuffed him none too gently.

"Ow! Take it easy, man! Aunt Scarlett, do something! Call somebody!"

"Quiet, young man, and listen to your rights,"

Vandegan said. "You have the right—"

Brady slumped as the other officer covered his head with his hand and lowered him into the police car. As Vandegan recited the Miranda rights again, Brady twisted in the seat away from everyone's stares, looking miserable. The officer slammed the door and hopped in.

"I'll meet you at the station," he told Vandegan.

"Go on and try to get some rest, ladies," Vandegan told Mamie and Carly as Scarlett talked on the phone. "I'll be in touch."

Exhausted after Babs's disappearance and the two arrests and then Carly's endless complaining about having to stay longer, Mamie opened her camper door, brought the dog in, and locked the door behind her. As she kicked off her shoes, she noticed a piece of paper curled in an empty coffee mug on her counter. She picked it up, and as she read the words scribbled in that now familiar handwriting, her heart seemed to stop. *Be careful what you wish for, honey. You may get more than you bargained for. More than you could possibly know.*

Chapter Twenty-Two

MAMIE CRUSHED THE note in her hand as she doublechecked the door to make sure it was locked and the outside light was on. She lifted the edge of the comforter where the mattress sat on its platform. In the tiny space between the mattress and the cabinet lay her pistol, in its usual spot. A breath of relief escaped her. At least the intruder hadn't found her pistol.

She knew it was loaded but popped the cylinder out just to be sure. Yes, there was a bullet in each of the five chambers. Hollow point bullets. The same ones that West had bought for her a few years ago, claiming they were deadlier than regular ones. She didn't want to know why. All she wanted to do was stop an attacker, not necessarily inflict a lethal wound. She shuddered as she clicked the cylinder back into place and carefully returned the pistol to its spot by the bed.

"I think we're okay," she said to Babs, but mostly to herself. As she undressed to change into pajamas, she noticed the note had fallen onto the rug. She picked it up, smoothed it, and secured it under a book on her dinette. "I wonder if I should call Nick?" she said aloud.

Babs looked up at her and wiggled the stub of tail on her bottom. After donning her pajamas, Mamie turned the covers back and let Babs tunnel underneath. She knew when it was bedtime. "No, I won't disturb him tonight. But you can bet I'll be talking to him first thing in the morning," she said.

The discovery of yet another threat called for a strong cocktail. Mamie opened the cabinet door to retrieve a small bottle of whiskey and then got a sparkling water from the fridge. The proportions were just right this time. She savored the burn as the drink rolled down her throat. Maybe it would take the edge off the anxiety and help her go to sleep.

She slipped under the covers and scrolled through emails and social media as she sipped. Finally feeling sleepy, she set her mug on the counter, turned off the light, and snuggled deep under the covers with her dog.

Sleep would not come as her mind went through every possible scenario with Brady and Howard Story. Why would they want to kill a lady camper? Two lady campers? Did they act together, or was one of them innocent? Did they know the women beforehand? Who left the cryptic notes? Was she next on the murder list? If so, why hadn't they already done it? They knew the ladies were leaving the campground the next day. Did they know she wasn't leaving with them? These questions kept repeating themselves until the whiskey finally relaxed her enough to allow sleep to take over, but not before she asked forgiveness for not depending on God instead of liquor to lessen her anxiety.

***

Mamie awoke with a start. Babs emerged from the covers, growled, and gave a low woof. They had heard something. She froze as she realized someone was jiggling the door handle outside, trying to get inside. She shook her head to try and shake the drowsiness off, and her senses went on high alert. Babs jumped off the bed and stood at the door, dancing and barking.

"Who's there?" Mamie cried, reaching for her

pistol.

There was no answer. The handle jiggled again.

"Who is it?" Mamie asked, pointing the pistol at the door.

The sounds of the metal trash can she kept outside clanging, an "Oof," and heavy running footfalls met their ears. She peered out of the closed jalousie windows but could only see a shapeless dark figure leaving her campsite through the frosted glass. Glad she had thought to leave the exterior light on, she flicked on the inside lights before picking up Babs to put her back on the bed.

Her heart racing, she slipped back under the covers and reached for her phone. Babs sat on top of the covers staring toward the door with an occasional growl. Unnerving growls. Mamie found Vandegan's number and a moment later a sleepy male voice answered.

"Nick," Mamie whispered.

"Mamie?"

"Yes," she whispered. "Nick, someone just tried to break into my camper."

"Make sure the door is locked. I'll be right there."

She nodded and sank into the bed, pulling the covers to her chin. "Nick's coming, baby. He'll be here in a bit. Everything's going to be okay." She stroked Babs' coarse black fur. At least she hoped so.

***

It was only a few minutes, but it seemed like hours when the flashing lights of Nick's cruiser arrived at her campsite. She peeked through the curtains to make sure it was him as he exited the car, and then she pulled West's shirt on over her pajamas.

"Mamie, it's me, Nick," she heard as he tapped on her door.

"Thank you," Mamie said as she unlocked and opened it. Babs jumped down barking, but then wagged her stubby tail as she realized who it was.

"Lock the door behind me," Vandegan said as he entered the tiny space. "Hey, Babs, how are you doing?"

"We're both scared out of our minds," Mamie admitted. She cleared several decorative throw pillows from the dinette bench and motioned him to sit down. "I found another note tonight when I came inside."

"So someone broke in again?"

She nodded as she pointed to the note on the table in front of him.

He brushed the dog down after she jumped up on him, sniffing.

"No, Babs." Mamie picked her up and placed her on the bed. "Stay."

Vandegan examined the note. "Looks like the same handwriting, doesn't it?"

"How could it be Brady if you arrested him?"

"He had time to leave it here before I arrested him, right? When you were at dinner? Maybe Babs got out when he was leaving the note, and he didn't notice until he found her behind the office."

Mamie nodded. "Maybe so. But what does he mean? What does he have against me? And who was just here trying to get inside my camper?"

"Good question. Brady must be working with someone else."

"But Howard Story was also arrested."

"There must be someone else besides those two."

Mamie stared at him. The absurdity of it all struck her as funny and she smiled. Here it was, three a.m., and she was in her pajamas in her camper with an attractive single man. Wouldn't the town gossip have a field day with this situation? She didn't even know who the town gossip was. Maybe there was a Three Gees gossip she hadn't met yet. Or a campground gossip. Anyway, if it wasn't such a serious situation, she would be laughing.

"What is it? Are you okay? Why don't you go back to bed? I'll stay outside in my car until daybreak so you can get some rest."

"No, no, I'm fine. I was just thinking how funny it is that I am in my pajamas in my camper with a handsome man for all the wrong reasons." She wished she hadn't uttered the words as soon as they came out of her mouth. Heat colored her cheeks.

Vandegan stood and pocketed the note, towering over her in the small camper. With its six-foot ceiling, he had to bend his head a bit. "What would be the right reason?" he asked, touching her arm and winking.

"Well, you know," she stammered.

"This?"

To her astonishment he leaned toward her, placing his lips on hers for a brief moment. She stared at him and smiled, forgetting her embarrassment. Placing her hands on either side of his face, she stood on tiptoe to return the kiss.

When she leaned back to look at him, his eyes softened as his arms went around her, pulling her close as his mouth covered hers. She felt as if she were floating in the air, as if her feet had left the floor and she were weightless. His kiss awakened feelings she had long forgotten—the thrill of attention, the excitement of being touched by a man, the joy of feeling attractive and desirable again. West had kissed her like this, once upon a time. *West.* What was she doing? She stiffened and pulled away.

"What's wrong?" Vandegan asked, his voice husky and low.

"I'm sorry. I can't do this," Mamie said, stepping back. "I was married for forty-one years."

"You're not married now, are you?"

"No, my husband passed away. I told you that, right? But I still can't do this. I'm so sorry." She turned away and sat on the bed, petting Babs, who sensed her mistress's anxiety.

Vandegan sighed and raked his hand through his dark hair. "Your husband wouldn't want you to be lonely, would he? Wouldn't he want you to move on?"

Mamie nodded and looked down, a single tear rolling down her cheek.

"You're tired and emotional, frightened by all this. We can discuss it later. I'll be outside in my car." He opened the door. "Try to get some rest. I'll see you in the morning. Lock the door."

She nodded, twisted the deadbolt after he shut the door, got into bed, and pulled the covers over her, not bothering to take off West's shirt. Rest is exactly what she needed. She touched her lips lightly with her index finger. There was no way she could rest after that kiss, though. She peeked through the curtains to see the squad car by her camper and, feeling safe in spite of it all, nestled down to try and sleep.

***

It seemed like she had barely closed her eyes when Babs woke her up, pawing at her face. Mamie groaned and rolled over, hoping the dog would leave her alone, but it wasn't to be. Babs needed to go out and she kept pawing at her owner.

"Okay, okay," Mamie grumbled, rolling out of bed and shoving her toes into flipflops. She fastened the harness on the wiggling dog and clipped the leash on it before stumbling out of the door. The patio mat and camp chairs sparkled with a thick layer of dew, and as she ventured toward the road, her toes became damp. There was Nick's car, parked in front of her campsite all night like he had promised.

Mamie followed Babs, guiding her toward the car. The dog dug her paws in just as they got about ten feet from the driver's side door.

"Babs, come on!" Mamie pulled on the leash, but Babs had stopped to do her business. "All righty, then."

The cruiser's door swung open and Vandegan gave her a sleepy smile. "Good morning, sleep well?"

"Fair. I'm more concerned with how you slept in that car."

"Not too bad. I'm kind of used to it, though I rarely have to do it in this town. Austin was a different story," he said, alluding to a previous job. "How about you? Did you get any sleep at all?"

"Maybe a little," Mamie said. It was the truth. She touched her lip absently. A knowing smile creased his face.

"I better head to the station and check on our suspects. I should also catch Sovern up on the latest. We may be back in a little while. You're not planning on leaving, are you?"

"That would be against orders, wouldn't it?" Mamie smiled. "No, I'm not going anywhere."

"Good. I'd hate to have to arrest you, too." But his eyes danced. He closed the door and rolled down the window. "I'll see you later."

"Yes, you will," Mamie said. Feeling flirtatious, she winked, and then she colored with embarrassment. She was acting like a silly schoolgirl.

"Please be careful, Mamie." Babs looked up from her sniffing to watch Vandegan's cruiser take off down the road.

"Come on, girl, we need to walk." But first, her pistol. Mamie led Babs back to the camper, stepped inside, and grabbed her weapon. It fit perfectly in her crossbody bag and gave her more confidence as she followed Babs down the road. Even with Brady and Howard Story in custody, there was still someone out there.

A pile of brown crinoline on one of her bench seats caught her attention. She had almost forgotten to return

Sissy's petticoat, boots, and hat. She stuffed everything into a trash bag and took it with her as she walked the dog.

She caught Sissy packing up and set the bag on the picnic table by her camper.

"Sissy, here are the things you let me borrow. Thank you so much."

Sissy looked up from where she was rolling up a water hose. "You're very welcome. I'm happy to have you in our group. Hope to see you again soon."

"Thanks, I enjoyed it very much, though it's probably been a little more dramatic than usual."

"To say the least." Sissy laughed. "Don't give up on us."

Mamie smiled. "I won't."

In the distance the lake was still. Several other ladies were up early, taking down camp and preparing for travel. As she passed their campsites, they waved. "See you down the road, Mamie! Be safe!" one said.

"You, too!" Mamie called back. As eventful as the camping weekend had been, it was sad to see it end.

A black SUV approached and Mamie led Babs away from the road to let it pass. It stopped next to them, sending her heart into overdrive. She fingered the pistol in her bag, praying she wouldn't have to reveal it. *Stop being so jumpy*, she told herself.

Chapter Twenty-Three

THE SUV WAS headed the same way Mamie was walking. As the passenger window slowly rolled down, and after everything that had happened that weekend, Mamie half expected to see the barrel of a gun pointed at her.

There was no gun. It was only one of her camping acquaintances stopping to say goodbye. The fact that she wasn't pulling a trailer had made Mamie think it was someone else, someone who might be a threat. This lady must have stayed in a cabin or shared an RV with another woman.

"Mamie, have a safe trip home. How far do you have to drive?"

"Thank you, Jillie. I'm only forty minutes from home. How far do you have to travel?" The woman's big smile had her relaxing for now.

"I'm about three hours away, not too bad. It was very nice to meet you."

"Likewise. Travel safe. I'll see you down the road, I hope."

Jillie waved and drove on ahead, leaving Mamie and Babs behind.

They walked past the clubhouse and continued until they arrived at the front entrance. Babs sniffed around the golf cart that was parked next to the office—Brady's golf cart. Mamie stepped up on the little porch where the ice machine was. She jiggled the doorknob and found that it was unlocked. Who was minding the office and grounds now that Brady and Mr. Story were both in jail?

Curiosity getting the best of her—again—she opened the door and stepped inside, Babs behind her.

"Pets are not allowed inside," came a stern female voice. As her eyes adjusted, Mamie saw a strikingly pretty woman standing behind the counter with a scowl on her well-maintained middle-aged face. Red lipstick outlined pursed lips as darkly lined eyes peered over readers perched on a small, straight nose. Scarlett Hayden. Mamie recognized her from the night before.

"I'm so sorry. Mr. Story allowed me to bring her inside."

"Mr. Story no longer works here." Scarlett looked Mamie up and down, making her feel like she was in the principal's office.

"Oh, I see. We'll leave, then."

"Who are you, anyway?"

Rude. "Mamie West."

Maybe Scarlett was angry about her help being arrested. Wondering if she had anything to do with the murders, Mamie thought maybe she should get to know the woman better, although that might be difficult since she was hoping to get to go home in a day or two.

She approached the counter and stuck out her hand. "Pleased to meet you. I've enjoyed the campground very much. The setting is beautiful, and the service is excellent. It's my first time camping and I can't imagine having been at a better place—"

"Uh huh," Scarlett replied. *Rude again.* "If you'll

please remove your animal now."

"Right." Mamie frowned as she led Babs out of the building. The woman was a piece of work. Nick might be able to tell her more about her.

***

They ended up back at the lakeshore. Nothing was going on at the clubhouse—in fact, it was closed—and there really wasn't much else to do except sit outside. Besides, it was more interesting watching activity on the reservoir than at her camper. She settled onto a bench overlooking the water. It was a partly cloudy day with fluffy cumulus clouds playing hide and seek with the sun. In a few hours it would be too warm to sit out in the sun. She would be hiding indoors with the a/c cranked up.

Mamie regretted not seeing Sheila, Tessa, and Lanie again, missing the opportunity to tell them goodbye. They had been entertaining and had gone out of their way, especially Lanie, to help her feel comfortable. She glanced at the wrist wrap she wore. Her wrist felt a hundred percent better than it had a couple of days ago when she had injured it. Still, she followed doctor's (or nurse practitioner's) orders by taking the anti-inflammatory medicine and keeping it wrapped. She hadn't really had the time to ice it, but the swelling seemed to have gone down on its own.

Babs finished sniffing and pawing and settled on the grass in the shade cast by the bench.

"That's it. We're just going to relax here for a while, sweetie. That mean lady won't have anything to say to us now." Babs glanced up at her and then laid her head on her paws and closed her eyes.

Who was Scarlett Hayden anyway? Was she some bigwig in Magnolia Bluff? How well did Nick know her? She felt a twinge of compassion for Brady having to put up with the woman as his aunt. Poor kid, having to spend time in jail. What if he wasn't the killer? He would have to carry this horrible experience the rest of his life. If he was the killer and was convicted of murder, he would most likely spend the rest of his life in prison. He had his whole life ahead of him. Why would he do something so stupid?

"Brady, Brady, Brady. You should be in college, not working at an RV park. Why wouldn't your aunt be sending you to college instead of letting you work here for nothing, or if not nothing, it couldn't be much."

She glanced around, wondering if anyone had heard her. But there were so many RVs leaving the park, and so many motorboats out on the lake that no one would be able to hear above the noise. Even Babs ignored what she said.

Her phone buzzed in her back pocket. Her daughter was checking on her.

"Hey, Junie."

"Mom, when are you coming home?"

"I've been asked to stay in case they need information for the murder investigation."

"How long? Is everyone having to stay?"

"No, just me and another lady. I'm not sure how long. I hope it's just for a couple more days."

"Seriously, Mom?" Junie's tone held disappointment and a bit of aggravation.

"Why? Do you need something?" Which was

usually the case.

"No, I just don't like the idea of you there alone. All the ladies except one left already? That leaves you pretty much alone in the campground."

Mamie glanced around her. "Junie, there are lots of nice people here." *I think.* She went on. "This is a safe place, and I'm keeping Babs and my pistol close." She wouldn't mention the notes, especially those left for her, or someone trying to break into her camper.

"If it's so safe, why have there been two murders there? Are you being honest with me, Mom? I don't think you're telling me everything."

"Junie, please. It's fine. I'm fine."

"Don't they have cabins there?"

"Yes, why?"

"I'm going to take off work and get a cabin there. You shouldn't be there alone."

"No, Junie, you don't need to do that."

"No, I'm coming. See you in a little while."

"Junie—" But her daughter had already hung up. When she got an idea in her head there was no use trying to change it. "It looks like we're going to have company," she told Babs, but the dog was snoring.

Mamie searched her phone for lunch options. She would have to drive into town to find something to eat. The campground grille was closed on Sundays and there were no friends around to share food with her. Maybe Carly would want to go into town with her. Except they weren't supposed to leave the grounds.

She reached down and rubbed Babs's fur. "Wake up, baby. Let's see if we can find Carly. We need to figure out lunch and I need to get that tee shirt from her."

Babs trotted along with her as she walked toward Carly's camper. Sarah's trailer was still sitting where it had been since Thursday when she had arrived, and it still had yellow police tape around it. She said a quick prayer for Sarah's family and wondered when the police would allow the trailer to be moved. Scarlett Hayden wouldn't want it around forever.

At first Mamie was afraid she had forgotten which campsite was Carly's. It was completely empty, trailer and car gone, all traces of its occupant gone. *Why had she been allowed to leave when I can't,* she wondered. Not fair. Not fair at all.

Nick would definitely hear about this. Speaking of Nick, a police cruiser had entered the park and was approaching her campsite, where she and Babs were sitting at the picnic table, trying to decide what to do for lunch. The cruiser stopped in front of her trailer and Vandegan got out. Mamie's breath caught at the sight of him.

"Hey," he said as he walked toward her.

"You're a sight for sore eyes," she said as he straddled the bench across the table from her.

"As you are." He winked, sending her stomach leaping.

"Let me guess. You have solved the case, and I can go home." She smiled.

"Afraid not." He shook his head.

"Anything you want to tell me? Or can tell me, then?"

"Nothing, not yet, anyway. I just wanted to make sure you were doing okay."

"I'm good, just wondering about lunch. Can you recommend anything in town besides the Silver Spoon and the coffee shop?"

"You can't leave the campground." His eyes were serious, his half-smile apologetic.

"Come on, Nick, why not? You have my phone number, and you know I wouldn't leave town without my camper. Besides, why did Carly get to leave?"

"She left?"

"Her campsite is clean as a whistle. No sign of her."

He raked his hand through his hair, leaned his head back, and gave a heavy sigh. "I asked her not to go anywhere. Excuse me."

He walked back to his car to report Carly missing. Mamie tried to ignore the sounds of her empty stomach. If he didn't let her go get food, he was going to have to bring some to her.

She watched him as he sat in the driver's seat and spoke to the radio. She couldn't make out what he was saying, but she didn't need to. When he was around, she felt safe. Even Babs was comfortable with him. After her initial greeting the dog settled on the ground beside her. She took the opportunity while Nick's attention was on his conversation to study his appearance. He was a little taller than West, but built much the same with broad shoulders, thick chest, and muscular arms and legs. He filled out his uniform nicely, just as her husband had. He had to be a lot younger than she was, though. He had to realize that she was much older, but he didn't seem to mind. She almost giggled out loud when she realized what her kids would call her—a *cougar*.

She watched him put the mic back, get out of the car, and walk toward her. She smiled. That walk of his. She couldn't believe she was having these thoughts so soon after West. But he would say it wasn't too soon. He would just want her to be happy. He had even told her to find someone else and not to live the rest of her life alone. She recalled those few conversations with a pang in her heart. He had always put her needs first.

"I have to go to the station. Sovern wants to go over some things. If we need to find Carly for more information, she's going to owe a hefty fine."

"I wouldn't want to be in her shoes." She stood. "When will you be back? I'm still hungry."

"I'll have one of the other officers bring you a burger and fries from the café. Will that work?"

"Yes, thank you."

"I'll be back as soon as I can. Be safe." He placed a quick kiss on her lips as she looked up at him.

She watched him leave, wanting more. What to do, what to do? It occurred to her that she had tucked a small notebook into a tote bag before she left on this trip. Maybe she should start on that novel she had always wanted to write. Thinking she had left the bag in the car, she fastened Babs's leash around the leg of the picnic table, grabbed her car keys from the camper, and unlocked the car. She was rummaging around in the cargo space of the

SUV with her back to the world when she sensed someone standing next to her.

Chapter Twenty-Four

"**O**H!" SHE CRIED as she straightened and turned.

It was the grizzled old man she and Babs had met on the trail the first day of the campout. He was standing way too close to her, a leering grin on his stubbly face. Tobacco juice rolled down his chin onto a stained, well-worn shirt that had seen better days. Salt and pepper hair in need of a haircut framed his thin craggy face. He leaned slightly on a wooden cane that looked like he had carved it from a tree branch.

"You frightened me!" Mamie said. Babs strained at her leash, barking and growling.

"Sorry," he said. "I know who the killer is." Several of his teeth were missing so it was difficult for Mamie to understand the words.

"I'm sorry, what did you say?" she said, unconsciously backing up. Remembering that she still had her pistol in her bag gave her a little more confidence.

"I know."

She frowned. "You know?"

"Yeah, who killed them women."

Mamie's heart leapt in her throat as she thrust her hand in the crossbody bag holding her weapon. She closed her fingers around the grip and fingered the trigger, ready to pull it if she had to.

"You do?" Where was Nick when she needed him? She glanced around quickly, hoping someone, anyone was watching. The way Babs was barking, surely someone would peek out of an RV to see what was going on. *Please, someone, look out your window!*

"Sure do. And it ain't who you think."

Her eyes widened. How did he know what she thought? Had he been spying on her, eavesdropping on her conversations?

"Who are you, anyway? How do you know who I might think it is, or even who it really is? How do you know anything?" Anger replaced fear as she glowered at him, stepping closer to him. He smelled about as good as he looked. Ew.

"Name's Pink. Live over that ridge in a trailer." He pointed in the direction of the trail she and Babs had walked that day. "I saw when them bodies was taken out of the campground and the lake. I saw the one killed 'em. I saw him do it in cold blood."

"Him? Brady Hayden and Howard Story were arrested. I guess you know that, too."

"Yep, but it wadn't them. I know who done it."

Why was he putting her in the middle of it?

"Have you talked to the police?"

"Nah." He spit tobacco juice on the ground, uncomfortably close to her shoe. "Don't trust the police. Them's crooks. I seen too many people brought down by them that were innocent."

"Then why tell me? What makes you think you can trust me?"

"I been watching you around here. You seem nice.

You seem honest. I don't want you to get hurt. And that killer, he ain't done." He peered at her. "You got one of them notes, too, didn't ya?"

Mamie shivered and nodded. Why was she letting him know that? It didn't seem to matter. He knew it, whether she agreed or not.

She turned as she heard a car coming toward them. It was a police car, maybe the officer bringing her burger. "I wish you would go to the police. Here comes an officer now." But when she turned back the old man was gone, and Babs had stopped barking. He had to know she would tell them about him, but he hadn't told her not to. And he thought she was next on the killer's list. Great.

***

Even though she was still shaking a little, she decided not to tell the young woman who had brought her lunch. She would wait and talk to Nick. Creepy that the old man had been lurking in the shadows watching her. Even creepier that he knew she had received the note. She almost wished Howard Story was in the office so she could ask him about Pink. Did Scarlett know him?

Mamie finished her burger, another delicious menu item from the Silver Spoon. Or maybe it tasted so good because she was so hungry. She grabbed Babs's leash and trekked back to the office, even though the dog wasn't welcome. There was no way she would leave her in the camper alone again. Someone had a key.

Good. She's still here, Mamie thought as she opened the office door and saw Scarlett behind the counter, TV on, magazine in hand. She peered over sparkly reading glasses when Mamie entered.

"The dog isn't welcome," Scarlett said, standing.

If she realized how that frown made her face wrinkle, she wouldn't be frowning, Mamie thought. "I know, but I have a question, and I dare not leave the dog alone in my camper. She was let out last night while I was at dinner."

"What do you mean, let out?"

"Someone stole the key to my camper out of my car and let her out."

"Did they take anything else?"

"No, but they left a threatening note."

"Is that why Brady and Howard were arrested?"

"I believe they are suspects in the two murders this weekend. Didn't the police talk to you?"

Scarlett humphed and shrugged her shoulders. "I don't believe a word they say. Bunch of bumbling Keystone Cops. They wanted someone to pin those murders on and Brady and Howard were handy. Stupid judge won't allow anyone to post bail." A tear rolled down her face, mascara dribbling in its wake, surprising Mamie, who had assumed this woman's heart was made of stone. "Poor Brady. I hate to think of what he is going through in that nasty jail."

"I'm sorry," Mamie said, feeling bad for her. She seemed a devoted aunt, after all.

Scarlett sniffed and dabbed her eyes with a tissue she pulled out of a box under the counter. "What is it you needed?"

"I just had an encounter with an old man who told me his name is Pink. Do you know him?"

"Did he look like a homeless person?"

Mamie smiled. "Yes, he did, in fact."

"He's harmless, wanders around the campground scaring people out of their wits, especially children. He lives in a rundown trailer house over the ridge behind us. I've asked him to stop hanging around, but he still does. What did he do?"

"Besides scaring me, like you said, nothing. But he said he knew who the killer was, and it wasn't Brady or Mr. Story. I just wondered if I should talk to Detective Sovern or Officer Vandegan about it."

"Probably wouldn't be a bad idea, although I figure it's just his way of getting attention."

"He knows about the notes left at each murder scene."

"Everyone knows about those. It was on the news."

"Right. I'll get out of your hair and get the dog out of the store. Thank you for talking with me." Mamie turned to leave.

"You don't have to worry about the dog. She's okay. I just don't like it when people bring in their dogs and they use the bathroom on the floor or tear open food packages on the low shelves and racks. Your dog seems well-behaved. She's welcome any time." A smile almost broke out on Scarlett's face until she stopped it.

"Aw, thanks," Mamie said, glancing at the dog who was standing next to her patiently. "The only thing she might do is shed a bit, but I figure you have to sweep anyway, right?"

Scarlett frowned, and Mamie steered Babs out

before she could change her mind. "Thanks again," she said as she closed the door.

So Pink was just an eccentric old man who just liked to hang around and scare people. What would Nick think about that? She didn't have to wonder long because his car pulled in just as she reached her campsite, following another cruiser already parked there.

Detective Sovern got out of the first one and waited for Vandegan before approaching Mamie, who unlocked her camper door and let Babs hop inside.

"Afternoon, Detective, Officer," she said, not sure if it would be appropriate to call Vandegan by his first name in Sovern's presence. She decided against it.

"Good afternoon, Ms. West. I'd like to ask you a few questions about Carly Hallmark."

"Of course. Shall we sit here?" She gestured toward the picnic table.

Sovern nodded. He and Vandegan straddled the benches as Mamie sat on the one on the opposite side of the table. She glanced at Vandegan, who winked at her, and she raised her eyebrows as she waited for Sovern to begin.

"I'd like to hear about your relationship with Carly Hallmark. How did you meet, how much interaction you had, anything she said that might be of interest in our investigation."

"Okay." Mamie took a deep breath and glanced at Vandegan again for reassurance. He smiled and nodded, encouraging her to go on.

"I didn't know her before this weekend. The first

time I saw her was when Sarah's body was discovered. She was very distraught, more than anyone else. She took offense at me for suggesting someone call 911 and then she was rude to me during dinner one night after drinking too much wine. I told her about finding the note at my camper and she became friendlier and seemed to want to help find the killer."

"Help you find the killer?" Sovern asked.

"I was trying to match handwriting samples with the handwriting on the notes, and I told her that and she said she was willing to help me."

"And did you match any handwriting samples with the notes?"

"Yes, the handwriting seemed similar to Brady Hayden's."

Sovern glanced at Vandegan. "That's what we've been going on?"

"It gave us a reason to look into Hayden and Story, yes. Without Mamie's, uh, Ms. West's conclusion it would have taken us longer to find the suspects," Vandegan said.

Sovern rolled his eyes.

"May I ask a question?" Mamie said.

Sovern nodded.

"Why was Mr. Story arrested? His handwriting was not a match."

"We're not at liberty to discuss an investigation, Ms. West," Sovern said.

"We don't think Brady acted alone," Vandegan said.

Sovern frowned, giving him a withering look.

Vandegan looked down at his clasped hands on top of the table.

But Mamie wouldn't be deterred. "What if I told you that someone else may know who the killer is?"

Chapter Twenty-Five

SOVERN LEANED FORWARD. "What do you mean?"

Vandegan frowned. "What are you talking about?"

Mamie proceeded to explain how she had met a man named Pink who had been lurking around the campground and claimed to know about the murders. Or at least he said he knew who committed them. Whether or not he had actually witnessed them he hadn't said.

"Who is this guy Pink?" Sovern questioned.

"I don't know. Babs and I had a scary encounter with him on the walking trail around the lakeshore on the first day I was here, and then he showed up again. He's creepy and he really scares me. He knows about the notes, too."

"You better check that out," Vandegan told Sovern.

"I'm on it." Sovern stood. "I'm going back to the station to run a check. You stay here and find out what you can."

Vandegan nodded. When Sovern had closed his car door Vandegan leaned toward Mamie.

"Did this joker threaten you?"

"No."

"Do you believe him?"

"Yes, I believe him. He's scrawny and unkempt, but he seems sincere."

"I guess I should question Scarlett about him. If

he's been hanging around here, she'll know him."

"I talked to her, and she didn't have much to say except that he's harmless. She keeps trying to run him off, but he keeps coming back. She said he scares the kids."

"I need to meet this guy. Is he homeless, or do you think he lives around here?"

"Scarlett said he lives in a trailer over the ridge."

"Okay, I know who this guy is. I've asked him to clean up around that trailer so many times I've just about given up. He's got a bunch of broken-down old cars and trucks over there, plus old tires and piles of junk. I think he used to be a mechanic but now he's just a hoarder. He's always outside tinkering with something. You said his name is Pink?"

Mamie nodded.

"I always knew him as Buford. I guess I thought that was his last name."

"Does he live alone?"

"Yes, his wife died years ago. I think he has a couple of kids but they never come around, or at least not that I've seen."

"That's sad. He's all alone. Maybe he hangs around here so much because he's lonely."

"Maybe so." Nick smiled and touched her hand as it rested on the table across from him. "You're more sympathetic than I am. I guess police work has hardened me."

"It's a woman thing," Mamie said with a smile.

"Would you like to go with me to talk to him? You

may think of questions I don't."

"Sure, I can do that," Mamie said, getting up. "If you'll give me a few minutes to walk Babs."

"I will. I'll wait in my car. There are a few things I need to catch up on with my tablet," he said, standing. To her surprise, he walked around the table and pulled her close, planting a kiss on her lips.

Feeling a tingle all the way to her toes, she smiled. "That was bold. What if someone saw us?"

"I don't care. There's no law against a tiny kiss while on duty."

"You might want to check that. I bet there is somewhere." She winked. "I'll be just a few minutes."

***

Just as Vandegan had described, Pink was out in front of his trailer tinkering under the hood of an old car. He didn't seem to notice when they drove up and got out of the cruiser. They walked over and as they got within ten feet of him, he looked up, tobacco juice running down his chin.

Mamie shuddered as her stomach turned. Didn't it bother him to have that nasty stuff on his face? Or in his mouth, for that matter? Didn't he worry about cancer?

"Hello, Buford," Vandegan said, offering his hand in a friendly gesture. The old man kept his hands in the engine compartment of the old beat-up car. The rusty hood and front fenders had seen better days, probably in the 1960s. Mamie wasn't sure of the make or model but it was vintage, for sure.

"Whatcha sneakin' up on an old man for?" Pink

barked, straightening and spitting on the ground. He wiped his chin with his bare forearm. Mamie shuddered again. Nasty.

"I'd like to ask you some questions if you have time." *That was polite,* Mamie thought. The man had nothing but time.

"I guess I can spare a few minutes," Pink said. He wiped his hands on a towel draped across the fender. "Wanna come inside? I got beer."

"No, no thanks. If you don't mind, I'd rather stay outside. This won't take very long."

Thank you, thank you, Mamie thought. No way did she want to go inside this nasty being's home. No telling what was crawling around in there, visible or invisible.

"Suit yourself. Howdy, ma'am." Pink nodded to Mamie.

"This is my friend Mamie West," Vandegan said. "I think you've met. She told me that you might know something about the murders at the campground."

"Oh, she did, did she?" Pink eyed Mamie, who swallowed, feeling uncomfortable. He had one eye that opened more than the other, reminding her of the cartoon character Popeye. Did he think she wouldn't talk to the police?

"I didn't feel right keeping the information to myself," Mamie said.

"What if I don't feel like answering any questions?" Pink said.

"Then I'd have to advise you to get yourself an attorney," Vandegan said. "We'd have to take it to a judge.

You can come to town with me now."

Pink uttered an oath and spat on the ground again. "All right then. Let's get this over with."

Vandegan pulled a small pad and a pen from his shirt pocket. "Let's start with the murder of Sarah Trenton. Where were you and what did you see?"

"I was up at the campground going through a trash can—you know, I get money for aluminum cans and people throw away good stuff sometimes. You wouldn't believe the things I've found that people throw away."

"Yes, and what did you see?" Vandegan prodded him.

"Well, I was going through the trash, you know, and I seen somebody walking up to that lady's camper and knocking on the door. She came out and they started yelling at each other. Then he ran to a pickup truck, shot her as she stood there yelling at him, and drove off fast."

"He shot her from the pickup?"

"Yep."

"You didn't try to help her?"

Pink spat on the ground again. "No way. I done got in trouble too much around here. If I showed my face they woulda pinned it on me."

Vandegan shook his head. *Disgusting,* Mamie thought. *The man is disgusting.*

"Then how do you think she ended up in the underbrush?"

"How am I supposed to know? I saw what I saw and then I hightailed it outta there."

"Maybe she dragged herself there, trying to get help," Mamie said.

"Maybe so, but why not toward the road where someone could see her? What else can you tell me about it, Buford? You didn't happen to get the license plate number, did you?"

"Nah, man, I had to get outta there."

"Okay, then tell me how you knew about the note."

"Note?"

"Yes, you asked Ms. West here if she had gotten a note."

"I heard them women talking about it, how somebody found a note that fell out of a book."

Vandegan looked at Mamie, who shrugged and shook her head. The guy had obviously eavesdropped on her conversation with Carly.

"All right, Buford. What do you know about the other murder?"

"That woman that was found in the lake?"

"Yes, that one."

"I saw her coming back to her cabin Friday morning after breakfast. That same guy that killed Sarah followed her inside. I didn't hear no conversation. I just figured she knew him. Next thing I know she turns up dead."

"So you really don't know who killed those women, do you? You did see Sarah's shooter and then you saw him go inside Holly Fuller's cabin, but you don't know for sure if he killed her. You don't know who the man is, do you?"

"I'd know him if I saw him again."

"Can you describe him?"

"I didn't get no good look at him, but he's average size, white, brown hair, beard."

Vandegan scribbled the information on his notepad. "I'll need you to come to the station, give a statement. How about tomorrow morning?"

"I guess I can do that."

"Good. I'll see you then. Thank you for the information, Buford."

"Yup." Pink turned back to his work under the hood of the car as Vandegan and Mamie walked back to the cruiser.

"I don't know whether to believe him or not," Vandegan said as he started the car.

"I don't think you have a lot of choice," Mamie replied. But if Pink was right, then who was the guy he saw? If not Brady or Howard Story, then who? Could it have been Sarah's husband?

Chapter Twenty-Six

JUNIE KEPT HER promise. When they returned to the campground, her car was parked in front of Mamie's camper. Mamie jumped out of the cruiser and met her daughter, who hopped up from her place at the picnic table.

"Junie! You got here fast!" Mamie said, giving Junie a hug.

Junie returned her mother's hug and then stepped back as she saw Vandegan approaching. Mamie turned and grabbed his hand while holding Junie's arm.

"This is Officer Nick Vandegan. He's a good friend and he's investigating the murders here at the campground. Nick, this is my daughter Junie."

"Nice to meet you," Junie said before turning her attention to her mother. "I've been so worried about you, Mom. Have there been any more murders besides the two I heard about?"

"Honey, I'm fine, and no, there haven't been any more murders. There's no need to worry. The police have two suspects in custody. And I have Babs with me," she added when she heard the dog barking inside the camper. "Look at that cute little face," Mamie grinned when she noticed Babs in the window.

"Yeah, I forgot about Babs. She would certainly be a deterrent to a killer." Junie's voice dripped with sarcasm.

"You'd be surprised at how much a deterrent a barking dog can be," Vandegan said. "Pleased to meet you, by the way." He extended his right hand to shake Junie's.

"I've enjoyed getting to know your mother."

Mamie smiled up at him as she squeezed his other hand. It was big and warm and surprisingly soft. Protective. Male. She had missed male contact much more than she had thought.

"I bet you have," Junie said, shaking her head.

"Junie! You're being rude. I taught you better than that."

Junie shook Vandegan's hand. "I apologize for my rudeness. I'm glad my mother has a friend in you. Thank you for helping her and protecting her. She may have mentioned my father was a policeman."

"Yes, she did. I'm doing my best, I can assure you. I'd like nothing more than to get to the bottom of all this and put the perpetrator behind bars for good. Or even see the death penalty given. Mamie, I'll be on my way now. I need to get back to the station and talk with Sovern about our meeting today."

"Thank you so much for asking me to go with you," Mamie said. "See you later?"

"I'll be in touch." He took a couple of steps while still holding her hand, then dropping it. Mamie's stomach fluttered as she watched him get into his car. Was she starting to fall for him?

"Earth to Mom," Junie said. "Can we talk?"

"Of course! Let me get Babs." She opened the camper door and fastened Babs's harness and leash on the little dog before allowing her to come outside. "She needs a walk. Come with us."

Junie rolled her eyes. "I need to lock my car," she

said. Mamie nodded and watched her daughter as she tossed her bag into the car and slammed the door.

"What is your problem?" Mamie asked.

"Other than you taking off pulling a trailer by yourself and then insisting on staying in a campground where there have been two murders in one weekend? And you've gotten involved with a younger man. And you broke your wrist, too?" She eyed Mamie's wrapped wrist. "Other than that, nothing."

"It's just a sprain. Junie, I'm a grown woman and your mother. I am perfectly capable of taking care of myself. Besides, I thought you were excited about me getting a trailer and going camping. As for being involved with any man, younger or not, that is none of your business. I did not tolerate disrespect when you were still at home, and I will not tolerate it now."

Junie fell into step with her mother and Babs as they headed down the road.

"I'm sorry, Mom. I didn't mean to be disrespectful. I'm just worried about you."

Mamie stopped and looked at her daughter. Junie was a younger version of herself—the same hair, same eyes, same height and build. Not only physically but in temperament and personality as well. She had the same drive and independence as her mother. But Mamie's generation graduated high school or college and got married. Junie's generation seemed to concentrate on careers more than marriage. As beautiful as Junie was, Mamie wondered why some young man hadn't snapped her up. She was a bit biased, of course. "I forgive you, honey, but please don't worry. As you can see, I'm just fine."

"I can see that. So, this Officer Vandegan. Did you just meet him on this campout?"

"I did, yes."

"Seems you hit it off."

"We did. Does that bother you?" Mamie said as Babs led them on.

"No, it really doesn't," Junie replied. "Tyler and I expect you to move on. We don't want you to spend the rest of your life alone and lonely."

"That's a relief." Mamie chuckled. "I promise you I'm not looking for a relationship. I still miss your dad, and I don't think anyone will measure up to the man he was. Nick is just really nice, and I like the attention, I guess."

"I don't blame you, Mom. I understand. I've got a new man in my life, too."

Mamie stopped and stared at her daughter. "Go on."

"His name is Brady Hayden and he's actually from right here in Magnolia Bluff."

Mamie almost dropped Babs's leash as she stopped in her tracks. "Who?"

"Brady Hayden. Do we need to look into hearing aids, Mom?" Junie laughed.

Could there be another Brady Hayden besides the one Mamie knew? The one who worked here at the campground and had been arrested for murder?

"Junie, not Brady Hayden."

"You know him?"

"Yes. He works here. He's the campground owner's nephew. He is in jail for the murders."

"What? No. You're joking. Although that would explain why he stood me up last night and hasn't returned my calls and texts."

"I wouldn't joke about it. He was arrested last night." It didn't matter, but she had to ask anyway. "How and where did you meet Brady?"

"Could we find a place to sit down, please? This is too much."

"Of course." They were near the beach area where the Adirondack chairs were, so Mamie led Junie there. The young woman sank into one of the chairs, and Mamie sat next to her with Babs on the leash at her feet.

"I was at a party a few weeks ago and my friend Bobbie introduced me to Brady. We talked and hit it off. We have a lot of common interests, and we've gone out a couple of times. He told me he graduated from Stephen F. Austin University and became a resort manager. He works here? Is he the manager?"

"No, honey, I mean, yes, he works here, but he works in maintenance. I don't think he's been to college yet."

Junie's eyes widened as she clapped a hand to her forehead. "Are you serious?"

Her mother nodded, her mouth forming a sympathetic line.

"What a fool I've been."

Chapter Twenty-Seven

MAMIE REACHED OVER and placed a hand on Junie's. The younger woman shook her head and sniffed.

"I have the worst taste in men. I pick 'em, don't I? I mean, Colin? Justin? Travis? I can't seem to find a good guy. Is it too much to ask? I mean, is God punishing me? What did I do wrong?" She stared at her mother with tears in her eyes.

"God is not punishing you. I don't believe that. Just be patient. The right man will come along, I promise. By the way, I liked Brady. He is a nice young man and was really helpful to me when I arrived here. I actually told him I'd like to introduce you two, but he said he had a girlfriend, which, as it turns out, was you. So I was fooled as well. Don't feel bad."

"But what if the right man doesn't come along, Mom?"

"Listen to me. You don't need a man to live a fulfilling life."

Junie rolled her eyes. "Didn't you, Mom? I'm not getting any younger, and I would like to have children someday. I need a man in my life to do that. So, yes, to be fulfilled, I need a man."

"Be patient, honey. I pray for you every day. You just have to wait. It will happen."

"But what if it doesn't?"

"Remember what I told you about 'what ifs?' They

do no good whatsoever. Give them to God. Tell Him your doubts. Trust Him to lead you. He knows what is best for you, whether that is children or not."

Junie made a growling sound in her throat as she stood. "You're not helping, Mom. I guess I've accomplished what I came here for. I was going to look Brady up but if he is in jail I would rather not."

"He's innocent until proven guilty, you know," Mamie said. She'd been under the impression that her daughter had come because she was concerned about her mother.

"There you go again with your platitudes. Even if he is innocent, he lied to me about graduating from college and about his job. I have better things to do than hang around with a liar. I'm heading back home." She waited for Mamie before walking toward the trailer.

"I wish you would stay until dinnertime. I thought you were going to get a cabin. Didn't you tell me that earlier?"

"I did, but I don't think I need to stay overnight after all. But could you go into town with me for dinner?"

"Nick told me earlier to stay put, so I would need to check with him."

"All right, do that. And ask him what place he recommends."

***

Following Vandegan's recommendation and clearance for Mamie to leave the campground for dinner, she and Junie enjoyed the Silver Spoon's chicken fried steak and gravy, mashed potatoes, green beans, salad, and their famous coconut pie for dessert.

"If I had too many meals like this, you'd have to roll me out in a wheelbarrow," Mamie laughed.

"I'm stuffed, but it was delicious. Please thank Officer Vandegan for recommending this place. I just love these small-town diners."

"I will. Thank you for the company. With everyone else already gone, camping by myself is pretty lonesome. I'm glad I have Babs with me. And speaking of Babs, I really should get back."

"I'll drop you off and then head back to Round Rock. Unless you want me to stay. I had planned to stay overnight."

"No, no, I'm fine. I don't need my daughter babysitting me. Yet." Mamie smiled.

"And I hope you won't for a very long time," Junie said. "I enjoyed the visit, Mom."

"Me, too. No more lectures from you, and I promise not to give you any, either."

"Deal," Junie said, chuckling.

***

Darkness was reaching its shadowy fingers through the campground when they returned. Mamie gave Junie a hug and sent her on her way before leashing Babs for a walk. The sign Nick had given her to put on the door warning of a security camera must have worked. Babs was fine. Mamie didn't really want to be out alone in the dark, but she stuck her pistol in her waistband and headed toward the clubhouse. She would make it a short walk. She wished Nick was with her. *Don't be silly,* she told herself. *You're being a baby.*

She knew what West would've said--not to go--but he also knew how stubborn she could be. He would be proud of her for carrying her pistol, though. Crazy how the least little noise made her jump. The leaves rustling in the trees, a bird fluttering in branches, someone closing a car door. Babs seemed unfazed, so that was comforting.

Then a twig snapped behind her. Her fingers closed around the pistol grip. Someone was following her. The fur on Babs's back stood on end as she whirled around and started barking. Mamie turned just in time to see the business end of a shovel coming at her. Then the world went black.

***

Her eyes fluttered open, her head pounding so hard it hurt to open her eyes, but she needed to figure out where she was. She reached for her pistol but it wasn't there. She was half lying on the wooden floor of a dark tool shed, propped against the wall, and she was alone. The smell of oil, gasoline, and dirt assaulted her senses. Where was Babs? What had they done with her dog? Panic seized her.

As she tried to sit up, searing pain shot through her head and she vomited on the floor. So much for the chicken fried steak dinner. At least she hadn't thrown up on herself. She dragged herself as far as she could from the smelly mess and tried to focus on her surroundings.

In the dim light of the moon and security lights spilling through the cracks in the rafters, she made out several garden tools in a corner with handheld tools covering a workbench. Paint cans, gas cans, bags of fertilizer and garden soil, a fertilizer spreader, and a weed trimmer were scattered around. A riding lawn mower sat on one side of the shed, which was barely big enough to accommodate it. She wondered how long she had been out.

I have to get out of here, she thought, but as she tried to stand, she sank to the floor. The door rattled as it opened, and a man she had never seen before stepped inside. He closed the door behind himself and squatted next to her.

Wait, I have seen him somewhere. Her head hurt too much to try and figure out where.

"Look who's awake. I thought I killed you. Glad I didn't. This way will be more fun." He grinned, his face inches from hers.

"What did you do with my dog?" She studied his face, trying to remember where she had seen him, with his long graying beard and bushy dark brown eyebrows. She couldn't tell much about his hair as he was wearing a ball cap.

"That yippy little thing? It bit me and I kicked the fire out of it. Probably still laying on the side of the road."

The tears that Mamie had been holding back finally squeezed out of her eyes and ran down her face. "Why would you hurt an innocent animal?"

"Innocent? It bit me, didn't you hear me?" He showed her the red bite marks on his hand. "Stupid animal deserved kicking."

"Oh, I'm sure," Mamie sobbed, strangely proud of

the little dog for defending herself in her last moments. "What do you want with me?"

"Are you gettin' more than you bargained for?" He laughed as he yanked her to her feet.

Her eyes widened as she realized where she had seen him. The coffee shop. Was he the killer?

Chapter Twenty-Nine

MAMIE WINCED AS she stood, shards of pain threatening to split her head in two. Unwelcome tears rolled down her face. She did not want to show any weakness. With her free hand she wiped them away.

He took the movement as an attempt to get away from him, so he yanked her arm harder. She cried out and he laughed. "Hurtin' ya, huh?"

"What, do you get off making women scream?" Mamie growled, anger replacing fear. This was the same man who had been watching her and Nick at the Really Good. "In your dreams. Where are you taking me?"

"Somewhere Vandegan and Sovern can't find you."

"You'll never get away with this. Officer Vandegan will be looking for me. Do you really want him to come after you?"

"Shut up." He pulled a roll of duct tape from the pocket of his fisherman's vest.

Her eyes widened. "No, please, I won't say another word."

"You're right. You won't." He let go of her arm, tore off a piece of the silver redneck fix-all and stuck it over her mouth from cheek to cheek.

I wonder if he's going to kill me like he did Sarah and Holly. I can't die like this. I can't. West, help me! God, help me! Her mind screamed as he grabbed her arm again and opened the door to the shed. *Please let someone see us,* she prayed as he pushed her ahead of him and outside. It was so dark there was little likelihood they would be seen. How long had she been out?

She then realized that the shed was in the back of the campground, well away from the RVs, office, and clubhouse. He was going to kill her and throw her in the lake just like he had Holly. She had to figure out a way to escape.

He dragged her to a rusty, beat-up old pickup truck and flung open the door to push her in. She kicked him in the shin, wiggled out of his grasp, and started running toward the RVs.

"Come back here!" he yelled. Cursing and limping, he took off running after her, but she ducked behind some trees before he could catch up to her. "You're going to be sorry for this," he shouted, trotting past her without seeing her. The darkness was on her side. She ran, weaving around trees and bushes until she reached the outermost campsite, and she darted behind the RV, thinking she heard him nearby. He walked past the campsite cursing.

The lights were on in the RV she was behind, so as soon as he had passed, she crept to the door and knocked softly enough that he wouldn't be able to hear. She hoped whoever was inside could.

The door opened a crack and an older man poked his head out. The sound of a TV program blared inside.

"Who is it, Ben?" came a feminine voice in the RV.

"Don't know yet. Can I help you?" he said with a deep East Texas accent she recognized from being around the West family whose roots were in the pine forests around Lufkin.

Mamie grimaced as she ripped the tape from her face. "Yes, please, someone is trying to hurt me and I need help." Tears rolled down her face as her eyes pleaded with him.

The man frowned. His wife, or the woman whose voice she had heard, joined him at the door.

"Well, let her in, Ben. She's scared to death."

"And what if whoever is trying to hurt her finds her here? What if it's a trick? What will they do to us?"

The woman grabbed his arm and pulled him out of the way, then opened the door wide enough for Mamie to enter the large RV.

"Come on in here, honey."

Mamie slipped in and the man shut the door and locked it as they saw the dried blood on her head and her disheveled appearance.

"Sit right here, dear," the woman said, gesturing to the sofa. "Can I get you something to drink? And maybe a cool rag for that nasty head wound?"

Mamie sank into the comfort of the couch with gratitude oozing from every pore.

"Yes, thank you. Water and a rag would be great," she managed, touching her scalp with a wince. The older couple reminded her of her parents when they were still camping. When the lady gave her a bottle of water, she drank three quarters of it right away.

"My goodness, dear, you were thirsty, weren't you?" said the lady, sitting next to her. "May I?" She dabbed the rag at Mamie's head.

"Yes, ma'am, thank you very much." The lady had a gentle touch.

The man closed the curtains and sat in a recliner opposite Mamie.

"Now why don't you tell us what is going on? Should I call the police?"

"Yes, please do," Mamie said, downing the last of the water. As the lady took the empty bottle, she continued. "I don't know if you've heard, but there were two murders here at the campground this weekend. A man knocked me out and put me in a tool shed. As he was taking me to his truck I got away, and now he is after me. I think he may be the one who killed those poor women."

"Ben. . ."

"On it, Fran." He pulled his cell phone from his shirt pocket.

As he punched the numbers for 911, Fran put her arm around Mamie's shoulders. "You're safe with us. We won't let anyone inside until the police get here."

"Thank you. Had you heard about the murders?"

"No, we hadn't, but we pretty much stay to ourselves. We're retired full-time RVers. We've been here about three months. We'll be traveling north at the end of this month. It gets too hot in Texas in the summer."

"It sure does," Mamie agreed. She didn't know whether she should tell Fran more about the murders. What good would it do these sweet people? They didn't know the ladies anyway. She decided to keep quiet.

"What else can I get you? Are you hungry?"

She was, but she didn't want to put these people out any more than she already had. She shook her head.

"Are you sure? Ben and I just had dinner and the chili is still hot. I can fix you a chili pie."

Mamie's tummy grumbled in response.

"I heard that." Fran hopped up and started bustling around the tiny kitchen area.

"I don't want to put you out," Mamie said.

"She lives for feeding people," Ben said, having finished his phone call. "You'll hurt her feelings real bad if you don't let her feed you." He chuckled. "The police are on their way."

"Thank you," Mamie said. The butterflies still fluttered in her tummy and would until the killer was caught. Who was that guy anyway, and what did he have against Vandegan and Sovern, other than not wanting to be arrested for murder? If he indeed was the murderer.

As she took the bowl of chili from Fran, a pounding on the door startled all three of them.

Ben reached into a cubby near his chair and pulled out a large revolver. "Who is it?" he thundered.

"I know she's in there. If she doesn't come out now, I'll tear the flimsy door off this rattletrap," came the raspy voice of Mamie's attacker.

Ben chuckled. "I'd like to see you try, buddy." Holding his pistol with his left hand, he lowered the recliner with his right hand.

"Don't get up," Fran whispered. "He might shoot

through the door. Does he have a gun?"

Mamie remembered her missing pistol. "I think he does," she said. The bowl of chili, cheese, and corn chips looked appealing but the knots in her stomach wouldn't allow her to take even one bite. She held it in her lap, watching Ben to see what he would do next.

The door handle shook violently as the killer tried to open the door. Then he started yanking on it. Fran dialed 911 even though the police had already been called. Ben aimed his pistol at the door, ready to fire if the man got the door open.

"Open the door!" The attacker's voice rose as he pulled harder on the door handle. It finally twisted and fell through the door to the outside, leaving a gaping hole. As he put his fingers through the hole to pull the door open, Ben grabbed his hand, pulled it inside, and twisted it toward the floor.

"Ahhh!" the man cried.

"Ben!" Fran yelled.

If the killer has my gun, now would be a good time for him to use it, except he might need his right hand, the one sticking through the door hole, Mamie thought. She held her breath.

Ben kept his free hand on the killer's arm, not seeming to care if the man was crying out in pain, and not seeming to care if the guy had a gun and managed to shoot.

"Let go of me!" the man yelled. "You're breaking my arm! I'll sue!"

Ben laughed. "I'll take my chances."

To Mamie's great relief, police sirens sounded in the distance and grew closer with each second that passed. The police must have been nearby. Maybe Nick had been near the campground when the call came in.

There was a commotion outside as the police arrived. Red and blue flashing lights illuminated the campground.

"Stay inside!" Mamie heard the shouts of the officers as they exited their cars. Likely other campers were poking their heads out of their RVs to see what was going on. She strained to hear Nick's voice.

In a few minutes, the attacker's arm had been pulled back through the RV door, and he was cuffed and tucked inside a police cruiser to be taken to the station. Ben went outside to speak to the officer as Fran stayed by Mamie's side until she stood, still gripping the bowl of chili pie.

"Here, dear, let me take that for you. Would you like some more water?"

"No, thank you. And thank you for everything. You and your husband are so kind."

"We were more than glad to help."

"I'll pay for the repair to your RV."

"Nonsense, dear. We have insurance. You just worry about you."

A familiar figure entered the open door of the RV, and Mamie gasped as she realized who it was. "Nick!" she cried, rushing into his arms. "You're here!"

He wrapped his arms around her and pulled her close, placing a hand on the back of her head as she nestled into his embrace.

"Thank you for your help, ma'am," he said to Fran. "You're going to be okay, honey," he told Mamie.

"Of course, Officer," Fran said. "Always glad to help."

A paramedic stepped up into the RV behind Nick. "I'm here to check her vitals," he said.

Mamie pulled back from Vandegan, shaking her head. "No, no, I'm fine. I'm just tired." Tears sprang to her eyes. "But I need to find my dog. She's hurt." She wouldn't allow herself to say the word *dead*. Babs had to be okay.

"First we have to make sure you are all right physically. Then I need you to tell me everything that happened." He looked at Fran. "Is it okay if we talk here?"

"Of course, yes. I'll just see about Ben." The older woman stepped out of the trailer, leaving Mamie alone with Vandegan and the paramedic. He asked her to sit and then used a penlight to peer into her eyes before wrapping a blood pressure cuff around her arm.

"Pulse and blood pressure normal. Slight abrasions on her arms and face. Nothing serious. Are you feeling any pain or discomfort?" He glanced at her wrapped left wrist. "Is this from an earlier injury?"

Mamie nodded. "I told you, I'm fine. Nick, I just want to find Babs. The man who kidnapped me said he kicked her and left her on the side of the road after he knocked me unconscious."

"You were knocked unconscious?"

Mamie rolled her eyes. "Yes, I think with a shovel, but I'm fine."

"I'd like to have you checked at the hospital."

"Okay, but not until we find Babs."

Vandegan glanced at the paramedic, who nodded. "She'll be fine until then, but she needs to go sometime tonight. If she has a concussion, she needs to be treated soon."

"All right, let's find your dog," Vandegan said.

Following the paramedic, he helped Mamie down the RV steps. The kidnapper glared at her from where he sat in the back seat of the cruiser, making her shudder. Her aversion was not lost on Vandegan.

"Get this guy outta here," he said, pounding on the hood of the cruiser with his fist. The driver, another officer and colleague of Vandegan's, nodded, slammed the vehicle in gear, and roared off, gravel flying.

"You okay?"

Mamie nodded, although she wasn't being completely truthful. She wouldn't be okay until she found her dog.

But her dog found her instead.

Chapter Thirty

"**B**ABS!"

The little black and white terrier jumped up on her owner's legs, demanding attention, her bottom wiggling madly. She whined and 'talked' as Mamie collapsed to the ground, wrapping the little dog in her arms while having her face licked over and over.

"Looks like she found you first," Vandegan said, grinning.

Happy tears flowed down Mamie's face as she checked the dog over for injuries, but there were no yelps from being handled, and the dog's behavior seemed normal.

"Shall we go to the hospital to get you checked out?"

"Only if I can bring Babs." She knew he wouldn't dream of saying no after what she had been through, because he nodded as he led them both over to his car and opened the back door. Mamie climbed in and Babs hopped in behind her. Before closing the door and getting into the driver's seat, he spoke to Ben and Fran.

"Thank you again for assisting Ms. West. She owes her safety to you. If you don't mind, please come down to the station in the morning and give your statements."

"It was our duty but also our pleasure, Officer. We'll be there in the morning," Fran said, not waiting for Ben to speak. Her husband nodded in agreement.

***

Vandegan waited at the hospital, charged with watching the dog, which hospital personnel had graciously allowed inside, while Mamie was examined. An off-duty nurse about to go home even volunteered to look Babs over.

"I worked at a vet clinic all through college until I decided I'd rather treat humans," she laughed.

"I'm sure her owner would really appreciate that."

Mamie and Babs both checked out fine and cleared to go home with the promise that they would be back if any symptoms cropped up. Vandegan popped them both into the cruiser to take them back to the campground.

"Do you feel safe going back to your camper?" he asked Mamie. She had laid her head back against the headrest and closed her eyes with Babs curled in the seat beside her.

"Um," was the response.

He pulled up to the campground office and used the key that Scarlett had given him years ago to let himself inside in case he needed to for security reasons. This night, though, he had another reason. A few moments later he emerged and got back into the car, noticing that Mamie was barely aware that he had stopped and gotten out.

A moment later he carried her through a doorway and lowered her gently onto the bed, then spread a light blanket over her. Babs jumped up beside her and curled up tight against her legs. He switched the lights off one by one until no light could penetrate her closed eyelids. Then he watched her troubled face relax as sleep overtook her. To be sure she was safe and not frightened when she woke up in strange surroundings, he settled on the loveseat for the night.

***

Mamie awoke to Babs licking her face. Sunlight teased her eyes open, and when she stretched, she saw Nick sleeping on a small couch near the door, his legs hanging over its arm. He was in full uniform, and he did not look comfortable. She glanced around, realizing that she was in a cabin. One of the cabins at the campground?

"Nick?" She pushed Babs away from her face.

He stirred and opened his eyes. "Hey, there. Sleep well?"

"Yes, I did. Where are we? And why?"

"We're still at the campground. I let us into one of Scarlett's cabins so I could keep an eye on you through the night. Good job I did of that, huh?" he chuckled. "Are you feeling all right this morning?"

"I think so. I'll feel much better when I've had some coffee and a little breakfast."

"I'll have Kristine bring us something from the Really Good." He pulled his cell phone out of his pocket and punched a number in.

There was no leash for Babs but Mamie figured she wouldn't run off after her misfortune the night before, so while Nick was on the phone she got out of bed and opened the door. Babs looked up at her for permission and when her owner nodded, the dog traipsed outside, did her business, and dashed back inside. Poor thing had just had a traumatic night.

Mamie went into the small bathroom and checked her appearance, aghast at her reflection in the antique mirror that hung over the sink. Sunken, mascara-smeared eyes stared back at her as a halo of unbrushed hair wildly framed her dirty, tear-streaked face. She cupped her hands full of warm water and splashed her face, wiping as much damage away as she could with a hand towel. She smoothed her hair with her fingers, hoping that helped some. What Nick must think. At least he had cared enough to stay with her through the night.

When she emerged from the bathroom, he was rummaging in the kitchenette cabinet and drawers. "I thought there might be some coffee. There's a coffee pot and I found some mugs. Aha! Coffee. We'll have some in a jiffy."

Mamie straightened the bed covers and sat down on the couch, Babs in her lap, while he prepared the life-giving liquid. He handed her a bottle of water, which she gratefully accepted, and then he thoughtfully placed a bowl of water on the floor for Babs, who lapped it up eagerly.

"Poor thing was thirsty," she said. "Thank you, Nick. What happens now?"

"With the suspect? He was arrested for kidnapping, aggravated assault, and breaking and entering. He'll be in jail until the judge determines bail—if he decides to."

"He wasn't arrested for murder?"

"As far as I know, there is no evidence tying him to the murders."

"Besides the fact that he singled me out?"

"Did he admit to anything? Did he talk about the other women?"

"No, but he quoted the words on the note."

"What did he say?

"He said I got more than I bargained for."

"That's a common phrase. I'm afraid that isn't enough to charge him with the murders."

A heavy sigh escaped her as she leaned her head on the back of the couch. If she hadn't been so quick to get away, maybe she could have had him talking, maybe even confessing. But then again, she was afraid he was planning to kill her.

"What is it?" Vandegan asked as he handed her a cup of steaming black coffee.

"Thanks. I was just thinking that if I hadn't escaped so soon I might have gotten him to talk."

He sat next to her, set his mug on the old trunk that served as a coffee table, took hers, and did the same. Then his arm went around her shoulders. "You did the right thing by getting out of there as fast as you could. He might have killed you. It could have been your body someone discovered floating in the lake this morning."

She shuddered. "I know. I just wish we knew if he was the killer so we could give the families closure and put him away for good."

"Chief Jager and I will be questioning him, and Detective Sovern will be searching for evidence. Do you remember where you were when you got away from him?"

"Yes, he had me in a tool shed at the back of the property. I think I remember where it is if you'd like me to take you there."

"I would like to see it, but I'll do that later, probably with Sovern. First we'll have breakfast as soon as Officer Combs gets here, and then I'll let you freshen up and get dressed. I'll walk you to your camper so you can get what you need from there."

"No need. I'll take Babs there and then I can use the campground showers."

"That's probably a good idea. I need to let Scarlett know I hijacked one of her cabins for the night. She'll need to get the cleaning crew to straighten up and change the sheets."

Mamie leaned her head on Vandegan's strong shoulder and breathed in his masculine scent. He kissed the top of her head and squeezed her shoulders. "Thank you for taking care of me and Babs and for staying with us all night. You probably didn't get much sleep with your arms and legs dangling off this tiny couch."

"Don't worry about me. I just had to make sure you were all right after such a traumatic night. We'll nail this guy, Mamie. And we'll find the killer if it isn't him."

"I know you will." She turned to gaze into his eyes and accepted the kiss he planted on her lips.

A sudden rapping on the door interrupted them just as the kiss deepened. Vandegan groaned as he stood to get the door, holding his hand up to keep Mamie from getting up, too. "Don't move. That's probably breakfast," he said, going to the door.

"Good, because I'm starved," Mamie said.

As soon as Officer Combs handed off a take-out bag and two coffees to Vandegan, she disappeared.

"Did she even see me?" Mamie laughed.

"I'm sure she did. She's a good cop and a better friend. She knows not to get in my personal business."

"You won't get in trouble, will you?"

"Sometimes the line between police business and personal business becomes blurry. I'm doing my job being here with you. That's all anyone needs to know," he said as he brought the bag to where she was seated on the couch. "Looks like we have plenty of coffee."

"Yes, but this is from the Really Good."

"Let's see what we have here."

They opened the bags and enjoyed breakfast tacos with hot sauce. Even Babs enjoyed a couple of pieces of egg and bacon from Mamie's taco.

"If you're sure you don't want me to walk you to your camper, I'll head home, clean up, and return to pick you up. You'll need to give your statement at the station."

"I don't need you to walk me back, and I'll be ready. Thank you for breakfast. For everything."

They both stood, Vandegan stuffing the taco wrappers into the bag and crushing it. Hot sauce dripped onto the floor.

"No, Babs!" Mamie cautioned the dog, who was already sniffing the spicy spill.

"Well, great. I thought I was cleaning up," he said with a rueful laugh.

"Here." Mamie took the bag from him. "You go on. I'll clean this up and see you later."

"Good, since I only seem to make a bigger mess." He kissed her lightly on the lips and headed toward the door. "Later, doggie," he said as he left. Babs wagged her bottom as Mamie used her foot to block the dog from licking sauce off the floor.

***

Babs trotted along beside Mamie as they walked the fifty or so yards to her camper. The dog didn't stray, even without her leash. What had happened to that leash, anyway? *I'll need to get another one,* Mamie thought as she unlocked the camper door. She was heartened by the welcoming space, her home away from home. Here it was Tuesday and she was still at Hayden's Resort. A three-day campout had turned into six. Glad she had brought more clothes than necessary, she gathered an outfit along with toiletries, locked Babs in the camper, and headed to the shower while praying for the dog's safety. She still needed to find out who had the extra key to her camper. Hopefully he was one of those behind bars.

She allowed the hot water to wash over her for a few seconds before lathering up, relaxing bruised muscles and lightly stinging skin abrasions on her arms, hands, and face. Careful to avoid getting her wrist wrap wet, she examined her skin the best she could. Bruises were already visible on her hips, legs, and arms. She was surprised she wasn't feeling more pain and stiffness. Maybe that would come later. She closed her eyes and enjoyed the warmth of the soothing spray.

After a few minutes, she reluctantly shut off the water, realizing if she didn't she wouldn't be ready when Nick returned. As she stepped out of the shower, she grabbed the towel she had brought from home. As she wrapped the cotton fluffiness around her, what appeared to be a piece of paper fluttered to the shower floor.

No. Not again.

Chapter Thirty-One

FEAR SEIZED MAMIE as her heart thudded in her chest. With shaking fingers she picked up the damp piece of paper and wiped her eyes with the corner of the towel in her other hand.

A laugh erupted from her throat as she realized what she had picked up. Not a piece of paper. A cardboard tag. The one from her towel. She had bought new towels for her camper and forgotten to remove the price tags. There was a folding chair next to the shower. Clutching the now soggy bit of cardboard, she sank to the chair, giggling with relief.

Her giggles segued into sobs and she cried until she was completely spent. The events of the past few days, especially the night before, had affected her more than she realized.

"Lord, I pray the man in custody is the one responsible for the murders, and that this is all over," she prayed. "Help the police as they do their jobs. Help the families of the ladies who were killed. Thank you for taking care of me and Babs, and please let us go home."

What about the suspect? She heard the Lord's words as if He had spoken them out loud.

"Yes, Father, I pray for the man responsible. I pray that you will give Him a new heart and faith to trust in You and turn from his wicked ways. Thank you for your abiding presence."

Vandegan rolled up to her camper just as she finished drying her hair. Wearing white capri pants with a turquoise linen tunic, she slipped her feet into white sneakers and fastened small silver hoops in her earlobes.

"I'll be back soon," she told Babs as she grabbed her purse. With the suspect behind bars, Babs should be safe alone. She had convinced herself that it was her kidnapper who had the extra camper key. She would have to ask Nick if they had found it. He was about to knock on her door when she opened it. "Perfect timing," she said with a smile. Shedding those tears and talking to the Lord had left her feeling lighter and even optimistic about the murder investigation. She had worried about it, cried about it, and now prayed about it. It had to be over soon.

***

The police station bustled with activity, busier than one would expect for a small town like Magnolia Bluff. The receptionist greeted them as they entered the station. "Good morning, Officer Vandegan."

"Hello, Gloria. Is Detective Sovern available?"

"I believe so. Just go on in."

As they passed by the counter, Gloria seemed to study Mamie, causing her to feel a bit uncomfortable. Wasn't this the same lady who had offered her a chair the last time she was here? "Is she always so friendly?" Mamie whispered before they entered Sovern's office.

"She wants me to date her daughter. She probably sees you as a threat."

"You don't want to date her daughter?"

Vandegan laughed. "Not hardly. Wait 'til you see her."

Mamie grinned. Warmth spread throughout her

being. He had mentioned the future. And it included her.

As they stopped in the hallway at the office of the police chief, Buford Pink was stepping out. She wrinkled her nose as his aroma followed him. The man needed a good scrubbing. Pink nodded and hurried past them. Vandegan held the door as they entered the office.

Giving her statement about what happened the night before didn't take long but it was emotionally draining. She had to relive every moment, and doing that was possibly even worse because she had to describe everything in detail that had happened. She had agreed to allow him to record her statement as she didn't think she could write everything down coherently.

Jager seemed to consider her feelings as he asked a few questions at the beginning and then allowed her to talk into the camera without interrupting her. When she finished, she wiped the tears from her face with the tissue Vandegan had given her from the box on Chief Jager's desk.

"Thank you for coming in, Ms. West. We'll do everything we can to bring the perpetrator to justice," the chief said.

"I hope so," Mamie said, feeling a bit unsteady on her feet as she stood. When she swayed, Vandegan caught her arm.

"Easy there."

"Ms. West, I believe this belongs to you." Chief Jager held out her pistol. "Your attacker had this in his position when we arrested him. I thought you would like to have it back."

"Absolutely. Thank you, Chief Jager," Mamie said as she took it from him and stuffed it into her purse.

"And does this belong to you?" He pulled something from his shirt pocket.

It was her camper key. Mystery solved. "Yes, thank you." Before dropping it into her purse, she held it up to Vandegan, who smiled and nodded.

When they were out of Jager's office, Vandegan led her toward the exit. "Are you okay?"

"I think so. That was brutal."

"I'm sorry you had to go through it again, but it's necessary if we're going to solve these murders."

"I know." She patted his arm and managed a smile. "All in a day's work. And I got my pistol back. And my camper key."

As they passed the counter, Gloria spoke to Vandegan. "Carly Hallmark called, left a message for you."

"Thanks, Gloria." Vandegan took the slip of paper, Mamie's curiosity piquing.

When they opened the door, the older couple who had rescued Mamie the night before was entering the station.

"Look who it is, Ben. How are you today, dear? Did you get some rest?" Fran asked.

"I did, and thank you again for helping me last night. You quite possibly saved my life." Grateful tears stung her eyes as she blinked them back. Would she be emotional all day? She felt like a teenager with PMS.

"Of course, honey. We're glad we were there to

help. Right, Ben?"

"Exactly right. We're going to give our statements and then have lunch. Would you like to join us at the Really Good coffee shop later?"

"Now, Ben, we really don't know how long this will take."

"We can text her when we're done, Fran. Get her number."

Mamie glanced at Vandegan and smiled. "I'd love to." She typed her number into Fran's phone.

"This nice police officer can join us, too, if you have the time, of course," Fran said. "It'll be our treat. We so appreciate our boys in blue."

"Thank you very much, Mrs. . ."

"We never properly introduced ourselves, did we?"

"Fran, let's get out of the doorway, so others can get in and out," Ben said, pulling her arm toward him.

"We're Ben and Fran Ratliff from Crosby, Texas."

"Thank you, Mrs. Ratliff. I'm Officer Nick Vandegan with the Magnolia Bluff police department."

"And I'm Mamie West from Leander. I'm so pleased to know you."

"Likewise."

"Come on, Fran, they've got things to do."

"Yes, dear. We'll be in touch when we're done here. See you in a little while."

With that, the Ratliffs entered the station through the door Vandegan held open for them. Mamie walked beside him toward his cruiser. "Are you going to tell me what that message from Carly says?"

He grinned. "Why?"

"Because I'm curious, although I guess it's none of my business," Mamie said, her cheeks coloring.

"I'm teasing. She apologized for leaving so abruptly. I guess she doesn't realize that she could be in trouble for that. I'm going to cut her some slack this time. She said she had a family emergency."

Mamie's heart swelled. Such a good man. "Good. I was surprised she would do that after wanting to help with the investigation. Will you be joining us for lunch?" she asked.

"You know what? I really need to get some work done. Why don't I call you later? You can tell me all about your dining experience with the Ratliffs. Would you like me to take you to get your car?"

"No, that's not necessary. I'll get them to take me back to camp. I'll walk around here and check out some shops until they're done. Or maybe I'll just relax at the Green with some coffee and do some people-watching."

"All right. If you get too warm, you can always go to the library where it's cool. Caroline McCluskey is the librarian and she's great. Just call me if the Ratfliffs can't give you a ride back. I'll see you soon." He glanced around them and then planted a gentle kiss on her lips that gave her goosebumps. She gazed at him as he walked back to the station entrance, wondering if their relationship would ever grow more intimate. She wasn't quite sure, but she believed she was ready. She cast her eyes toward the heavens with the uncanny feeling that West was smiling down at her.

***

Mamie wandered through a couple of shops, the boutique she had visited earlier with Sheila, Tessa, and Lanie—the shop even had cute dog collars and leashes so she grabbed a leash for Babs—and then bought a cup of coffee from the Really Good before she wandered over to a bench on the edge of the Green. The streets of downtown Magnolia Bluff were busy with cars speeding up and down Main Street as people scurried up and down the sidewalks on their lunch breaks. This must be the busiest time of day for this small town, except when school was in session and let out in the afternoon. She'd seen quiet little towns become large traffic jams during dismissal time.

A rag-tag man wearing worn-out overalls she recognized as Buford Pink came out of the bakery chewing on a pastry, saw her, and ambled in her direction. It was too late to act like she hadn't seen him, and it would have been rude to get up and walk away, so she pasted a smile on her face.

"Hello again, Mr. Pink."

"Howdy, there, ma'am. I noticed you ain't left the campground yet. All them other ladies done did."

"Yes, well, I'm needed for the murder investigation, I suppose."

"You git anymore them notes?"

"What do you know about those notes, Mr. Pink?"

"I know they show up when a body is found, and I know there was one at your camper."

"I think the police have the suspects in custody, so there shouldn't be any more notes."

"I done told you that boy and that office guy weren't the ones."

"But the notes were written in Brady's handwriting," Mamie countered, wondering why she was allowing him to draw her into conversation about the notes and murders.

"He was forced, don't you know. Ever thought of that?"

"Forced? By whom?"

"Pauly Brown."

"Who is she?"

"He is the man that almost killed you last night. He made Brady write them notes."

Mamie gasped. How did he know all this?

"I saw Pauly get in Brady's face one day in the bait shop parking lot, so I snuck around behind Brady's truck and heard ever word they said."

"Go on."

"Seems Brady knowed something about Pauly and Scarlett and he was gonna tell his aunt. Pauly found out somehow. He musta overheard Brady talkin' to Howard Story about it. Anyhow, Pauly told Brady—and I heard this from Pauly's mouth—that if he didn't write them notes for him he would tell Scarlett that Brady had been robbin' the store for pot money."

"Pot money? That's ridiculous. Brady would not rob his aunt's store, and especially not to buy drugs." But she couldn't be sure, especially after he had led Junie to believe he had graduated from college. He might not be the bright upstanding young man she had believed him to be, after all.

"You can believe what you want, ma'am, but I'm tellin' you the truth."

"Why won't you go to the police?"

"Because Pauly has eyes and ears everywhere. He'll know I had somethin' to do with turnin' him in. I don't want to be in his crosshairs."

"How do you know you aren't already there? He's been arrested. He's in jail as we speak."

"Yep, but that ain't my doin.' That's yours. Better pray he don't get out no time soon, or he'll be comin' after you."

She swallowed. "Did he kill those women, Mr. Pink?"

"Yep, I just as good as seen him do it."

"But why? And you have to go to the police."

Pink sat on the bench next to her, her nose wrinkling at his pungent odor. It was obvious that old trailer he lived in didn't have running water. If it did, he didn't avail himself of it.

"I'll tell you all about it if you want to know, but then you'll be in more danger than you already are."

Chapter Thirty-Two

MAMIE RECALLED BEING grabbed and dragged to the shed where she was tied up and left alone in the dark. She shuddered as she stared at Pink's stubbly tobacco-stained face. With the killer in custody there was no reason she should be afraid. He couldn't get to her. And Brady and Howard Story were still in custody as well, although they should be able to post bail any time now if the judge would let them.

"I think the threat is over now that the suspect is behind bars," she told Pink. "Please just go ahead and tell me."

"Don't say I didn't warn you," Pink said before launching into his report of a wronged man who believed the only way to get revenge was to kill the one responsible. Sarah had apparently refused his advances at LouEllen's Lounge the night before she was murdered. He had threatened her and the other woman had overheard. He thought the only way to rectify the situation was to shoot Sarah dead and strangle Holly. But Holly had come late to the campout. How had she been at LouEllen's?

"How do you know any of this?" Mamie said. "And what about Hunter Trenton, Sarah's husband? And Holly came late to the campout."

"I got eyes and ears and I'm stealthy as a fox," Pink bragged with a toothy grin. "That husband didn't have nothin' to do with it. Yep, but she was at the lounge that night. I seen her."

"You must tell the police. What if I have Officer

Vandegan meet us here and you just tell him what you told me? You won't be in any trouble."

Pink eyed her with distrust and spat on the ground. He didn't answer.

She took that as a yes and punched Vandegan's number. "Nick, I'm with Buford Pink at the Green across from the Really Good. He has some information I think you need. Okay, see you in a bit."

Pink rose from the bench, but against her cleanliness instincts Mamie grabbed the side loop on his overalls to keep him from going anywhere. His frown was menacing, but it didn't deter her. She held on as he tried to take a step.

"What are you doin'?" he asked.

"I'm keeping you here until Officer Vandegan gets here. Please, Mr. Pink? I'll buy you anything you want from the bakery."

A toothy smile graced his unshaven face. "I like the cinnamon rolls."

"I'll buy you half a dozen. Please just stay here until Nick gets here."

He sat down on the bench and leaned back, produced a piece of straw from his front chest pocket, and stuck it in his mouth. He stared across the Green, seemingly lost in his own thoughts.

Mamie tried not to stare at him, but he fascinated her. What was his backstory? Was he originally from Magnolia Bluff? She might never know. The only thing she really needed to know he had told her.

A police siren disturbed her thoughts as

Vandegan's cruiser slid to a halt on the street behind the bench. He hopped out, tablet in hand.

Mamie dared not get up in case Pink decided to bolt. She gripped his arm just to be sure.

"What's this I need to hear?" Vandegan asked as he approached them.

"Woman thinks I need to talk to you, but I ain't got nothin' to say."

Mamie rolled her eyes and gave him a disgusted look.

"Ms. West, why don't you tell me what he told you, and he can confirm or deny?" Vandegan moved so that he was standing directly in front of Pink, so close the man wouldn't be able to get up if he wanted to.

She nodded and retold the story as she had heard it from Pink, staring at the ground as she concentrated on recounting every detail. When she finished she looked up at the officer.

"Is that everything, Pink?" he asked the old man.

"That about does it," he replied. "Am I under arrest?"

"No, but don't leave town. We'll have to do some more investigating and questioning of our suspect."

"What about my cinnamon rolls?" Pink asked Mamie.

"Cinnamon rolls?" Vandegan asked.

"I told him if he would cooperate I would buy him his favorites from the bakery."

"I see. Pink, you head on over there and I'll call

Noonan so they'll have them ready for you."

"I told him I would buy him half a dozen."

Vandegan looked at her, incredulous. "Okay, then." He punched a number into his cell phone. "Yeah, it's Officer Vandegan. Can you put together half a dozen cinnamon rolls for my friend Buford Pink? He should be there about now. Okay, just give him all you have. I'll settle up next time I'm in. Thanks."

"I'll pay you back," Mamie said as they watched Pink enter Bluff Bakery.

"If this information solves the murders, I'll be more than happy to expense them. Want to go back to the station with me, or do you want me to take you back to the campground so you can head home? I think you've given us all the information we need, and I can always call you if I need more. Unless you want to hang around and have lunch with the Ratliffs."

The words *head home* saddened her a bit. Would he be sad when she left town? "If you don't mind, I'd like to hang around a little bit longer. I haven't heard anything from the Ratliffs, but I'd like to see where this goes. Unless you're getting tired of seeing me in the same clothes."

Vandegan put his arm around her shoulders and squeezed before kissing the top of her head. "You could wear the same thing every day for a year and I wouldn't mind in the least."

She grinned up at him before they walked to the car and climbed inside. Tyler would be so jealous. He had always wanted to ride in the front of a police car, and now she had done it several times. The thought of her son made her smile.

"What is that smile about?" Vandegan said as he backed the car into the street.

"I was just thinking about my son Tyler," she replied.

"Is he older or younger than your daughter?"

"He is older than Junie. He has a son himself, my grandson." She glanced at Vandegan to see his reaction.

He looked at her. "Do they live far?" Still no reaction, and this was the second time she had mentioned she had a grandson. She decided to bring it out into the open.

"Nick, you don't blink an eye when I mention I have a grandson, and this is the second time. You knew I have a grown daughter and a grown son. It's obvious that you are much younger than I am. Does it bother you to date a grandmother?"

Vandegan pulled into his usual parking space at the station, shoved the gearshift in park, and turned to look at her. He placed his right hand on her neck and stroked her cheek with his thumb. Shivers ran through her as she anticipated what he was about to say.

"Mamie, I'm not interested in you because of whether you have grown children or grandchildren or because of your age. I'm interested in you because you're beautiful inside and out, you're inquisitive and smart, and I love spending time with you. It has nothing to do with those other things." He leaned toward her and placed his lips on hers, sending her senses into a flurry. The car suddenly became too warm.

"We better go inside before I get carried away," he

chuckled, turning the key to the OFF position. "Are we good?"

"We're better than good," Mamie replied, grinning from ear to ear. Her heart suddenly felt full. Could the ache that West's death left be easing? She couldn't wait to find out.

Chapter Thirty-Three

AS VANDEGAN AND Mamie entered the station, the icy gaze of Scarlett Hayden, who was standing at the front desk, greeted them. Mamie didn't know whether to say hello or nod or just ignore her. She didn't have to worry about it long.

"Perfect stranger comes to stay at my property, cozies up to my nephew and office manager, and then has them arrested for murder. Just what is it you're trying to accomplish here in Magnolia Bluff, city lady?" Her voice dripped with condescension.

The few people in the waiting area and behind the desk riveted their attention to Mamie, waiting for her reaction. Scarlett scanned her from top to bottom and rolled her eyes. Mamie suddenly felt as if she didn't measure up, but why should she care?

"Now you've got our Officer Vandegan wrapped around your little finger, don't you?"

Mamie glanced at Vandegan who shook his head slightly, indicating that she shouldn't take the bait, but Mamie West had never allowed students or anyone else to railroad her, and she wasn't about to start now. Scarlett was almost the right age to have been one of her students back in the day. Mamie opened her mouth to speak, but Vandegan interrupted.

"Good morning, Ms. Hayden. Now if you'll excuse us, we have business to take care of." He pulled Mamie's elbow toward the hallway, stepping around Scarlett in such a way that kept Mamie out of reach.

"I bet you do. And since when am I Ms. Hayden? You've always called me Scarlett, Nick." Scarlett turned to the receptionist. "How long does it take to post bail anyway? What is taking so long?"

Gloria colored and picked up the phone. Before Vandegan could lead Mamie down the hall, Brady and Howard Story came sauntering through some double doors that she figured must lead to the jail. They were escorted by two other officers.

"We're releasing these two men into your custody, Ms. Hayden. See that they don't leave town before they see the judge," one said.

"I'm not in custody of anyone. It's their business whether they leave town or not. Find your own way home, gentlemen." With that, Scarlett turned and walked out, her three-inch stiletto heels clickety-clacking down the sidewalk.

Brady gave Mamie a look of regret. Considering his friendliness and helpfulness versus his lies to her daughter, she was torn between sympathy and anger and turned away. He hung his head and followed Story out of the building, both looking at the ground as they walked. He couldn't know that Junie was her daughter. Yet.

At the desk in the room he shared with the other officers, Vandegan picked up the phone handset, staring at Mamie as he dialed. She shifted in her chair, waiting to see what he was doing. He told someone he was going to visit the prisoner and replaced the handset.

"Would you mind waiting here? I'm going to talk to this Pauly Brown."

She nodded and watched him walk out of the

office, shutting the door behind him. She pulled her phone out of her purse to do a long overdue check of her email and social media, but it didn't take long. No messages, no tags. *Nobody likes me, everybody hates me, I think I'll go eat worms.* She smiled, remembering the words she used to hear her grandmother say when she didn't get any mail in her mailbox.

Did Nick expect Pauly Brown to admit involving Brady and Story in his crimes? Had Brady told the police the truth, that the reason he had written the notes was because he and Story had been threatened?

There was a knock on the office door, but before she could figure out what to do—whether to answer the door or remain quiet—the door flung open.

"I'm sorry, I didn't know you were here. I have some information for Vandegan that can't wait. Do you know where he is? Sorry, I'm Hans." He extended his hand.

She shook it. "Pleased to meet you. I'm Mamie West. Nick went to talk to the prisoner."

"Thanks." The door shut and he was gone. Did the information he had relate to the murder cases? She itched to follow him but knew she would be stopped. *Patience*, she told herself.

By the time Vandegan returned, her stomach was telling her it was way past lunchtime, and she hadn't heard a thing from the Ratliffs. It was half past one according to her phone, so why hadn't they texted? Were they still there at the station?

Vandegan sat at the desk and wiggled the computer mouse to wake up the computer. He seemed to read her mind—or had he heard her tummy? "Weren't you supposed to have lunch with that nice couple who came in to give their statements? The Ratliffs?"

"Yes, but I haven't heard from them. Did Hans find you?"

"Yes, and he and the Ratliffs gave me some information I think will close this case. The license plate on that pickup also checked out. I'll see if they're still here."

He picked up the phone again and spoke to someone, and in less than a minute, there was a knock on the door. Ben and Fran entered when Vandegan said, "Come in."

"Ready to go eat?" Fran asked Mamie.

"More than ready," she replied, glancing at Vandegan with her brows raised. She was dying to know what they had revealed.

"You go ahead, Ms. West. I have to make a report. I'll meet you at the restaurant. The Really Good, right?"

"You got it. See you there," Ben said, grinning. He offered his hand to Mamie as she rose from the chair. "Let's get something good at the Really Good," he said, laughing. "We'll see if it's really good or not."

"I need a really good cup of coffee after this morning," Fran said with a wink.

***

Mamie enjoyed a hearty chef salad and a cinnamon dolce latte as she learned from the Ratliffs what piece of information they had given to the police. It had been their habit since they became full-time RVers to install outdoor cameras at the campsite. They had video footage of Pauly Brown shooting Sarah from the cab window of his pickup the night she was killed. They also had footage of Brown dragging a heavy, rolled-up blanket down the lakeshore in front of their site. Another piece of footage revealed Brown standing next to Brady's golf cart, shaking his finger in Brady's face, obviously threatening him. It was everything a jury would need to convict him of the murders. Brown hadn't taken camper video surveillance into consideration.

Neither had he considered video surveillance by the campground itself. She later learned from Vandegan, who called her as she was riding in the Ratliffs' car, that he had also secured camera footage of the office from Scarlett, which showed Brown slamming a notepad onto the counter and arguing with Howard Story. Brady had then entered the office and Brown turned on him and shoved what appeared to be a notepad at him. What looked like a brief argument ended with Brown exiting and Brady and Story standing there staring after him. It was obvious that Brown was forcing them to do something against their wills.

She was indeed a happy camper when the Ratliffs dropped her off at her campsite that afternoon. So was Babs, who hopped in gleeful circles and wiggled her bottom as Mamie finally got her new leash clipped onto her harness.

"We have time for a short walk, sweet girl. Then Nick's coming to see us when he gets off work."

But all Babs cared about was trotting along the edge of the campground road, sniffing every new scent and squatting to relieve herself. She was turning into a good camper, after all. Even though the afternoon air was heavy with humidity, Mamie felt as if a weight had been lifted from her shoulders. The sound of children laughing had her looking in the direction of the campsite where Sarah's trailer had been sitting. It was gone, replaced by a shiny silver Airstream trailer. In front of it two little boys used a bubble wand and pail to send bubbles floating past her. Life went on, as it would for Sarah's and Holly's families. Maybe the tragedy would spur Hunter to get help and finally fully recover from drug abuse.

As Mamie and Babs headed toward the beach area, Brady appeared next to them in his golf cart. When Mamie realized who it was, she kept walking, not really wanting to talk to him after what Junie had told her.

"Mrs. West, could we talk, please?" he said, rolling beside them.

She glanced at him, shaking her head. Babs tugged at the leash, wanting to greet Brady. Could he be all bad if Babs liked him?

"Please, Mamie?"

She stopped walking and faced him. "What do you want to talk about? You're a murder suspect, Brady."

"Not anymore. Didn't Officer Vandegan tell you? They found security footage. Howard and I were threatened by Pauly Brown. We had to do what he wanted us to do."

"Okay, yes, he did tell me that. But that doesn't excuse your lies to my daughter."

"Your daughter?"

"Yes, Junie West is my daughter. You've been

dating her."

Brady's eyes widened. "Junie's your daughter? Junie's your daughter!" He clapped his palm to his forehead. "Of course! West!"

"Yes, she's my daughter. And you lied and told her you graduated from college and ran this resort."

"I can explain."

"I sure hope so. She's hurt and thinks she attracts losers. I didn't think you were a loser, Brady. I was so impressed with you. You were polite and helpful and patient with us lady campers. You seemed to be the kind of young man a mother would want for her daughter. Then you turn out to be a liar and a criminal."

"I'm not a criminal, and I lied because I didn't think Junie would date me if I told her I had decided not to go to college yet and work at my aunt's campground. She's classy and I was afraid she wouldn't have anything to do with me if I told her the truth. She would think I'm too young for her."

"Age isn't an issue, Brady. What is the issue is that you thought you had to lie to make her like you. Lying is never the answer, young man." She felt her heart softening toward him. Maybe Junie should give him another chance.

"Do you think she would understand if I explained and apologized?" Misery wrote itself all over his face as a tear escaping down his cheek surprised both him and Mamie.

"I can't speak for her, but an explanation and apology would be a good place to start."

"I'll do that." A smile broke through the misery. He pressed the gas but then stopped the cart suddenly. "Mamie, will you forgive me?"

"I'm working on it, Brady. I'm glad you're not responsible for the murders, and I'm glad to see you back at work. I will be going home in the morning. Maybe we'll cross paths again soon." She smiled. "Good luck with Junie. Remember, respect and trust have to be earned."

"I hope I can earn it back, with both of you. Thank you, Mamie. Bye, Babs." He stepped on the gas again and wheeled the cart away.

Mamie watched him and then she and Babs headed to the beach area to find a lounger to sit on. It would be a miracle if Junie forgave him, but time would tell. A young family picnicked at one table while an older couple sat in loungers facing the lake. Several children of different ages played frisbee, built sandcastles, and splashed at the water's edge. She chose a lounge chair away from everyone else and sank into it, enjoying the warm sunlight on her face. Babs plopped beside her on the grass. She wasn't panting yet, so she was good in the summer heat.

They would need to pack up and leave in the morning. What would Nick say when he arrived? Did he want to question her more about the murder case? Would he be interested in seeing her again after she left Magnolia Bluff? She recalled the kisses they had shared. Would there be more? She drummed her fingers on the flat arm of the Adirondack chair she occupied. This was a perfect time and place for a fancy drink with an umbrella sticking out of it. Too bad there wasn't a waiter and a bar around. She leaned back and closed her eyes, soaking in her last moments at Hayden's Resort.

"Mind if I join you?" came a familiar masculine voice. There was no sound from Babs.

Mamie smiled and opened her eyes. She was getting used to this voice. She hoped she could look forward to hearing more of it, but she was about to leave Magnolia Bluff. Did he feel the same way? Did he want to take measures to grow their relationship, or was this the last of it?

"Of course, not. Please sit down."

Vandegan dragged a nearby lounger closer to hers and folded himself into it, his long legs stretching out beyond. Babs's bottom wiggled as she wagged her nonexistent tail. She liked this man, too.

"Penny for your thoughts?" He lightly touched the top of her hand, sending a shiver up her arm.

"I was just thinking that this is my last night in Magnolia Bluff. I'll be pulling out tomorrow and going home to Leander. I'm ready to be home, but I'm going to miss my new friends." She gazed at his handsome face with a question in her eyes.

"Are you now?" He grinned and squeezed her hand.

"Will you miss me?" she asked, deciding to get straight to the point.

His eyes went skyward as his other hand rubbed his chin. "Hm, let me think about that one."

She punched his arm playfully. "You rat."

He grew serious as he straightened—as best he could in an Adirondack-style lounger—and studied her face, his eyes boring into hers. Had she noticed how strikingly blue they were? The sunlight made them even more stunning, and they were fixed on her.

"I will miss you just like I miss you now when you're away from me. I miss you when we are not together. That will not change. I hope to continue seeing you. I'd like to come to Leander and see you if it's okay."

Mamie's heart swelled. "Of course it's okay! Yes! I was so hoping you would say that. I couldn't bear it if we stopped seeing each other. I—"

Her words halted with a kiss as Vandegan leaned over and pressed his lips onto hers. His hand caught in her hair as he lingered there, sending a jolt of pleasure all the way down to her toes. She gave a little moan of happiness and desire as she lost herself in the kiss. It had been so long since she had experienced this feeling.

It's okay, darling, she heard West say in her heart. *I always wanted you to be happy, and that will never change. Be happy, my love.*

Babs ended the kiss abruptly as she hopped on Vandegan's lap, dancing and wiggling her bottom.

"Do you approve, Doggy?" he laughed.

"I think she does," Mamie said, tears of joy wetting her face. "And West does, too."

Vandegan glanced upward. "I'll take good care of her. You can count on that."

Mamie wiped the tears from her face with the back of her right hand and then reached for Babs. Her heart was full. *Thank you, God,* she breathed. He had never failed her, and He never would. The words from Hebrews

13:5 popped into her mind. ". . .for He hath said, I will never leave thee, nor forsake thee." She nuzzled Nick's neck. God would take care of her. Now and forever.

The End

Acknowledgements

I'd like to thank the Underground Authors, especially Linda Pirtle, for inviting me to join the Magnolia Bluff Crime Chronicles writers and enter the marvelous fictional world of Magnolia Bluff. It was so sad to lose the talented and prolific author who founded the group, but I'll be eternally grateful to Caleb Pirtle III for providing this opportunity. What a mentor he was to aspiring writers! You are sorely missed, Caleb.

A huge thank you to my beta readers Rachel Bates, Lydia Holley, and Linda Pirtle. Thank you for catching my errors, holes in the story, unanswered questions, and suggestions for improvement. You ladies rock! I'm indebted to you for your help with this project. The same goes to members of my critique groups: Tom Collins, Woody Edmiston, Lydia Holley, and Patricia La Vigne (ETWG); and Joe Congel, C.W. Hawes, and Linda Pirtle (UA). Your opinions matter, even though they hurt sometimes. I think the stab of a keystroke can sometimes hurt worse than a knife, but I thank you anyway. Something good always comes out of the initial pain.

And last, but certainly not least, praise goes to Almighty God. I wrote this for Him and through Him. Without Him, I can do nothing. (John 15:5)

About the Author

Award-winning author April Nunn Coker has been writing since she was old enough to hold a pencil. She penned stories for her friends in school, was published in her high school's creative writing magazine, and became editor of her high school newspaper. Intending to become a television news reporter, she set off to college with a major in journalism, soon finding out that she lacked the aggressiveness to be a reporter. She changed her major to pre-med, soon discovering she was too squeamish to be a doctor, which led her into the field of education.

After teaching high school English and science and directing an alternative school, she retired after thirty years in public school service and returned to her first love of writing. Her school career had offered opportunities to write for her campus faculty newsletter and to write for professional association newsletters, but in retirement there was more time for writing.

Her first book, *I'm Dreaming of a Black Christmas: A Holiday Survival Guide* was a tongue-in-cheek handbook on saving money and one's sanity during the holidays. Next came *Night Keeper*, a romantic suspense novel about zookeepers who work at night, based upon her late husband's experiences as a night keeper supervisor at Caldwell Zoo in Tyler, Texas. Soon after losing the copyrights to those books when her publisher sold out, she decided to self-publish and released *The Keeper*, a faith-based Christian romantic suspense novel about night zookeepers also inspired by her husband's zoo career. *Keeper II: The Storm* and *Keeper III: Blackout* soon followed, along with *Ellie and the Alphabet Zoo*, a children's book featuring a character from the Keeper books and her pet hedgehog.

April was honored to be asked to join the Underground Authors and to write Magnolia Bluff Crime Chronicles book #25.

If you liked this book, please consider leaving a review on Amazon and/or Goodreads, and any other book review website you like.

You can contact April at her website

www.aprilnunncoker.com or email her directly at april@aprilnunncoker.com. She would love to hear from you. Thank you very much for reading *Just Dying to Glamp*, and look for its sequel, coming in March of 2025.

ENJOY THIS EXCERPT FROM THE NEXT BOOK IN THE SERIES:

CATCH A TIGER BY THE TOE

Magnolia Bluff Crime Chronicles, Book 26

By Joe Congel

Chapter One

Brandon Turner pulled his truck into the Magnolia Bluff high school parking lot. It was important that he made it there by four o'clock. This was the last baseball game of the school year and he'd made a promise to Jason, so he wasn't about to let him down.

Joyce was showing a client a home on the other side of Burnet Reservoir and wouldn't be able to make the game. Turner felt it was important that he was there to support her son, so he'd told them both he would be in the stands cheering for the team.

It was a beautiful afternoon for a baseball game. It was hot. But it was always hot. Over the last year since he'd migrated south, he'd adapted to the climate of the Texas Hill Country, making the heat slightly more bearable than when he'd first arrived.

A small price to pay to be able to live his life without constantly looking over his shoulder. Something that had become increasingly difficult right before retiring from the NYPD and moving to Magnolia Bluff.

Turner clicked a leash on his three-year-old Labrador and the two made their way across the parking lot to the bleachers on the home team's side of the diamond. They climbed up to the first row and took a seat on the wooden bench.

Max barked, which caught the attention of Jason, who was warming up on the sideline. "Looking good," said Turner as the boy jogged over to where they were seated.

"I really like the new uniforms. The blue Bulldogs logo on the white jersey is sharp."

"Yeah, I do too," replied Jason. He leaned over the railing and gave Max a pat on the head. "The white top with the blue pants looks a lot better than the all-blue look we had last year." His lips stretched wide into a grin. "The girls like it better, too."

Turner nodded knowingly and smiled. "Just keep in mind what I told you," he said.

"Make sure I remember to plant my foot when throwing to first."

"Exactly. You'll generate more power, and your throw will almost always beat the runner, no matter how fast he is."

Jason grinned. "Unless I bobble the ball."

Turner laughed. "Just have a great game," he said, shaking his head.

"Thanks, I will." Jason turned as the coach called out to him. "Well, I better get over there. Coach wants to have a huddle before we hit the field."

He's a good kid, thought Turner as he watched Jason join his teammates so they could listen to the coach's pregame pump up.

Ever since he'd started dating Joyce, Jason had become an important part of his life. They shared an interest in sports, especially baseball. Turner had been the starting second baseman back in his high school days, just like Jason was now on his high school team.

He wanted to be respectful of Denny, Jason's dad, but since his father lived in Austin, Turner had stepped into more of the day-to-day role of helping Joyce raise her son.

At sixteen years old, the kid could be a handful at times. But they'd managed to find a middle ground they all could live with, allowing Turner to function as a mentor for the boy over the last year.

He loved helping Jason work on improving his baseball skills, and he knew Jason appreciated it as well. The boy was a natural athlete and already a good second baseman. Turner liked to believe that the drills they worked on over the weekends helped him to become an even better overall ballplayer.

Everyone stood as Ms. Caroline McCluskey sang the national anthem, as she did for every home game. When she was through, the umpire yelled, "Play ball!" and the game was underway.

It was a pitcher's duel right up through the bottom of the fifth inning. That changed with the first pitch in the top of the sixth when the visiting team's third baseman connected with a fastball and drove it over the left field fence.

The Bulldogs answered in the bottom of the seventh when Jason scorched a three-run homer that bounced off the scoreboard high above center field, putting them up three to one.

The home team held on in the ninth for the win when a ball was hit to the shortstop, who flipped it over to Jason, who stepped on the bag, planted his foot and fired to first completing the double play to end the game.

Turner and Max excitedly jumped up along with the rest of the crowd while the Bulldogs whooped and high-fived each other as they ran off the field in victory.

The kids were busily packing up their bats, gloves,

and other assorted equipment. Turner and Max waited over by the backstop while Jason finished gathering his gear and stuffed it inside his bag. Several of the other players were still laughing and enjoying the win while their parents waited and chatted about work and life.

Turner watched as a woman pushing one of those small umbrella-style strollers came marching across the playing field from the visitor's side of the diamond. She was frantically whipping her head from side to side and crying hysterically. She stopped right in the center of the pitcher's mound and began screaming, "Has anyone seen my baby? Has anyone seen my baby?"

A crowd formed around her as other parents came running over to see what was wrong. The scene quickly became chaotic as everyone spread out and combed the immediate area for the woman's missing child.

Turner fished his phone from a back pocket of his jeans and dialed 911 as he rushed over to where she was standing. Once he'd reported what was happening, he clicked off his device and tried to calm the woman down. "Ma'am, my name is Brandon Turner. I am a former police detective. I want you to take a couple of deep breaths and exhale slowly. The police are on their way."

The woman was shaking but did as he asked. She continued to breathe in and out and after a minute, she began to settle down a bit.

"Good, good," he said in a soothing voice. "What's your name?"

"My baby is missing," she said as her voice crumbled and she started crying again.

Turner reached out and took her hands in his and

looked her in the eyes. "What's your baby's name?"

"Emily. My baby's name is Emily," she said between sobs.

"Good," said Turner. "How old is Emily?"

"Sh-she's only two years old. I have to find her. Please help me find her."

"The police will be here any second. Can you tell me what happened?"

"It's my fault," she said. "I was arguing with my husband… my *ex*-husband. Emily must have wandered off while I was on the phone." Her chest heaved up and down and she screamed. "I wasn't paying attention. Oh God, I was too busy bitching at Jerry, and I wasn't watching Emily."

Turner tried to keep his voice even and calm as he spoke. "Was your daughter sitting in the stroller?"

Her chest heaved again as she sucked in air and tried to fight back her tears. "Yes. Emily must have climbed out." She shook her head, clutched her stomach, leaned over and threw up. She used the back of her hand to wipe her mouth, then looked up at Turner. "How could I not notice she was gone? What kind of mother does that?"

Sirens blared and lights flashed as a white and green trimmed four-wheel-drive police SUV, followed by an unmarked cruiser, drove through the parted crowd and up onto the field. Chief Tommy Jager climbed out of the vehicle, fastened his hat securely on his head, and walked over to where Turner and the woman were standing. Right behind him, Detective Reece Sovern emerged from the cruiser and joined the chief.

Turner pulled them aside and filled them in on what

was going on. "She appears to be a single mother who was on the phone with her ex when her two-year-old child disappeared. She might have wandered away and is lost. It might be something worse. Either way, the kid, whose name is Emily, is missing."

"Thank you for the update," Sovern said, stepping around Turner so he could see the woman. "We'll take it from here."

Turner looked over at the chief. "Tommy, the mother is hysterical and blaming herself. Her child is missing. I think you should talk to her before letting your detective loose on her."

Detective Sovern turned back toward him and scowled. "What the hell is that supposed to mean, Turner?"

"I just meant that she doesn't need to be interrogated right now. You have to call in more officers and comb the area for the child. You can pepper her with your questions later."

Tommy pulled the microphone from his shoulder and radioed for Winkler and Vandegan to get out to the high school pronto.

Sovern was working on the remnants of a soggy cigar. He pulled it from between his lips, turned his head and spit. Then he returned the stogie to its resting place in the corner of his mouth. "You said she was talking to her ex on the phone when she noticed the child was gone. Do you believe her? She might think he took the kid and for some reason is covering for him."

Turner looked at the detective and then at Tommy. The chief understood and nodded, then glanced over at

Sovern. "There'll be plenty of time for speculation, Reece," he said. "I've got Hans and Nick on the way. Meanwhile, let's spread out and find this woman's child."

Turner brought the chief over to the woman and introduced him. She told him her name was Dawn Harding. He also found out that Emily had light brown hair and was wearing pink shorts and a white top with a hummingbird on the front with the words *sweet as nectar* underneath the bird graphic.

Sovern was already leading a group of parents toward the outfield when Officers Nick Vandegan and Hans Winkler arrived. The chief and Turner quickly briefed them. Then they rounded up the parents who were still there and began walking the entire school grounds in a grid pattern.

Turner told Jason to throw all his gear in the back of his truck and then join him and Max. He had his dog sniff all around the seat of the stroller, and then they headed off to join the search party.

After about twenty minutes, Max dragged Turner and Jason over to the far corner of the parking lot, where the buses were lined up for the evening.

He noticed that the door on the bus at the end farthest from the school building was wide open. Max pulled on the leash hard enough that he had to let go. The dog bolted for the open door, with Jason running right behind him.

Turner called out after the boy. "Jason, do not go inside that bus without me."

Max ran up the steps and entered the school bus. Turner broke into a full sprint when he saw Jason follow the dog through the door.

He stepped onto the bus and walked to the back, where Max and Jason were standing. As he got closer, he could see Max licking the little girl, and bile rose from his stomach up into his throat.

Jason turned to him and said, "She looks so peaceful cuddled up with her stuffed animal. Like she's sleeping."

Turner knew better.

"Please go find Chief Jager and bring him back here."

Jason nodded and went to find the chief.

Turner stared down at the little girl and sighed. She looked so innocent. He would've believed she was sleeping if it wasn't for the note pinned through the hummingbird graphic on her shirt.

He pulled out his phone and took a picture of the note. Then he dialed Sovern's number. "I found the girl," he said when the detective answered. "You can send all the parents home and tell Winkler and Vandegan they can head back to the station, then come around to where the buses are all lined up. I sent Jason to go find Tommy."

Turner and Max sat on the school bus near Emily until Sovern, Tommy, Jason, and the girl's mother arrived. He glanced up at Jason. "I need you to wait outside for now."

The boy's face scrunched into a frown. "But I already saw her. I helped find her."

"I know you did. And we'll talk later. But for now, I need you to wait outside." He reached over and handed him the leash. "Here, take Max with you."

Jason let out a sigh and reluctantly took the leash. "Come on, Max," he said, pulling the dog down the aisle with him as he left.

Chief Jager and Sovern walked the mother over to where her daughter was lying. "I know this will be hard for you, Dawn," Tommy said gently. "Is this Emily?"

She nodded. Her knees buckled and she fell forward into Tommy's arms. "My baby," she whispered as tears flowed down her cheeks. "My baby." She buried her head into Tommy's shoulder and wept.

Turner watched Tommy interact with the woman. The chief's bedside manner surprised him. He didn't peg Tommy as a guy with much empathy. But he wrapped her up in his arms and let her cry for as long as it took for her to get it all out.

Once she quieted down and the shivering subsided, he pulled back from her. Turner could tell from his expression that the chief was ready to get down to business and ask a few questions.

Tommy found her eyes. "Dawn, do you recognize the handwriting on the note?"

She took in a deep breath and looked down at her little girl. The tears started to flow again.

"Take your time," he said.

Turner looked over her shoulder and read the note again: *Eeny, meeny, miny, moe.* He tilted his head and wondered what the significance of a children's nursery rhyme could be.

Dawn sniffled, closed her eyes, and took a deep breath. She opened them as she exhaled and took another look at the note. She slowly shook her head. "I-I have no idea what it means." She turned and stared directly at Turner. "Why would someone pin this on my Emily's shirt? It makes no sense."

"I'm not sure why," he said, trying to console her. "But the police will find out." He smiled gingerly at her. "At least Emily still had her stuffed toy to comfort her when she passed."

The woman looked up, her eyes darting between the three men. "That's the thing," she said. "That doesn't belong to Emily. I've never seen that stuffed tiger before in my life."

Made in the USA
Columbia, SC
20 June 2024